PRAISE FOR ROCHELLE ALERS'S PREVIOUS ARABESQUE TITLE *HIDEAWAY*

"This is Alers at the top of her form! The sensual love scenes are the best in genre writing."

—Vivian Stephens
Founder, Romance Writers of America

"Rochelle Alers is a compelling storyteller who has the ability to weave romance with the delicate subtlety of Monet."

—*Romantic Times*

"A vivid portrayal of family secrets, revenge and a love not to be denied. *Hideaway* ignites from beginning to climactic end with red, hot passion and hold your breath suspense. Not to be missed."

—Donna Hill
author of *Scandalous*

"Fantastic! Pick of the month! Thanks for a great book!"
—Jacquelynne Lovejoy
Manager, Covina Book Store

"*Hideaway* is SUPERB. Rochelle Alers is an author of immense talent who once again pens a love story that sparkles with sensuality, and whose action-packed excitement and intrigue keeps you turning the pages."

—Brenda Jackson
author of *Tonight and Forever, Cupid's Bow,*
and *Whispered Promises*

TIMELESS LOVE

Look for these historical romances in the Arabesque line:

BLACK PEARL by Francine Craft (0236-0, $4.99)

CLARA'S PROMISE by Shirley Hailstock (0147-X, $4.99)

MIDNIGHT MOON by Mildred Riley (0200-X; $4.99)

SUNSHINE AND SHADOWS by Roberta Gayle (0136-4, $4.99)

HIDDEN AGENDA

Rochelle Alers

Pinnacle Books
Kensington Publishing Corp.
http://www.pinnaclebooks.com

PINNACLE BOOKS are published by

Kensington Publishing Corp.
850 Third Avenue
New York, NY 10022

First Printing: April, 1997
10 9 8 7 6 5 4 3 2 1

Printed in the United States of America

To Nadia Gabrielle Gonzalez—
with love from Grammie—
and
Nancy Westall—
for a lifetime of friendship.

Now, Lord, you know that I take this wife of mine not because of lust, but for a noble purpose.

Call down your mercy on me and on her, and allow us to live together to a happy old age.

—Tobit 8:7

Chapter One

"I'm a fool," Matthew Sterling whispered under his breath. He could not understand what had made him agree to operate in his own backyard. He refused to think of it as a challenge, because it wasn't. Try as he could, he couldn't come up with a plausible explanation.

Maybe it had something to do with the woman sitting by herself at a small, round table in the dimly-lit supper club. He had spent the past two days watching her, and she had spent the past two days waiting for him.

Rising smoke from the thin, fragrant cigar in a marble ashtray lingered in his nostrils, but he made no attempt to pick it up. Watching the dark, slender woman was much more pleasurable.

He knew why Eve Blackwell had flown to Mexico City and checked into his hotel, but he wondered if she knew that she was to become an actress in a much more complicated plot than the one which involved her abducted son and ex-husband.

* * *

It began with Harry Blackwell's unexpected visit to Lubbock, Texas. Matt had escorted Harry out of his parents' home, his face a glowering mask of rage. He could hardly wait to confront him as to why he had left his shadowy, gray world in Virginia for West Texas.

"What the hell do you think you're doing, coming to my folks' place?" he'd questioned Harry. "*I* came here to become godfather of my sister's daughter, and, whatever your reason for invading my privacy, I don't intend to engage in any dialogue about undercover intelligence operations."

Harry Blackwell's impassive expression did not change as he endured Matt's tongue-lashing. An eerie silence surrounded them as he took a deep breath of dry Texas air. Thrusting both hands into the pockets of his trousers, he said quietly, "I need you."

"Forget it, Blackwell," Matt retorted. He bit the tip off of a thin cigar and leaned back against the side of a barn. The sound of a match against the wood was angry, mirroring his mood. As he cupped his hands around the flaring flame the tobacco caught, and the fragrant smell mingled with the sweet aroma of freshly cut hay.

"Dammit, Sterling," Harry countered. "I wouldn't have come here if I didn't need you, and you know it," he continued in a pleading tone Matt had never heard before.

Matt shook his head. "I'm out of it. Finished." The cigar was clamped tightly between straight white teeth. The sun setting behind the flat landscape fired a pair of golden eyes in a sun-browned face that stared out at land that had belonged to Sterlings for more than one hundred years.

"I've bought some land," he continued in a soft tone. "I've decided to set up a horse farm."

Harry took several steps, then waited for Matt to follow him. Turning, he glanced over his shoulder. "This one is for *me.*"

Matt stared at the tall, gray-haired man who had provided him with the means for amassing a small fortune.

The money he had earned bought him a luxury hotel in Mexico City and the six-hundred acre ranch in New Mexico. He wanted to be known as Matthew Sterling, horse breeder, not as an independent operative for individuals who paid generously for his special skills.

Harry's dark gaze held his. "This one is different. It involves my niece and . . ."

Matt flicked an ash off the cigar and placed a booted foot over the dying ember. "Your niece and who else?" he questioned when Harry did not complete his statement.

"Alejandro Delgado."

He whistled softly under his breath. He knew there would be a catch. Delgado he knew about. Blackwell's niece was another matter. "What's the connection?"

This time when Harry began walking, Matt fell in step beside him. "Delgado is her ex-husband. They were divorced early last year. Six months ago he snatched their son and took him back to Mexico."

Matt arched an eyebrow. "It should be easy for you to get the child back."

"I want the child *and* Delgado. We have to stop him— *now*."

"Have you uncovered his contact on this end?"

Harry shook his head. "For starters, we've only identified someone at The Metropolitan Museum of Art in New York who may have been in on the theft of the tapestries; but he's only a small fish in this pond. What we want is Delgado's contact with the Costa Rican rebels. Stolen artifacts are one thing. Using the proceeds from the thefts to purchase weapons stolen from U.S. military installations in order to finance a private army is another matter. I want you to get to Delgado, interrogate him about the art thefts and the gun smuggling, and get Eve's son back to the States."

"How did your niece get involved with Delgado?"

Harry kept his gaze on the ground. Lack of rain had burned the grass, leaving a layer of dust which seemed to settle onto everything. "She married him before we fingered him as the mastermind, and the money behind the rebels."

"Did she know about his double life?"

Again, Harry shook his head. "I doubt it. The man's too wily to trust a woman, even his wife. It was infidelity that destroyed their marriage."

"His or hers?" Elegant, controlled Harry Blackwell muttered a savage expletive. "All right," Matt conceded. "Delgado wasn't content to just sleep in his own bed, so he tried a few others," he offered as an apology. "How old is the boy?"

"Three."

The two men continued walking in silence, both lost in their private thoughts. Harry was an even six feet in height, but he still had to look up at Matthew Sterling. The man was tall and muscular and possessed uncanny strength, yet moved with the stealth of a large cat. He smiled. He could hear him thinking. Matt was not only good; he was the best man Harry had ever utilized in the twenty-five years he had worked for the bureau.

"How would I pull this off?" Matt asked.

"As Mateo Arroyo, you have no problem establishing a cover in Mexico. The only problem you may encounter is convincing Eve to marry you."

Matt stared at the other man, complete surprise freezing his features. His luminous eyes widened in astonishment seconds before he flung his half-smoked cigar to the ground. Walking over to the burning ember, he ground the heel of his boot on the cigar and into the rain-starved soil. One spark could send a raging inferno across the dry Texas plains, destroying everything in its path.

"Stuff it, Blackwell!"

"You don't have to remain married," Harry said to Matt's broad back. "After you snare Delgado and get my grandnephew back you can annul the marriage."

Matt spun around on his heel. "What do I get? Your

niece gets her kid back, and you get a smart-ass who has been thumbing his nose at the United States for years. Do you actually think waving your niece in front of me as a perk will get me to change my mind?''

Harry closed the distance between them. "Touch my niece and I'll blow your cover." The threat was cold and deadly.

Reaching out, Matt grabbed the front of Harry's shirt and lifted him off his feet. "Don't ever threaten me, Blackwell," he warned from between his teeth. He shook him like a small child before releasing him. "Now get off my folks' land, and forget who I am."

You can annul the marriage.
The statement haunted Matt. Harry gave him time to cool off and, rather than pay him another visit, he called. The call had come through his private line at the hotel, and he knew Harry had had him under surveillance. He hadn't been at El Moro for more than thirty minutes before the call came in, and Matt found himself agreeing before he reconsidered the consequences.

The black and white photograph of Eve Blackwell had been delivered to the hotel three days before his arrival, and the large, serene eyes of the woman appeared to leap off the paper and torment him with something he was unable to identify.

Motioning to a waiter standing near his table, Matt whispered instructions to the man, handing him a bill. The waiter surreptitiously pocketed the money, nodding.

He glanced over at Eve Blackwell, then stood up and left the room.

Eve was certain the waiter could hear her sigh of relief as she followed him to an elevator. She was to have met Matthew Sterling two days before, and her patience had worn thin, along with the short fuse on her temper. She had been ready to give him one more day before calling her uncle and reading him the riot act for her futile trip to Mexico City.

Stepping into the elevator, she retreated to a far wall. There was a slight fluttering in the pit of her stomach at the swift ascent to the top of the towering structure. The feeling was the same one she felt whenever a jet picked up speed before it was airborne. She hadn't conquered her fear of flying, but she had taken a giant step when boarding the plane in New Orleans for her connecting flight to Mexico. Only Harry Blackwell knew why she was taking the trip. She couldn't afford to trust anyone else.

The elevator doors opened and Eve stepped out into a room enclosed by walls made entirely of glass and allowing for a panoramic view of the beautiful city. This suite was nothing like the one she had checked into.

"Breathtaking, isn't it, Miss Blackwell?"

Eve turned and stared up at the tall man who had spoken. She nodded rather than trusting herself to speak because she was totally unprepared to interact with this flesh and blood man she assumed was Matthew Sterling.

Looking at him reminded her of black and brown velvet with warm, sparkling citrines. The blackness of his long, wavy hair and mustache, the sun-browned darkness of his skin, and the strange golden eyes, all stirred a ripple of uneasiness.

He's a cheetah, she mused, recalling the story her uncle had related to her of Matthew Sterling. There was no doubt Uncle Harry had told her the truth. This man was a large, powerful, dangerous, male predator.

"Eve Blackwell," she said in a remarkably calm voice, extending her hand and smiling.

Matt decided he liked her. She was direct and breathtakingly beautiful. She claimed the slimness and the grace of the cats the Egyptians worshipped and immortalized in their hieroglyphics.

"Matthew Sterling, Miss Blackwell," he said, introducing himself as he took her small hand, his thumb caressing the soft flesh over her knuckles. As he lowered his head, his lips replaced his thumb, and he tightened his grip the instant he felt her attempting to extract her fingers.

His head came up slowly. "Have you had dinner, Miss Blackwell?" Gold-green eyes met and captured a pair so dark, so black, that he couldn't see into their depths.

"I'm not hungry." Eve's reply was soft, calm.

Matt released her hand. "The lady and I will dine here tonight, Esteban," he informed the waiter lingering in the elevator. Esteban pushed a button and the doors closed.

"I said I wasn't hungry," Eve insisted between her teeth.

"Make yourself comfortable, Miss Blackwell. You and I have a great deal to talk about, and I make it a rule never to discuss *business* before I dine."

Eve's black eyes narrowed and she swallowed back an angry retort. She had come to Mexico to talk to this man about getting her son back, not socialize. As it was, she had wasted two days waiting for him to contact her.

"You've been in Mexico for more than forty-eight hours. Another hour won't change things, Eve," Matt remarked glibly, reading her mind.

Her delicate jaw dropped. "You've kept me waiting!"

Matt's fingers grasped her elbow firmly as he led her over to a sofa and eased her down to sit beside him. "Don't act so put out. You'd wait until hell freezes over if it meant getting your son back."

Eve went rigid, her gaze sweeping over his face. Thick black eyebrows curved dramatically over his large eyes. How oddly beautiful they were. Matthew Sterling's eyes were a dark jade green ringed in amber-brown, and glowed with a wild intensity that reminded her of a jungle cat's.

Pressing her back to the plump cushion, she nodded. "You're right," she admitted. "I'd wait forever to get my son back."

It was Matt's turn to nod. He hadn't realized he had

been holding his breath as he examined the narrow, delicate, face of Eve Blackwell. Her luminous eyes, the color of black velvet, tilted upward in an exotic slant; her hair, equally black, was cut short and worn in a curly natural. Soft, glossy curls hugged her small, round head like a cap. Her nose was short and straight, and her mouth was full and lush in a face the color of golden oak dusted with a fine sprinkling of soot. He wondered what bloodlines she claimed, other than her obvious African heritage, that made her the most exquisitely exotic woman he had ever met.

The soft chiming of a telephone shattered the pregnant silence, and Matt excused himself as he rose to answer it. The doors to the elevator opened again and Esteban reappeared, pushing a serving cart.

Matt picked up the telephone on a table behind the sofa, listening intently to the voice coming through the receiver while watching Eve. She left the sofa and walked over to look through the glass, where millions of lights sparkled over the city.

He stared openly at her with a naked hunger she would have no trouble interpreting as lust. Her face was as perfect as her body. Having given birth to a child hadn't caused her breasts or buttocks to sag, as with some women. The fabric of the black, silk, wrap dress caressing her slender body confirmed his assumption.

Eve turned, her attention directed at the tall figure dressed in a raw silk, tan jacket over a white shirt, open at the throat, and a pair of black, tailored slacks and imported slip-ons. This costume of modern elegance did not camouflage the primitive, savage ruthlessness which followed Matthew Sterling's reputation as a modern day soldier of fortune.

Her uncle insisted that was what Matthew Sterling liked to call himself, while others labeled him a mercenary or bounty hunter. It didn't matter to her what he was; she wanted him to find the son her ex-husband had kidnapped and hidden away somewhere in Mexico.

She felt some of her tension easing as she walked around the large room. The sofa and armchairs of twisted, natural rattan were covered with plump cushions in beige cotton. The tables were a matching rattan with beveled glass tops. Each piece in the expansive suite had been selected to conform with the country's tropical climate; the area resembled a rain forest, with leafy green palm and banana trees in large straw planters.

The man Matt had addressed as Esteban completed setting a table in an alcove with silver, china, stemware, and several covered serving dishes.

Matt replaced the telephone receiver on the cradle and Esteban nodded to him. "Dinner is ready, Señor Arroyo," he announced softly. "Would you like anything else?"

"No thank you. *Mil gracias,* Esteban."

"De buen agrado, Señor Arroyo." He inclined his head, then made his way over to the elevator.

Crossing the room, Matt extended his hand to Eve. She took the proffered hand and he escorted her to the table in the alcove.

Chapter Two

Matt seated Eve, lingering over her head. She was like the perfume she wore—alluring. Smiling, he spread a pristine linen napkin over her lap. Straightening, he walked around the table, taking a matching chair opposite her.

"Do you speak Spanish?" he asked, watching her intently.

Eve returned his stare. "A little. Alex hired a Spanish-speaking nanny for our son, and I managed to pick up a few words and phrases."

Matt frowned at her reply, his mouth tightening noticeably under his mustache. He had to make certain she knew enough of the language if they were to travel throughout Mexico together. His frown disappeared as quickly as it had formed. He filled two crystal goblets with a pale yellow liquid from a chilled pitcher and handed her one.

The overhead light cast a golden glow over her obsidian head, and for the first time he detected a liberal streaking of silver in the raven-black curls. Eve was graying prematurely. He knew her to be only thirty-four. He was thirty-eight, and his hair was still free of any traces of gray. Not that he hadn't earned them. The escapades he had been involved in were enough to turn his hair white *and* give him cardiac arrest.

He took a sip of his drink, then leaned back on his chair, flashing a wide grin. His teeth appeared white against the thickness of the black mustache.

"I suppose you know most of the curses."

"But of course."

Eve gave him a warm, open smile for the first time. Seeing her slanting eyes crinkle and her lush mouth soften delighted him as he leaned closer.

"Did you learn the curses from the nanny?"

She wrinkled her delicate nose. "I learned the curses at a prison that was licensed as a school."

"I take it you attended a boarding school?"

Her jaw hardened and the brilliant lights in her eyes faded. "It was more like a prison than an exclusive school for girls."

"How many years did you attend?"

She gave him a cold stare. "Twelve. My stepmother insisted that the school was what I needed to turn me into a respectable lady. She claimed I embarrassed her because I preferred baseball games to high tea, wrestling matches to ballet, and Aretha Franklin to Leontyne Price."

"I assume you and your stepmother did not get along too well," Matt concluded, concealing a smile behind his napkin.

Eve speared a small portion of cold fish salad, shaking her head. "She despised me, and the feeling was mutual." Her gaze was fixed on her plate. "My father married Janice less than a year after my mother's death, and she played her role well as the adoring stepmother until she had to compete with me for my father's attention."

Her head came up slowly, and she stared across the table at Matt. "My mother developed multiple sclerosis within three months of my birth, and her health deteriorated rapidly over the next five years. I didn't know it until years later, but my father and Janice were having an affair during this time. She waited until my mother died, then legalized her claim on Floyd Blackwell.''

"What did your father say about her sending you away?"

"Nothing." The single word was flat, emotionless.

Matt leaned forward. "I can't believe he said nothing."

Eve swallowed painfully, meeting his topaz gaze. She was angry with herself because she'd revealed more than she wanted to. "I came to Mexico to ask you whether you would accept payment to return my son to me, not to give you a familial overview."

Resting an elbow on the table, Matt glared at her. "Miss Blackwell, you need me." His voice was deceptively soft. "I want you to try to remember that, because I sure as hell don't need you, or the pittance you're prepared to offer me."

She felt her face burn. Pittance. What she was going to offer Matthew Sterling was all of the money she had left. She had spent practically all of the proceeds from the sale of her Washington, D.C., gift shop hiring investigators to find her son and bring him back to the States, and here this pompous pig was calling her offer a pittance even before he heard the amount.

"Maybe to a man of your means twenty-five thousand dollars would seem like a pittance, but I've heard stories where people were hired to eliminate others for a lot less," she snapped at him.

Matt hadn't missed her slender fingers tightening on the handle of her knife. He smiled.

"Twenty-five thousand dollars would just be enough to cover the bounty on one of my ears, Miss Blackwell," he crooned, and the drawl of West Texas was distinctly noticeable in his speech pattern for the first time that night. "The word is that the last time I left Colombia the price for my ears was up to fifty thousand." He placed a large brown hand over his heart in a gesture of remorse. "So you wound me, lovely lady, with your paltry offering."

Her knife clattered noisily to the delicate china plate. Eve stood up, not knowing whether her quaking knees would support her body. It was over before it began. This man was her only hope; her last hope. Her anger did not begin with Matthew Sterling, but with her uncle. He had lied to her.

"Sit down," Matt ordered.

"No!" she shouted.

Her rage shocked him. He hadn't expected the outburst. In the two days he'd sat watching, Eve Blackwell revealed an elegant, composed woman. But then, he had to remind himself that she was related to Harry, and he had witnessed the man's violent temper on several occasions.

"Please sit down, Eve." His tone was soft, conciliatory. "There's no need to get hysterical."

"I'm not hysterical, Mr. Sterling. I'm just mad as hell at myself. I've been had. By you and my uncle."

Matt rose to his feet. "I'll look for your son, Eve."

"How much?" she demanded.

He frowned in confusion. "What?"

"I said, how much do you want?"

"I don't want your money."

A frown creased her smooth forehead. "What do you want?"

"I want you to marry me," he stated in a calm voice, surprising himself after he said it.

Eve blinked several times, shaking her head. Her mouth dropped open, but no sound came out. Her heart pounded uncontrollably, and she prayed she wouldn't faint. A jumble of confused thoughts and feelings assailed her as she played his offer over and over in her head. He didn't want her money, but he did want her to marry him.

Sinking down to the chair, she gripped the edge of the table to steady herself. *I want you to marry me.* There was no mistaking his proposal.

"I need my son, not another husband," she insisted quietly, forcing the words from the back of her throat.

Matt pressed his attack. "Marry me or there's no deal."

She ran a trembling hand over her high, rounded forehead. "Why—why can't you look for my son without me becoming your wife?"

Matt reclaimed his own chair. He hated to deceive her, but he wasn't given a choice. He'd promised Harry that he'd rescue his grandnephew and deliver Alejandro Delgado, and that could only become a reality with Eve Blackwell as the lure.

"You and probably three other people in Mexico are the only ones who know what I do when I'm not executing my duties as owner of El Moro," he began solemnly. "I'm known in Mexico as Mateo Arroyo, not Matthew Sterling."

Her confusion intensified. "Which are you? Sterling or Arroyo?"

He smiled. "Both. My father is an African-American from Texas. My dad's family trace their roots back to Texas when it was still a republic, and also to southern Louisiana. I claim my Mexican heritage from my mother. She came to Texas to attend college, met my father, married him, and stayed in the States. And because my mother is an Arroyo, I'm Mateo Sterling de Arroyo in Mexico."

Pulling her lower lip between her teeth, Eve closed her eyes, trying to comprehend what she was hearing. Matt did not want her money, yet he was willing to look for her son, but only if she married him.

Opening her eyes, she stared across the table at him. He returned her steady gaze, a slight smile playing around his mustached mouth. He seemed very pleased with himself. He knew she needed him, and he was content to play a cat and mouse game with her.

"So, if I marry you, I'll be known as Eve Arroyo?" Matt nodded. "And after my son is returned to me, what happens to us?"

He stared over her head before replying. "After I return to Mexico City I'll file for an annulment."

Eve wavered again, trying to comprehend what Matt told her. "Why marry at all?"

"I'm a respectable Mexican businessman with a number of respectable Mexican relatives. If you travel with me, how do I introduce you? Do I say, 'Please meet Eve Blackwell. She's keeping me *occupied* while I'm on holiday?'" He noted her downcast gaze.

She glanced up at him from lowered lids. "I thought I wouldn't be involved when you began your search for my son, that's all. My uncle told me you usually work alone."

"I do," he confessed. "But Alejandro Delgado is a former high profile government official and a member of Mexico's privileged social elite. I'm certain we'll receive more than our share of invitations to these soirées so that everyone can catch a glimpse of Delgado's ex-wife and her new husband, once the word gets out that we've married."

He didn't tell her of his need for a cover once he began his assignment for Harry Blackwell. Eve would be the perfect foil, because it would be the first time he had ever operated within his mother's native country.

He would be above suspicion whenever he visited friends and relatives if accompanied by a beautiful American wife. He would be permitted one, and only one, opportunity to execute and complete his mission; to not complete it meant not only failure, but death.

Eve watched numerous expressions cross the lean, dark face. Matt didn't appear to be pleased with the idea of marrying her. Well, it wasn't as if she wanted it any more than he did. Being married to Alex had given her her fill of being some man's wife, and she did not look forward to repeating vows with another one—even if it was temporary.

"Can't we pretend to be married?" she questioned.

A frown settled between Matt's eyes. "No," he retorted. "Any pretense would very easily be discovered with a single telephone call from Delgado." Propping his elbows on the table and lacing his fingers together, he glared at her. "No marriage, no deal."

Running a slender finger down the side of the icy goblet, Eve shrugged her shoulders in resignation. "It looks as if I'm not allowed any options, am I? You're saying that if I don't marry you or pretend I'm your wife, then Alex will be alerted as to why I'm here. Or better yet, he will wonder about your association with me, and perhaps make *another* telephone call to initiate an investigation of exactly who Mateo Sterling de Arroyo is."

Her delicate jaw tightened, and she tilted her chin as her dark eyes filled with determination. "You've got yourself a deal, Mr. Sterling. Or should I say Señor Arroyo?"

Chapter Three

Matt raised his glass in a half-salute. He wasn't going to pat himself on the back for achieving a quick victory in convincing Eve to marry him. Instinctively, he knew she would agree to anything to get her son back. Harry Blackwell had underestimated his niece.

"If we're to be married you'd better get used to calling me Matt or Mateo, and forget the formalities."

Eve swallowed her rising apprehension. The enormity of what she had agreed to rendered her speechless. How was she to pull off the farce that she and Matt were in love enough to marry? She wondered how many other times he had done something like this.

"How many other women have you married to complete an assignment?" she questioned, finding her voice.

The hooded lids and the thick, black mustache concealed the amusement in Matt's eyes and the smile curving his mouth. "You're the first, Eve. I've never been married before." Turning the full force of his golden gaze on her surprised features, he stared at the lushness of her parted lips.

A slight frown creased her smooth forehead. "If you don't want any money, then what is it you're hoping to get out of this?"

"I owe Harry Blackwell, and this will be my way of repaying him," he explained softly, his Southern drawl more pronounced than before.

He did not disclose the sum of money her uncle had offered him on behalf of the United States government. The payment he would earn from this assignment and the proceeds from the expected sale of El Moro would afford him financial independence for the remainder of his life.

If you live to enjoy it, a silent voice taunted him. A chill shook Matt's body, numbing his brain. *Fear.* An emotion he had not felt in years made the blood run cold in his veins.

It had been a rescue mission in the jungles of El Salvador. The fear had been like a breath of air—he imagined it, felt it, but he couldn't see it until he lay close to death. It had swallowed him whole like the blackness of the jungle night.

A gasping, choking sound shook Matt from his reverie and brought him to his feet. Tears flooded Eve's eyes as she held a hand over her mouth.

He was beside her in seconds, pressing his napkin to her mouth. The heel of one hand thumped her back. She clung to him, and would've fallen if he hadn't supported her sagging body.

"What—what did you put in that drink?" she gasped breathlessly.

If he hadn't been so turned on by the soft body molded to his, he would've burst into laughter. His fingers cradled the curve of her waist as the heat and feminine sweetness of her hair and skin created a quiet storm in his loins. Releasing her and stepping back, he watched Eve blot the moisture staining her cheeks.

"Tequila." He flashed her an irresistibly devastating grin. "Welcome to Mexico."

She sniffled loudly, her eyes crinkling in a smile. "I can do without the welcoming committee."

Matt held out her chair, seating her again, and for the second time that evening he lingered over her head. No wonder Harry had threatened him. Eve Blackwell was sexy, and he suspected she didn't know just how sexy she was.

She touched the corners of her eyes with her fingertips. "Tequila and chili definitely top my list of do not sample."

He smiled at her, taking his seat. "I must admit they take some getting used to."

"Count me out," she countered with a grimace.

Eve examined the contents of her plate, and only after recognizing most of the vegetables and different varieties of fish did she begin to eat. She hadn't realized how hungry she had been until she ate most of what was on her plate.

It had been a long time, too long, since she was able to eat without food sticking in her constricted throat. Most times she could only swallow a few forkfuls before feeling full. Falling asleep and sleeping undisturbed throughout the night were as foreign to her as nuclear physics, too.

The insomnia and her lack of appetite had begun with the realization that Alejandro Delgado was not going to return the little boy she had dropped off to spend two days with him. What was to have been a festive Halloween weekend celebration became a living nightmare when she waited Sunday evening for Chris's return.

The calls to her ex-husband's residence, the Mexican consulate, the Washington, D.C., police, then finally the F.B.I., manifested the fear she'd carried from the moment the divorce court judge granted her sole custody of Christopher Delgado, while permitting Alejandro Delgado liberal visitation privileges.

Her vocal protests and those of her attorney had prompted a stern warning from the judge that they could be held in contempt. He then rendered his decision to permit Alejandro Delgado the right to visit with his two-year-old son two weekends each month, and a full month during the summer school recess.

The feral look in Alex's eyes should've warned Eve that she would pay for initiating the divorce proceedings. She had been aware of her ex-husband's vindictiveness, but she never thought he would kidnap his own child just to get back at her.

She glanced across the table at Matthew Sterling. His impassive expression revealed nothing. It was as if his offer to marry was something he did often, even though he confessed that he had never married.

She wondered just what it was he owed her uncle. She shrugged a slender shoulder. Whatever it was it no longer mattered, because she was willing to enter into a pact with anyone if it meant getting her son back.

"When do you want to marry?" she asked, breaking the comfortable silence.

He put down his fork. "We'll marry the end of next month."

"Next month!" The two words exploded from her. "I can't afford to wait a month."

Matt pressed his large, well-groomed hands together, bringing them to his chin. Only the flickering of the gold glints in his eyes revealed the foreign emotions attacking him. Eve Blackwell was the first woman in a very long time who elicited a rush of desire in him, because she was so female. She was the most sensual female he had ever encountered.

"You don't have a choice, Eve," he replied in a soft, even tone. "If we're to pull this off it must look good. We'll announce our engagement, accept whatever social invitations are extended to us, and then we'll marry."

She couldn't wait another month. As it was, her life was in limbo. It was now the last week in March, and each time a page on the calendar revealed a new month she weakened a little more. The hope which had burned so brightly within her diminished with each day she was separated from her child.

There were times when she wondered if Chris remembered her. Would he recognize her face, the nursery rhymes she used to sing to him, and their quiet times together when she read him his favorite books?

Eve captured Matt's golden gaze, unshed moisture glistening in her eyes. "I can't wait a month, Matt. I don't know if I can survive waiting—"

"You can, and you will," he countered firmly, interrupting her. "I will get your son back. I give you my word on that."

His mouth tightened as he berated himself. He didn't know what made him promise Eve that he would return her son to her. His usual statement was that he would *look* for the missing person.

"What if we say that we met in the States some time ago, and I came to Mexico City to marry you?" she said, hoping to get him to change his mind about waiting a month.

Matt shook his head slowly. "I'm sorry. Either you agree to do it my way or you can go back to the States and continue to give your money away to people who don't have the remotest idea how to find your child. And even if they do manage to locate him, how do you think they'll get him away from Delgado? I'm certain I don't have to tell you of the man's clout here in Mexico."

She covered her face with her hands. She was so close, yet so far; she was certain Chris was hidden away somewhere in Mexico, and she still couldn't claim him.

Matt moved fluidly from his chair and pulled Eve up and into the circle of his embrace. He registered the fragility of her slender body and the slight trembling she was unable to control. She floated against him, her curves molded to the solid hardness of his larger body.

"It's going to be all right," he stated quietly, confidently. "A month is nothing compared to the length of time you'll have with your child once you get him back."

Eve melted into Matthew Sterling's massive bulk, her fingers gripping the rock-hard biceps straining against the delicate fabric of his silk jacket. "It's been so long," she breathed into his chest, "that I'm afraid I won't ever see Chris again."

He curved a forefinger under her chin, raising her face to his, inhaling sharply. His gaze moved slowly over her features. Eve's black velvet eyes were filled with tears and fears, while her full, lush lips were compressed with anxiety.

"I need you to trust me," he said, exhaling and relieving the tightness in his chest. "And that means you can't question what I do or say."

Closing her eyes, she nodded, unaware of the vulnerability softening her delicate features. "I'll trust you, Matt."

She opened her eyes and he smiled. A lone tear flowed down her satiny, dark brown cheek. Lowering his head, Matt pressed his lips to her jaw, catching the salty moisture on his tongue.

"It's going to be all right, Eve."

She heard the deep, crooning voice, inhaled his masculine aftershave and the lingering aroma of tobacco and registered the unyielding power in Matthew Sterling's body, feeling her despair easing. Something strange and unknown communicated itself, telling her that she would get her child back.

"I believe you," she whispered against his hot throat.

She was tired, too numbed, to argue and fight with him. She felt as if she'd been arguing for years. A whirlwind courtship and marriage to a stranger had taken its toll, and had drained her of her rebellious spirit.

After Alex abducted Chris, Eve had almost lost the will to survive. But survive she did, because the drive to survive was as strong as the love for the child she longed to hold to her breast. She could not and would not give up.

Matt's left hand dropped while his right rested against the small of her back, his fingers caressing the curves along her rib cage and spine. "It's time I got you settled in."

She tilted her chin. "Where are we going?"

"*You* are going to stay with a cousin of mine. You'll live with her family until we marry. After that we'll travel south."

Applying the slightest pressure to her back, he steered Eve toward the elevator, the strength and warmth of his hand searing her through the fragile fabric of her dress. He did not remove his hand once they stepped into the elevator, and the brass doors closed behind them. His long fingers lingered loosely around her waist but she pulled away, moving out of his reach. The muted overhead light shadowed his eyes, but not the tensing of his jaw.

"We'll only have a month to get used to each other," he stated in a low, ominous tone. Shifting, he stood behind Eve, and his moist breath feathered over the back of her neck while his fingers curved over her shoulders. "It will be for real," he whispered in her ear. "And that means we'll have to look like the loving couple. I expect you to respond to my kisses and caresses when we're in public, and not cringe like a frightened virgin every time I touch you. And when we visit relatives, be prepared to share a bed with me." Reaching over, he pushed a button on the panel and the elevator began its descent.

Eve turned and stared up at him. Heat suffused her high cheekbones and darkened her eyes. "You forget why I'm here. I *want* my son. You won't have to worry about me playing the part of the adoring wife. I've had more than my share of experience."

Matt slapped a button on the panel, stopping the elevator. "If that's the case, then kiss me," he challenged in a hoarse whisper.

Her breath faltered before rushing through her parted lips. She watched Matt lounge lazily against a wall. Why was it she felt degraded having to please him because he had paid her? And he *had* paid her, once he agreed to look for Christopher. She was expected to perform sexual favors in return, only he sought to legitimize everything by marrying her.

"Please don't make me repeat myself," he warned in a soft, no-nonsense voice.

Eve struggled to contain her temper. She hated herself for the position she had been forced into. Matt didn't believe she could play out her role as the loving wife.

Her life had become a rerun. She could not count the times she and Alex appeared in public as the genteel couple after they'd traded vicious, scathing barbs only hours before.

Moving closer to Matt, she felt the searing heat from his large body as his fingers brushed over her shoulders, then slid slowly down over her breasts. Everywhere they touched they burned her flesh, and she closed her eyes rather than allow him to see her reaction. His thumbs swept over her breasts, and the nipples strained and swelled against the lace of a matching black silk slip. She missed his smug grin. He knew she was not wearing a bra.

His mustached mouth pressed against the sensitive flesh of her exposed neck, leaving a trail of moisture as his tongue tasted her ear before moving on to the hollow of her throat.

"Good," he moaned, his hands slipping down to her hips and bringing her thighs to his. "You and I are going to get along just fine."

Eve thought she was prepared. Matt's eyes blazed with liquid fire seconds before his mouth claimed hers. His left hand held her hips prisoner while the right moved up, searching for the pulse along the column of her neck which began to flutter erratically under his callused fingertips. Her lips parted and she permitted him to inhale the moistness of her breath with his own. Her heart pounded wildly in her chest and she pressed closer, molding every curve of her body to his. His searching tongue extinguished the very last fragile thread of resistance, and her dormant fire raged out of control when her arms swept from his shoulders to wind around his neck.

Matt was shocked at her response, and his own. The pleasure he'd derived from Eve's mouth was euphoric. Beneath the dark, fragile beauty, Eve Blackwell was an inferno.

Raising his head, he stared down at her. Her eyes were large pools of polished onyx, while her mouth was pouty and swollen from his passionate kiss.

He cupped the back of her head in one hand, smiling. She was perfect. "We're going to make a helluva couple, Eve Blackwell. No one will suspect that we've just met."

Releasing her, he reset the button on the panel, and the elevator continued its descent.

Eve glanced up at his profile. He appeared totally unaffected by what had just occurred between them, while her heart pumped wildly against her rib cage. Matthew Sterling was too virile, too potent, to shrug off or ignore as a man, and he was the man she had to pretend she loved enough to marry.

It's only temporary, a silent voice reminded her. They would marry, find her son and bring him back to the States. Then they would go their separate ways, to live their separate lives.

The elevator stopped at the hotel's lower level and Matt grasped her hand firmly and led her down a narrow corridor and out to an underground parking area. "Your clothes have been packed and are in the trunk of my car," he informed her. "You can't stay here with me."

Eve took quick steps to keep up with his longer strides. "Why can't I stay here?"

"It's not proper. Some of my very conservative family members will assume that I've been sleeping with you, and that our hasty marriage indicates that you're *embarazada.*"

"Embar—"

"Pregnant, Eve." He glanced down at her. "What are you smirking about?"

"Somehow I didn't think you would be that concerned about propriety."

He pushed open a door, and they stepped out into the warm night. "What did your uncle tell you about me?"

"Not much," she confessed.

"Sure, I bet."

She studied his bold profile. "Do you really care, Matt?"

He stopped suddenly, facing her. "Yes!" His gaze caught and held hers in the brightly lit parking lot. "I care very much," he added in a softer tone.

She touched his arm. "He said you're the best. He also said there is something wild, almost savage, within you that will not permit you to acknowledge fear. And it is this lack of fear that makes you a winner, over and over again."

Matt caught her wrist in a firm grip. "Harry Blackwell is a liar. He thinks he knows me. No one will ever know the real Matthew Sterling."

Eve withdrew from him without moving. Whatever closeness they had shared vanished quickly.

Chapter Four

There was an uncomfortable silence as Matt drove through the crowded streets of nighttime Mexico City. Twenty minutes later the streetlights dimmed and the traffic thinned as he maneuvered his spacious Lincoln sedan along a winding mountain road.

At the higher elevation Eve barely made out the sparkling lights of the city that reminded her of New York City. Mexico City refused to go to sleep, although the blazing sun had long sunk behind the mountains, ending the day.

She tried to, but could not ignore the man sitting beside her. Matthew Sterling's double life intrigued her, and she wondered how he was able to shed his everyday persona once he went undercover.

There was so much she wanted to know about him and so much she didn't need to know about him.

She chanced a surreptitious glance at him. Again, she encountered his impassive expression, wondering what was going on behind his mask of stone. How was she to pretend she loved this enigmatic man? Would she feel comfortable enough to spend a month with him, then feign passion after they married?

A month! The time Matt had set for their courtship and length of engagement startled her into awareness. "I'm scheduled to return to Virginia on Thursday," she informed him quietly.

"That's impossible," he replied quickly, concentrating on the dark road in front of the automobile.

Eve felt a rush of heat in her face as she leaned forward, straining against the seatbelt restraint. "I have things to take care of—"

"Your uncle can take care of your *things,*" he countered, interrupting her.

"I need clothes," she insisted.

"I'll buy you what you'll need. We'll go shopping tomorrow."

Easing back against the leather seat, she closed her eyes in resignation. It was only then that she realized her life was not her own to plan or control. It was as if she had surrendered her future to Matthew Sterling, a stranger, who would dictate every phase of her existence until she was reunited with her only child.

An emotion swept through her, and she recognized it as rebellion. She had always felt the need to rebel—against her father and stepmother for sending her to the boarding school, and against Alex for his blatant infidelity.

Alex had sought to absolve himself of guilt by blaming her for his infidelity. Every time he came home with the scent of another woman's perfume clinging to his clothes, Alex had reminded Eve that he couldn't make love to her after he'd witnessed the birth of their son; she found it impossible to comprehend that he was repulsed by his own wife's body though he slept with other women who had given birth to children.

She told Alex to seek professional help in overcoming his aversion to her body. He'd laughed, declaring there was nothing wrong with him, even though she'd threatened to leave him if he continued with his adulterous affairs. The threat became a reality when she moved out of their opulently decorated house and into a small apartment in Alexandria, Virginia. The day she moved, Alex was served with divorce papers.

"How did you meet your ex-husband?" Matt queried, breaking into her musings, and again reading her mind.

The dossier her uncle had forwarded to him revealed substantial details of her childhood. However, entries about the adult Eve Blackwell were sketchier. It was as if she had become more guarded, mysterious.

And, despite the information he'd gleaned on her, he wanted and *needed* to know more about her. If she were to become his wife, he had to be able to react to every facet of her personality. He had to know what she liked, didn't like, what frightened her, and whether he could trust her to not disclose his double life.

He had become involved with only one woman after he accepted an assignment in the past, and the distraction nearly cost him his life. A muscle in his lean jaw twitched noticeably. This was to be his last mission, and Eve Blackwell would be the last woman he would permit himself to become involved with as an independent agent for the U.S. government.

"I owned a gift shop in the D.C. area, and Alex would come in whenever he needed something," Eve began, her voice low and soothing in the cloaking darkness of the luxury sedan.

"What did he buy?" Matt questioned.

"Collectible figurines. Lladrós."

"Who did he buy them for?"

She smiled in the comforting darkness. "His mother."

Nodding, he filed away this information. "What else did you carry in your gift shop?"

"Fine china, crystal, silver, and estate jewelry. Most of the business was generated through our bridal registry."

"How long did you know Delgado before you became involved with him?"

Her head spun around, and she stared at Matt's profile. He looked as if he had been carved out of granite, the distinctive features of his Mexican ancestry quite obvious. The jutting of his bold, aquiline nose, high cheekbones, and strong, square jaw complemented the darkness of his skin and heavy, wavy hair.

"What do you mean by *involved*?"

He glanced to his right, his sensitive hearing picking up the increase in her respiration. "Sleep with him," he said before directing his attention back to the road.

Eve bit down hard on her lower lip, feeling the heat stealing up her neck to her face. She'd tried for years to control the reaction. She was grateful for her dark coloring, because a lighter hue would have revealed her uneasiness immediately.

Taking a deep breath, she said, "Alex came into the shop for almost a year before he asked me out."

A small smile softened Matt's mouth under his mustache. "How soon after he *asked you out* did you marry him?"

"A month." The two words were barely audible.

Throwing back his head, he roared with laughter. It was the sound of undeniable masculine triumph. "A month," he repeated in a high falsetto, mimicking her. "I can't wait a month, Matt." he continued. Glancing over at her averted face, he sobered. "It is apparent you couldn't wait to become Señora Alejandro Delgado."

He didn't know why, but he was annoyed that Eve would marry Delgado after dating him a month, while openly balking at his offer of marriage.

As a Sterling he exemplified stability. His family heritage claimed an important link in Texas and Louisiana history, with slaves, ex-slaves, and free people of color adding to its past and present; and with his recent purchase of land in New Mexico, where he intended to breed thoroughbreds, he would sink Sterling roots deep within another state.

"There's a big difference between meeting someone for the first time and agreeing to marry them," Eve argued. "And more importantly, to marry someone who earns his money the way you do," she continued, not caring whether he heard the censure in her voice.

His eyes burned amber liquid fire in the dimness of the car. Taking a deep breath, he said, "I don't ever want to hear you say that to me again for as long as we're connected to each other." His voice was soft *and* lethal. "Do I make myself clear?"

Her fury almost choked her. "Don't tell me what to say."

"Eve!"

The sound of her name exploding and vibrating in the automobile shocked both Matt and Eve, and there was a strained, uncomfortable silence.

Her anger dissolved into shock before old fears and uncertainties surfaced. Matt sounded exactly like Alex.

"Matt, please don't ever raise your voice to me again," she warned quietly.

He glanced up at the rearview mirror, signaled, and maneuvered off the road to an unpaved shoulder. Unbuckling his seatbelt, he pushed open the car door and stepped out into the blackness of the Mexican night. A sprinkling of stars, a slip of a last quarter moon, and the steady beam of the Lincoln's headlights provided the only illumination.

He walked around the car, opened the passenger side door, and in one motion unbuckled Eve's belt, eased her gently off the seat, and pulled her up close to his chest.

"Let's get something straight, Miss Blackwell, before we go another kilometer. Don't ever mention how I earn my living outside the States, and I won't yell at you again."

Matt's hold on her upper arms was loose enough for her to break, but for some foreign reason she wanted him to hold her. Despite her disastrous marriage she needed to feel a man's strong, protective arms around her. It had taken her a while to realize she had substituted Alex for her father.

However, that would not happen with Matt. He would become her husband in name only. There would be no promise of love, no passion, and no protection.

Leaning heavily against him, she nodded. "Okay."

Gathering her closer, he dropped a kiss on the top of her head. "Good. I hope this means that we understand each other."

Eve nodded again. "Yes."

They returned to the car and there was an unspoken agreement and a comfortable silence until Matt turned off the road. A large house, surrounded by outdoor lights, loomed in the distance.

"Is your cousin expecting us?" she asked him.

Matt drove into a driveway and turned off the engine. "No."

"But—"

"It's all right," he cut in. "Remember, you're my *novia*. My fiancée," he translated quickly.

She gave him a skeptical look, permitting him to help her from the car and escort her through a courtyard and loggia, and to the entrance of a two-story, Spanish Colonial style villa.

Towering cactus and piñon trees surrounded the pale adobe walls, and even in the velvet darkness of the night the structure's beauty was obvious.

"What's your cousin's name?" Eve queried, hoping Matt's relatives wouldn't resent her unplanned stay at their home.

"Alma Sterling-Navarro."

"Sterling?"

"Our fathers are brothers," he explained.

Ceiling fans turned slowly from a deep overhang of cypress in the loggia, while wrought iron lanterns attached to the adobe walls bathed Matt and Eve in a soft, flattering light as their gazes met and held. Night sounds shattered the stillness of the warm spring night. She inhaled the fragrance of the different flowers blooming and creeping up one wall near a massive, decoratively carved iron door.

"It begins *now*," Matt whispered.

A frown furrowed Eve's high, smooth forehead as a rush of unanswered questions attacked her. How could she have forgotten?

"What if your cousin asks about us? How we met? Shouldn't we at least get our stories together before we go in?"

He smiled down at her. "Don't worry so much. There's no need to rehearse a script. Just follow my lead." Reaching for her hand, he squeezed her fingers gently. "Ready?"

She hesitated, studying his shadowed features. "Let's do it." Her voice was steady and filled with newfound confidence.

Matt shifted a thick, black, arching eyebrow. He knew Eve Blackwell was ready. She was ready to play any role assigned her to hold Christopher Delgado in her arms again.

He pulled the chain to the clapper attached to a large bell beside the iron door. A dull peal echoed melodiously before fading. Unconsciously, Eve moved closer to his side, and his left arm went around her waist.

A massive, inner oaken door opened, spilling more light out onto the loggia. A slender young woman with chemically-straightened, chin length black hair and velvety dark brown skin peered at them through the elaborate swirls of iron.

"Matthew?"

"Please close your mouth, Alma, and open the door," Matt ordered in a teasing tone.

Alma unlocked the iron door, blinking rapidly. "I hardly recognized you without the beard," she continued in a Southern drawl reminiscent of Matt's. "You're beginning to look civilized, dear cousin."

Leaning over, Matt kissed Alma's cheek. "And hello to you, dear cousin," he teased.

Alma patted his lean jaw. "The mustache makes you look like a *bandido.*"

"I am a bandit, Alma. I steal the hearts of all beautiful women. And that includes you, *prima.*"

Matt shifted slightly and Alma noticed Eve for the first time. The shock at seeing her American cousin garnered all of her attention as her dark eyes now darted from Eve to Matt. "Have you stolen this one's heart?" she questioned in rapid Spanish.

His arm tightened around Eve's waist. "This is Eve, *mi novia.*"

Alma's eyes widened in surprise. "You're going to marry him?" she asked Eve, switching smoothly back to English.

Eve, smiling, peered up at Matt. "Yes, I am."

Alma crossed herself and rolled her eyes upward. "My prayers have been answered." Stepping aside, she motioned for them to enter the house. "Please come in."

Following Alma, Eve glanced up at a two-story skylighted atrium. A plaster, low relief above the archway was complemented by a tile wainscoting and floor, lending a Hispano-Moresque ambience to the area. Ebony Anglo-Indian armchairs and gray-blue upholstery on the sofa, lounge chairs, and several ottomans added to the eclectic furnishings.

Matt's left arm curved around her waist in a natural gesture of affection and she stiffened, feeling the bite of his strong fingers against her ribs. Inhaling deeply, she relaxed against his side.

"Alma, this is Eve Blackwell, my fiancée. Eve, Alma Navarro, my American cousin," he stated, introducing the two women.

Alma extended a hand, smiling. "Welcome to the family."

Eve took the proffered hand, returning the warm smile. "Thank you, Alma."

The other woman was about an inch shorter than Eve's

five foot, seven inches, and a loose-flowing red and gold caftan artfully concealed the roundness of her thickening waist and belly. Her haircut was simple yet sophisticated. Bangs were feathered over her forehead, while the blunt cut ends curved gently along her delicate jawline.

Alma's gold-brown eyes crinkled as her smile became a wide grin. "Matthew has chosen well. The two of you will have magnificent children."

Eve's smile faltered momentarily before it was back in place, while Matt's laughter rumbled deep in his chest, adding to her apprehension.

"Let us marry first before you start counting children. Speaking of children," he continued smoothly, "how are you feeling?"

Alma cradled her belly with both hands. "Much better. At least I don't have to spend all day in bed. Please make yourselves comfortable while I pull Carlos away from his paperwork long enough to share in your wonderful news," she said quickly, not pausing to take a breath.

Turning gracefully, the silk of the gold and red caftan sweeping around her bare feet, Alma made her way up a staircase with an assortment of Portuguese tile stair risers and an elaborately carved iron railing.

"Come, Eve," Matt urged softly. "Sit down and relax." He led her to the sofa, sitting and pulling her down beside him.

She moved closer to him as he draped an outstretched arm over the back of the sofa, her right hand reaching over and covering his right one. She studied his hand, finding it large, well-formed and well-groomed; and she knew his hands were no strangers to hard work, because his palms and fingertips were covered with thick calluses. They were large, strong hands that could probably bring a smaller man to his knees with one blow; large, strong hands that were gentle and masterful when they explored her body in the elevator.

Closing her eyes, she relived the drugging feel of his

mouth on hers. In those few seconds Matthew Sterling made her recall the passion she hadn't experienced in years; an all consuming passion she maintained before she'd become pregnant.

Her desire for her husband had waned and then diminished entirely with the physical and hormonal changes in her body, but returned several months after Christopher's birth. By that time it was too late—their roles were reversed. Alejandro Delgado no longer desired his wife.

Matt covered the delicate hand caressing his, a half-smile curving his generous mouth. The fingers of his left hand trailed along the side of her neck, and as Eve raised her chin to stare up at him he winked at her. A slow smile parted her lush lips. Leaning over, he placed a light kiss under her ear, increasing the pressure until she trembled.

"Matt," she gasped, her warm breath searing his exposed throat.

The sound of her husky entreaty shattered his entrancement. He didn't know what it was about this woman that made him lower his guard and become a little too reckless for the mission they were about to embark upon.

Pulling back slowly, he stared at her, his gaze traveling over her face and searching the depths of her eyes. Her eyes reminded him of a well deep enough to drown in.

The strange sensual longing he'd felt the moment he saw Eve Blackwell for the first time was replaced by the need to protect her as he recalled the telephone conversation he'd had earlier that evening in his hotel suite.

Eve was unaware that she was to become involved in an even more complicated plot than the first plan her uncle outlined to him. Harry's telephone call revealed that Alejandro Delgado was now heavily involved in drug smuggling and money laundering. The former Mexican diplomat, who had been a staunch ally of the United States, now headed their F.B.I.'s Most Wanted List.

Harry verified that Delgado had orchestrated The Metropolitan Museum of Art thefts, selling the priceless tapestries to private collectors. Delgado had also arranged for the money from the illegal art sales to be used for arms to fight a socialist war in Central America.

The bureau had gotten word to Delgado that Mateo Arroyo was interested in doing business with him. The time for their meeting was to be set up by a third party who was on the payroll of the U.S. Department of Justice.

Matt's amended directive was to rescue Christopher Delgado, convince Alejandro Delgado that Mateo Arroyo was interested in a joint venture for the purpose of smuggling drugs out of Mexico, *and* identify who was organizing the Costa Rican rebels.

Lines of tension ringed Matt's mouth when he thought of drug smugglers, the people who sold death.

They were a different breed from those who stole and sold priceless works of art, or those who were in the business of stealing and selling black market weapons. Drug traffickers were immoral and ruthless, and spared no one who wandered into their path. And that included innocent women or children.

The bounty on his ears was the result of his rescuing a DEA agent whose cover had been blown after the agent gathered enough information on a Colombian army colonel who'd alerted heads of several drug cartels of scheduled raids by the military and local police.

Matt had given Harry his word: he would interrogate Alejandro Delgado, find Christopher Delgado, and make arrangements for the child and his mother to return safely to the States.

Then he would get his own affairs in order. He would finalize the sale of El Moro, leaving Mexico and Mateo Arroyo behind him. In New Mexico he would be known as Matthew Sterling, marry, father a couple of children, build a horse farm, and breed champions to rival the three-year-olds who raced at Churchill Downs on the first Saturday in May. His father bred champion bulls, and *he* intended to breed a Kentucky Derby winner.

Eve's velvet-black eyes, so large and trusting, caressed his face, and his tension eased as he lowered his head for the second time. He registered her warm breath seconds before he captured it. His thumb moved under her chin, making her his willing captive as he tasted the sweet, moist, lushness of her erotic mouth.

Eve's skin prickled from the heat of his touch. She melted against the massive warmth and strength of his embrace. She was an actress in a role, and she intended to give a winning performance. Matthew Sterling wanted a loving and passionate wife and he was going to get one. She would never give him a reason to doubt her ability to play the part she had been given.

Her hands moved up his hard chest to his face, and she cradled his cleanshaven cheeks between her palms.

"I hope you aren't going to have a long engagement, Mateo," intoned a masculine voice, filled with laughter.

Eve and Matt pulled apart abruptly. They met the amused smiles of Alma and her husband. Carlos Navarro, tall, thin, and serenely elegant, with a head of wavy, snow-white hair, cradled his much younger pregnant wife at his side.

Eve's gaze was downcast as she held onto the hand Matt extended; he stood up, pulling her to her feet. Her embarrassment was short-lived when Carlos released Alma, grasped her free hand and placed a light kiss on the knuckles.

"Welcome to Mexico and to the family," he said softly in lightly accented English.

She was charmed by the man, whose dark eyes burned like blazing coal in a weathered face the color of golden, aged tobacco.

Carlos extended both arms to Matt. *"Congratulación, primo."*

Matt slapped the older man on the back, causing Carlos to wince slightly. *"Gracias."*

Alma looped an arm through her husband's. "When are you getting married?" she asked her cousin.

"In a month," Matt answered. "And Carlos, I'd like you to do the officiating."

Alma's gaze widened. "You're not getting married in Texas?"

Matt shook his head. "It's going to be a couple of months before I get back to Texas, and I wanted a commitment from Eve before she changed her mind."

Eve, curving an arm around Matt's waist inside his jacket, smiled. "He's right. He's lucky I agreed to a month. If it were up to me I'd marry him tonight."

"As a federal magistrate I can get a special license for you," Carlos offered solemnly.

"That's all right," Eve protested, smiling up at Matt. *"We* can wait a month."

Carlos inclined his noble white head. "If that's the case, then I'll be more than willing to marry you."

"Carlos, we're forgetting our manners," Alma scolded in a soft whisper.

"Of course, *Niña.*" He waved his hand. "Let's sit out on the loggia and open a bottle of prized sherry to toast this very special occasion."

It has begun, Eve thought as she followed Matt out to the loggia. It was so simple that it frightened her. Matt had fooled his cousin, and she wondered how many others they would deceive before the curtain came down on their staged performances.

Chapter Five

Matt stood behind a seated Eve, sipping a glass of smooth Spanish sherry, his left hand resting lightly on her shoulder. He felt the warmth of her flesh through the fabric of her dress and the delicate bones of her collarbone as he savored the hypnotic fragrance of her perfume.

Una mariposa, he thought. Eve Blackwell was a fragile, velvet brown and black butterfly.

He wondered if he would have been as attracted to her under another set of circumstances, if Harry Blackwell had not forced them into a liaison. The notion of being attracted to Eve summoned thoughts about women from his past.

For one thing, she was taller and slimmer than the others; she was also less submissive. He had known her for less than three hours and he already knew Eve Blackwell would challenge him over and over, despite her promise to follow his orders.

A wry smile lifted the corners of his mouth as he stared at Alma and her husband. His American cousin had found happiness with a man old enough to be her father, and

in another three months Alma would make Carlos a father
for the very first time.

His fingers curved around the slender column of Eve's
neck, causing her to shift slightly and stare up at him.
There was enough light in the loggia to note her questioning glance.

"Carlos, Alma, I'd like to impose on your hospitality,"
Matt began in Spanish before he remembered Eve was not
fluent in the language.

"What is it you want?" Alma questioned in English.

"Can Eve stay with you and Carlos instead of her living
at the—"

"Of course," Alma interrupted. "There's no need to
ask, now that Eve is going to be family." She made an
attractive moue. "Being in love has changed you, *primo*,"
she teased.

"Wait until your wife's belly swells with child," Carlos
said, gathering Alma closer to his side. "Then you'll
become a . . . *cómo se dice marshmallow en Español?*"

"Marshmallow!" Matt and Alma said in unison,
laughing.

"*Sí*," Carlos stated solemnly. "That is what I have
become. A marshmallow."

Alma dropped an arm over Carlos's shoulder. "A marshmallow I love beyond description," she admitted openly.

Carlos cradled Alma's face between his hands, kissing
her mouth in a tender gesture. "I love you too, *Niña*. But
I must get back to my papers before I go to bed." He rose
slowly to his feet, extending a hand to Matt. "Mateo, Eve,
please excuse me." Leaning down, he pressed his lips to
Eve's forehead. *"Buenas noches."*

She smiled up at him. "Good night, Carlos."

Alma stared at her husband's retreating figure before
picking up a crystal decanter filled with sherry. She noted
Eve's glass. She hadn't drunk her wine. "Matthew?"

"No thank you," he replied, declining another glass.
He had to be sober for the drive back to the hotel as well

as clearheaded, once he replayed the tape of Harry's latest call. Every call that came in through his private line was recorded, and erased within hours. He memorized everything he needed to know or do, eliminating the risk that someone would uncover his double life.

Alma refilled her own glass with cranberry juice, then settled back on a wicker loveseat. Her alert gaze missed nothing. She noted the surreptitious glances Eve and Matthew exchanged and she also noted the possessiveness of his touch. Each time his hands grazed a part of Eve's body they said *mine*.

"Alma, I'd like you to help Eve with her Spanish," Matt said, breaking the comfortable silence.

"I'd love to," she agreed.

Eve gave Alma a warm smile. "Did your mother teach you Spanish?"

"No," Alma replied. "Matthew's mother taught me. I spent more time at Matthew's house than I did at my own. Becoming bilingual paid off, because I decided to major in Spanish once I entered college. I taught at a junior high school in Lubbock for eight years before applying for a position to tutor the children of wealthy Americans and Europeans, who either lived or vacationed in Mexico. I moved here permanently six years ago, and now call it home."

"How long does it take to become fluent?" Eve queried.

Alma took a sip of her juice. "It all depends how much you truly want to learn. It always helps if you fully immerse yourself in the language. In other words, think in Spanish rather than in English. The words may come haltingly at first, but after a month you'll find yourself doing it unconsciously."

Matt squeezed Eve's shoulder. "Don't concern yourself too much, *Preciosa*. Alma is the best." Leaning over, he placed his wineglass on a wrought iron table. "I'm going to get your luggage from the car, then I'll be on my way."

Eve and Alma rose simultaneously, smiling at each other,

and Eve knew she had found a friend in Alma Navarro. Living with Carlos and Alma would help soothe the month's wait before she and Matt married. Her confidence spiraled upward as her smile widened.

One more month, an inner voice crooned. One more month and she and Chris would be reunited.

Matt returned with Eve's luggage and followed her and Alma into the house and up the curving staircase to the second story. The bedroom and adjoining bathroom selected for Eve were spacious and filled with furnishings reflecting the country's Spanish and Indian influences. Shuttered windows opened out to vistas boasting mountains and valleys.

He walked over to the windows, drawing the shutters and concealing the nighttime sky. Turning, he met Eve's steady gaze and smiled. Her expression was serene and trusting. She wore the same expression the photographer had captured in the black and white photo her uncle had sent him.

Alma watched the silent exchange between her cousin and his future wife, slowly backing out of the room. It was apparent they wanted to be alone. "I'll see you in the morning, Eve. Matthew, you before you leave."

Matt waited until Alma left, closing the door behind her, before he extended his arms. A wide grin displayed his straight, white teeth. "We did it," he said softly.

"Thank you, Matt."

He tightened his hold on her slender body. "You should accept the accolades. You were perfect."

What Eve didn't know was that she was going to make his last mission a lot easier than he had expected.

"I'll see you for breakfast," he continued. "After that we'll go shopping."

She yawned delicately, placing a hand over her mouth.

"Please excuse me. I don't know what it is, but I can't keep my eyes open."

"You're excused," Matt countered, noticing her drooping eyelids. "You're on a different time zone, and with the change in altitude you probably need as much sleep as you can get." He released her. "Do you need help unpacking?"

Eve yawned again. "No, thanks." Tilting her chin, she stared up at Matt peering intently down at her. His nearness made her uneasy, made her senses spin, as a rush of heat burned her cheeks.

An emotion she hadn't felt in a long time and did not want to feel swept through her. She had to fight the rush of sensations that made her want to remain in Matt's arms as he offered his protection and strength.

Her delicate jaw tightened. "Good night, Matt." There was no mistaking the underlying coldness in her voice. She had just dismissed him.

The dismissal was apparent to Matt. His body tensed, then relaxed. *She's exhausted,* he thought, noting the slight puffiness under her eyes. And he had no doubt that the strain of playing his intended was also stressful.

His brilliant jade and gold gaze slowly caressed her face. "Good night." Turning on his heel, he walked out of the room.

Eve sank down onto the mahogany four-poster bed at the same time the door closed behind Matt's departing figure. Staring up at the intricately crocheted lace canopy, she counted the pounding beats of her heart.

She and Matt had fooled Alma and Carlos, but she did not want to think about her reaction to the man who pretended to love her enough to offer marriage; and she did *not* want to remember the alien feelings she had locked away forever.

A smile eased her strained expression. The curtain had come down on the first scene of the first act.

* * *

Matt lay sprawled on the sofa in the darkened living room, smoking and staring out at the lights blinking over the city. El Moro had been built close enough to the center of the city so that the monument *El Angel* was clearly visible in the center of *Paseo de la Reforma*. The impressive monument had been dedicated in 1910, rising above the Paris-styled avenue and celebrating Mexico's centennial of independence from Spain.

Exhaling a cloud of smoke, he smiled. A Spanish monument in the center of a French-styled avenue. Like the towering luxury hotels and modern office buildings, the teeming city life, the slower, surrounding provincial village activity, and the mixture of its people, Mexico City was diversified and exciting.

He dropped the cigar in an ashtray on the floor and drew in a deep breath. Within a month he would be leaving it, with Eve Blackwell-Arroyo.

Finding her son, if he actually was still in Mexico, would be easier than solving a child's riddle compared to what he had to go through for Harry and his people.

Grimacing, he wondered how his Mexican grandparents and his other cousins would react if they learned of his clandestine operations. He had earned a great deal of money from his covert missions, and even after he'd invested a small fortune into the once nearly bankrupt hotel and purchased the land in New Mexico, he still had enough to invest in other ventures.

Each mission had been his last . . . until the next time. However, the risks and the lure of excitement had proven too much for him to decide to retire and take over running the horse farm. Now, operating openly in Mexico went beyond daring. It had become a deliberate flirtation with exposure *and* death.

His conversation with Harry washed over him: *"Don't*

worry, Blackwell, I'll send her back just like she arrived—safe and beautiful. I suppose we can call it even after this one is over?"

"I don't think so, Sterling. Get my niece's son back and I'll owe you. I'll make the arrangements for their departure. Adios, amigo, *and* buena suerte."

"Good-bye and good luck to you, too," he'd whispered to the dial tone.

He needed more than luck. Eve's ex-husband was a Delgado-Quintero, and that meant he was a member of one of the most influential families in the country. It was no wonder Eve couldn't get the American or Mexican governments to cooperate with her. Not even her uncle's influence reached that far.

Closing his eyes, he planned what needed to be done to accomplish his missions—both of them. Somewhere between the time when most of the lights dimmed over the city and when the sky brightened beyond the mountains in the distance, Matt slept. His thoughts were untroubled. He had mapped out everything necessary to give Harry and Eve what they wanted. Not once did he ever think of what he wanted.

Whenever he accepted an assignment from Harry Blackwell he never thought of himself. To do so would make him subjective and vulnerable. Becoming too involved meant he could lose his life, and he had lived on the fringes too many times to brazenly or openly tempt fate. He wasn't ready to die—*not yet.*

Chapter Six

Eve stirred on the bed and shifted her prone position as ribbons of sunlight seeped through the shuttered windows, threading their way across her neck, cheek, and forehead. The heat penetrated her body through layers of silk, bringing with it a wave of moisture.

Her lips parted as she struggled to open her eyes. Another surge of heat and an oppressive weight held her captive, not permitting her to move or escape.

"No," she groaned, struggling to free herself from whatever was holding her prisoner.

"It's all right," crooned a soft, masculine voice.

Eve came awake immediately, her senses stimulated by the warmth of the hard male body, the subtle yet sensual fragrance of aftershave, and the firm grip of Matt's hands on her shoulders.

Rolling over onto her back and peering up at him, she frowned, discerning the brightness of the morning sun through the shutters.

"What time is it?" Her voice was low and husky from sleep.

"It's nearly eleven," he replied.

She tried scrambling from the bed, but he tightened his hold on her arm. "Why did you let me sleep so late?"

"You needed the sleep." Shifting her effortlessly, Matt pulled her across his lap, cradling her cheek to his shoulder. "I can assure you that once we share a bed you won't have to worry about oversleeping," he teased.

Her head came up quickly and her fathomless dark eyes widened in surprise. Then, his mocking statement forgotten, Eve stared numbly at him. If it hadn't been for his startling, hazel-colored eyes and the drawling Southwestern cadence in his speech she would not have recognized him.

His hair had been cut so that thick, black strands lay close to his scalp, barely grazing his forehead. The thick mustache was also gone, revealing a strong, sensual mouth. His top lip was firm, while the lower was fuller, and drooped with enough petulance to make it hypnotically attractive.

"Is there something wrong?" he asked, his lids lowering slowly over his brilliant eyes.

Eve lowered her chin, smiling. "I almost didn't recognize you."

Matt ran a hand over his head. "I thought I'd affect a different look for our official engagement photo session."

Her head snapped up again. "What photo session?"

"The photograph we'll send to all of the daily and weekly newspapers announcing our upcoming marriage," he explained, gently easing her off his lap. He stood up, walked over to the windows, and opened the shutters.

Matt didn't have to turn around to see Eve's stunned expression. She still had not come to terms with their upcoming nuptials. He didn't know why, but her reluctance to marry annoyed him. Did she see him as a monster? Or—did she see him as beneath her? Would she have preferred him to come with foreign service credentials, like her ex-husband?

Turning slowly, he noted her slightly tilted chin and her

dark eyes filled with contempt and another emotion he couldn't identify. His own eyes narrowed as a realization shook him to his very center. Eve Blackwell was spoiled and used to giving orders, not taking them.

The boarding school she claimed was a prison without bars was one of the most exclusive in the northeast. And he knew enough about the private Harry Blackwell to glean the prominence of the Blackwells of Virginia and Connecticut.

The Sterlings of Texas may not have had the progeny of the Blackwells, with their ties to politics and the foreign service, but on the other hand Matt's father, grandfather, and great-grandfather had made names for themselves throughout the States with their knowledge of animal husbandry. His father, Clayton, had bred a milk cow that was resistant to most bovine diseases while yielding lean, tender beef.

His anger spiraled. Eve Blackwell reminded him of another woman he once thought himself in love with and had offered marriage. She'd laughed in his face, saying she didn't want to spend the rest of her life on a farm wearing flannel instead of silk and smelling of fertilizer rather than imported perfume. It was the last time he had asked a woman to share his life—*until now*—even if it was only temporary.

His sensual mouth, no longer hidden under a mustache, tightened. "Now that you're up, get dressed and be ready to leave within the hour," he ordered. "We have a lot of things to do *today*."

Eve frowned, confused. She stared at Matt as he stalked out of her bedroom, slamming the door behind him. What was wrong with him? What had she done or said to make him growl at her? And he had ordered, not asked, that she get dressed.

Their so-called marriage was in trouble even before they exchanged vows. If Mateo Arroyo thought she was his chattel, then he was seriously mistaken. She had no intention of being ordered about; he would find out quickly, very quickly, how difficult his life would become.

Matt's hand halted filling a cup with strong Mexican coffee the moment he spied Eve approaching the table where he sat on the loggia with Alma. Without warning, his pulse quickened and his gaze narrowed. Seeing Eve Blackwell in the full light of day was astounding, and he was momentarily paralyzed as well as speechless. The startling effect of her dark beauty dazzled him once he finally rose to his feet.

All of the gold in his eyes vanished, leaving them a deep verdant green. He smiled his approval. *The wait was worth it.*

Eve was fully aware of the impact she had made on Matt. She'd washed her short hair, applied a styling gel and brushed the naturally curly strands off her forehead, molding them to her scalp and showing off the delicate bones that made up her exquisite face. Her subtly applied makeup, white linen, short sleeve blouse and tailored black linen slacks, her imported lizard-skin loafers and matching narrow belt around her slim waist, were all classic and elegant.

Grasping her hands, he pulled her closer and pressed a kiss at the side of her mouth. "You look beautiful," he said softly, but not softly enough. Alma had overheard the caressing compliment.

Eve smiled, patting his lean, cleanshaven jaw. "Thank you, Darling." She permitted him to seat her. "Good morning, Alma."

Alma glanced down at the watch on her wrist. *"Buenas tardes. Cómo está?"*

"Muy bien, gracias," Eve replied quickly.

"Bueno," Matt complimented, pleased that Eve hadn't hesitated to reply to Alma's greeting in Spanish. "I don't

mean to rush you, *Preciosa,* but we must leave as soon as possible. I'd like us to do some shopping before the *siesta.*"

Eve noted the thin gold watch on her own wrist. "What time is *siesta?*"

"Usually two to four."

"Do I have time for coffee?"

Matt hesitated and Alma smiled at him. "Lighten up, Matthew, and let her eat something, or else she's going to faint in this heat."

"She's not pregnant," he countered, glaring at his cousin before his gaze dropped to her rounded belly.

"You don't have to be pregnant to faint, Matthew," Alma shot back. "In case you've forgotten, Eve's not used to this altitude, or our polluted air. Here, Eve," she persisted, pushing a plate full of freshly baked rolls across the table. "Eat."

Matt clenched his teeth. It wasn't that he didn't want Eve to eat. He'd delayed having his own breakfast because he wanted to share the meal with her. He'd planned to take her back to the hotel and introduce her to a variety of breakfast and lunch foods before they visited the upscale boutiques in the *Zona Rosa.*

He hadn't known until he'd watched her sleep earlier that morning that he wanted to spend as much time as he possibly could with her. There was something silent, mysterious, and almost hypnotic that drew him to her; and he wanted to find out what that *something* was.

Reaching into the pocket of a pale gray linen jacket on the back of his chair, Matt withdrew a flip-open cellular phone. He punched in several numbers, spoke rapid Spanish, then pressed a button, terminating the call. His conversation lasted less than ten seconds.

Alma's embarrassment was apparent. "I'm sorry, Matthew. I had no idea you'd made plans to eat with Eve," she apologized.

Matt's fiery gaze was fixed on Eve's face. "How soon you

forget, Alma," he stated quietly. "Sterling men always take care of what belong to them."

This time Eve did not misinterpret Matt's statement. He didn't see her as chattel, but as someone he had promised to protect, and that was what she'd sought all of her life—to feel safe.

Her father had taken care of all her material needs, withholding what she wanted most—nurturing protectiveness. She had wanted him to hold her—when she woke up crying from her nightmares, when she fell and skinned her knees, when the boy she worshipped from a far treated her as if she had a contagious disease, and most of all when Alex openly flaunted his affairs in her face. She'd wanted Floyd Blackwell to put his arms around her and tell her that everything would be all right, and that he would never let anything harm his baby girl.

But she was no longer a little girl. She was a thirty-four year old woman who had her own child. A child she'd carried to term, nurtured and loved. A child who was wrested away from her, and hidden where she couldn't find him.

Recalling his statement, Eve smiled at Matt. *Sterling men always take care of what belong to them.* Even though they weren't married, she knew he would take care of her; he would protect her *and* return her son to her.

"We'll have the rest of our lives to breakfast together, Matt."

He stared at her, complete surprise freezing his features. He knew her words were spoken for Alma's benefit, but for him there was a hidden meaning. Just for a brief moment he'd wanted to believe her. This beautiful, sensual woman with whom he would exchange vows within a month made him forget that they were only playing a game. A game where, he prayed, there would be *only* winners.

He nodded, not trusting himself to speak.

Alma pushed back her chair, rising to her feet. "I'll tell Mariana to prepare something."

Matt rose to acknowledge his cousin's departure, his gaze never leaving Eve's face.

It was apparent that Eve Blackwell was a much more accomplished actress than she realized. More adept than he'd ever been or would be.

The labels on Eve's new wardrobe equaled the ones which once hung in her closet in Washington, D.C. As a diplomat's wife she'd been expected to make the rounds of the endless parties in the capitol city.

The elegant little shops in the trendy *Zona Rosa* carried creations by Von Furstenberg, Givenchy, Ungaro, Missoni and Chloé, and a larger shop yielded leather treasures of Gucci, Bally, and Cole-Hann.

She tried on dresses, suits, and accessories, giving her approval and not permitting herself to succumb to the excitement of being graced with exquisite, eye-catching fashions many women dream about.

Matt escorted her into a jewelry store, unaware that her monosyllabic responses were due to heat exhaustion. Her body hadn't adjusted to Mexico City's unusually high spring temperatures.

"What kind of ring do you want?" he questioned, grasping her hand and helping her sit on a delicate chair in a corner of the shop.

She tried smiling. "It doesn't matter."

"Diamond, ruby, sapphire, emerald. It's your call."

She stared at him, marvelling at how he still appeared alert and unruffled by the extreme heat. His white cotton shirt was crisp and wrinkle free. He hadn't removed his jacket in any of the shops or made an attempt to loosen his tie.

All of the upscale shops were air-conditioned, but once they stepped outside onto the overpopulated streets with the smog and thermal inversion, she experienced difficulty breathing normally.

Matt took a chair beside her and she placed a hand on his arm. "You make the selection."

He arched an eyebrow. "You trust me?"

Her smile was spontaneous for the first time in more than two hours. "Of course."

He splayed one hand possessively at the small of her back while gesturing for a salesperson. Eve waited as the salesman measured her finger, listening as Matt described his preferences. He favored rubies set in yellow gold, and she lost count of the number of rings slipped on and off her finger.

They listened to the salesman extolling the superior quality of a two-carat oval ruby surrounded by a double row of channel-set diamonds. She spread her outstretched fingers under a lamp on the antique table, admiring the flawless quality of the blood-red stone.

Matt cradled her fingers in his larger hand. "I'll take it."

Her gaze lingered on his face. "You like the color red." It was more of a statement than a question.

He leaned closer, his warm breath sweeping over her ear. "Only on you. It complements your beauty." Their gazes met and held. The rich, vibrant color emphasized the gold undertones in Eve's flawless skin.

"Thank you." The two words were so simple, yet conveyed all of the appreciation she felt for Matt at that moment. It wasn't the clothes or the jewelry—she had had those with Alex. It was Matthew Sterling—the man.

He was offering her hope.

Chapter Seven

The onset of *siesta* began in practiced precision as shopkeepers closed their doors, dimmed lights, drew shutters, and unfurled awnings.

Eve and Matt walked out of the jewelry shop, stopping abruptly. A blackened sky and large drops of rain greeted them. Pedestrians quickened their pace to get out of what was certain to become a torrential downpour.

"Wait here," Matt suggested. "I'll bring the car around."

Eve moved closer to him under the shop's awning, curving an arm around his waist. His car was parked three blocks away.

"No. I'll go with you."

He stared down at her bowed head. "You'll get wet."

"I don't care." She didn't want him to leave her.

He hesitated, then said, "Okay. Let's go."

Holding her hand, he half-jogged along the sidewalk, skirting others in their rush to get out of the rain. Eve, quickening her pace, followed Matt's lead. Both of them were soaked by the time they were seated inside the Lincoln, the sounds of their heavy breathing reverberating in the confined space.

Matt glanced over at Eve and went still. Her thin white blouse was plastered to her chest, clearly outlining her bare breasts. His body reacted swiftly and he groaned aloud. He had almost forgotten that she did not wear a bra.

He'd scrutinized her after she'd tried on formal and casual dresses, slacks, blouses, skirts, shoes, and accessories, but he had given her complete privacy when she selected her intimate apparel.

Gritting his teeth, he had hoped there would be at least *one* bra in the purchases scheduled for delivery at the Navarro residence later that evening.

"Are you cold?" he asked her, unable to pull his gaze away from the outline of her dark areolas.

Eve saw the direction of his gaze, and liquid fire ignited her face, spreading to her chest. His gaze traveled slowly upward over her face, then retraced its path down her body just as slowly.

The tingling in the pit of her belly inched lower, becoming an intense, heated throbbing; a throbbing, raging force that spread and scorched the essence of her femininity.

No! she screamed inwardly. She couldn't let it happen; she did not want a physical attraction between herself and Matt. This was a game they were playing and she wanted no memories once they separated.

"No, I'm not cold," she replied in a choked voice. Turning her head, she stared out the side window.

Matt also glanced away, starting up the car. His features were deceptively composed as he tried not to concentrate on what was happening in his groin. His reaction to Eve was so swift, violent, and totally unexpected that he wanted to make love to her—right in the car!

He wanted to taste her swollen nipples and kiss her sexy little mouth until she begged him to stop.

But it would not happen, because he'd promised her uncle that he wouldn't touch her. He would marry Eve, perhaps even share her bed, but would never consummate their union.

"Why aren't we going back to Alma's?" Eve asked Matt as he maneuvered the car into his private parking space at El Moro's underground garage. It was the first time she'd spoken since they left the *Zona Rosa*.

He turned off the headlights and the ignition, not bothering to look at her. "The local roads are dangerous when it rains. We'll stay here until it stops."

"I need dry clothes."

"You'll get dry clothes."

She folded both hands on her damp hips. "From where?"

Matt slipped from behind the wheel, came around the car, and opened her door. Reaching in, he helped her out. The tenuous rein on his temper snapped.

"Why do you always have to question me, Eve? I told you I'd get you something to wear."

Her temper also ignited. "I question you because you bark demands as if I were a trained pet, *Mateo Arroyo*. You never ask or explain anything."

She was right. He did bark orders at her. It wasn't his style, but Eve had no way of knowing what she was doing to him. She didn't know how difficult it was for him to pretend he felt nothing for her when just being with her disturbed him.

There had been times earlier that afternoon when he actually enjoyed watching her emerge from the dressing rooms wearing dresses or gowns that flattered her figure. It filled him with pride when he noticed other men staring at the woman who was to become his wife.

A little voice had taunted him, saying: *She belongs to me. She is mine. And only mine.* He didn't know where the rush of possessiveness had come from. All he knew was that he

wanted Eve Blackwell, and wanted her for more than the
lust she summoned from him.

"I live by my own set of rules, Eve," he began in a hushed
tone. "And because I do, I've managed to stay alive. I *will
not* risk losing my life because you refuse to listen to me.
You're going to have to get out of the habit of being
Daddy's spoiled little princess. I—"

"In order words, you want me to *obey* you," she interrupted.

He nodded slowly, a smile replacing his frown. "I think
you're beginning to understand me."

"What I understand is that you want a puppet."

Moving closer, he lowered his head, their noses only
inches apart. "I want you to be *anything* I ask you to be.
I'll take an obedient, affectionate, and passionate fiancée
for starters." He noted the narrowing of her eyes and knew
she wasn't going to concede without an argument.

"You forget that I'm the one who's been married. I
know how to play the game, Matt, and that means I'm much
more experienced when it comes to making concessions. It
can't be all your way," she argued.

Matt straightened; his smile becoming a wide grin.
"You'll be given the opportunity to 'play the game,' as you
say, later tonight. A business associate has invited me to
his home to celebrate his daughter's acceptance into
Spain's most prestigious school of classical dance. The
timing couldn't be more perfect to introduce my friends
to *mi novia.*"

Eve's delicate jaw tightened in frustration. She didn't
want to attend a party; she wanted to find her child.

"I can't go anywhere looking like this," she snapped,
refusing to relent, and glaring challengingly at Matt.

Crossing his arms over his chest, he stared back at her.
"What do you need?"

She noted his tender expression, the total absence of
gold in his luminous eyes, and for the first time she realized

his eyes reflected his mercurial moods; she preferred the deep jade-green to the fiery amber sparks.

"I usually have my hair and nails done before a social event."

"You *will* have your hair and nails done," he stated with quiet finality. Turning, he made his way along the corridor to the private elevator, leaving Eve rushing to catch up with his long strides.

She preceded him into the elevator, averting her gaze. She knew very little about Matthew Sterling, but she'd discovered that he wasn't as unaffected by her presence as he pretended. What his lips did not say, his eyes did. They told her he enjoyed the roles they'd opted to play. They also missed nothing. She was certain he could recall every dress, formal gown, and shoe she had tried on.

"What do you want me to wear tonight?" she queried, deciding to test his memory.

His eyebrows inched up in surprise. "You want me to decide for you?"

Biting down on her lower lip, she concealed an emerging smile. "These people are your friends, Matt. I don't want to embarrass you."

Matt studied her for a moment and they exchanged subtle looks of amusement. First she lashed him with the whip she called her tongue. Then she purred like a satisfied kitten.

"I'd like you to wear the burgundy dress."

Eve was pleased. It would've been her choice. "Thank you for the suggestion."

"You're very welcome, *Preciosa.*" They shared a smile, he shaking his head. He knew the time he would spend with Eve would never be boring. However, what he didn't want to do was become too comfortable with her; he didn't want to miss her once they parted.

The elevator doors opened to Matt's suite and Eve followed him into the air-cooled space. Wrapping her arms around her body, she shivered noticeably.

"You'd better get out of those wet clothes," he suggested, hanging his own soggy jacket on the back of a chair in the dining area. "Use the bathroom in the bedroom. You'll find a bathrobe on a shelf that will fit you."

She walked to the far end of the suite and into his bedroom. Her gaze swept over the neatly made king-sized mahogany bed, large masculine dresser, and matching armoire. She barely remembered the pearl gray and white color scheme of the wall-to-wall drapes and bed dressing by the time she stepped into the bathroom. The entire space was covered with smokey gray mirrors. Even the ceiling was mirrored!

She slipped out of her shoes, slacks, and blouse. Every time she shifted she caught a glimpse of her naked upper body.

"Hedonist," she whispered. Whoever had designed the bathroom had to have been a hedonist.

Glass shelves cradled thirsty towels and an ample supply of thick, white velour bathrobes in varying sizes from mens' extra large to womens' petite.

Eve wondered how many other women had selected robes from the supply in Matt's bedroom when he conducted liaisons in the privacy of his hotel suite.

Well, there was one thing she was certain of—she would *not* be one of Matt's women.

Chapter Eight

Eve reentered the living room and found Matt in the dining area staring out the wall of glass. The sky had darkened so much that it was impossible to tell the hour.

He hadn't changed his clothes and his damp shirt clung to his back, outlining the brown flesh through the finely woven fabric.

A roll of thunder shook the heavens, followed by an ear-shattering crash of lightning, and the distant mountains were brilliantly highlighted by the flash of atmospheric energy. Placing a hand over her mouth, she'd hoped to cut off her scream of terror, but she wasn't quick enough.

Matt turned, his eyes large and questioning. He was beside Eve in less than a half dozen steps. "What's the matter?"

Her fingers trembled against her equally quivering lips. She tried speaking, the words refusing to come from her constricted throat.

Grasping her shoulders, Matt shook her gently. "Eve!" He pulled her to his chest, and she collapsed. The fear in her eyes was so vivid that he couldn't imagine what had put it there. She continued to mumble incoherently against his chest. Lowering his head, he kissed her forehead. "What is it, Darling?"

"Close the drapes. Now!" Desperation vibrated in the demand.

He seated her on the sofa, then turned and made his way to the windows. Within seconds the panoramic view of Mexico City was hidden behind a wall of pale silk.

Retracing his steps, Matt stood over Eve. She lay face down on the sofa, her arms crossed over her head; he sat down beside her and pulled her trembling body into his strong embrace, pressing her face to his shoulder.

"I've closed them, Eve. Look," he urged.

Eve chanced a look at the drawn drapes, her heart rate slowing. The fear she should have overcome as a child had continued to haunt her into adulthood.

"Thank you, Mateo." Her voice was a breathless whisper. Resting her head on his chest, she closed her eyes, absorbing his warmth and strength.

In the instant she'd whispered his name, Matt had learned more about Eve Blackwell than in the past twenty-four hours or than her dossier had revealed. She only called him *Mateo* in anger or in fear, and he'd seen her fear—stark and vivid.

Holding her gently, one hand caressing her back, he pressed his lips to her moist hair. "Tell me about it, *Preciosa.*"

Eve felt a momentary wave of panic, then it subsided. How could she tell Matt about something so fearful, so trenchant? And what saddened her was that she connected the only thing she remembered about her mother with fear.

"Eve, you must learn to trust me. I have to know how to protect you."

She had sought to erect a wall of resistance against Matthew Sterling. She wanted their encounter brief and uneventful, not one which meant involvement with this mysterious, complex man.

But she would become involved; and her involvement would be as his wife!

"I don't remember too much about my mother," she began quietly, unshed moisture glistening in her eyes, "except that she always wore perfume. I used to tell her that she smelled good enough to eat. She'd laugh because she knew how much I loved candy. She used to threaten me, saying that if I didn't stop chewing bubble gum and eating candy I'd grow up with bad teeth and an acne-riddled complexion."

Matt tightened his grip on her waist. Eve's mother was wrong. She had beautiful teeth and a flawless complexion. What he wanted to tell her was that she, also, smelled good enough to eat. The perfume she favored was light and feminine, the fragrance blending sensuously with her own body's natural scent. His sensitive nostrils detected the essences of jasmine, rose, ylang-ylang, sandalwood, and vetiver.

"Do you look like your mother?" he asked, his voice soft and soothing.

Eve's smile indicated sadness as she remembered the photographic images of her mother and father on their wedding day. "Everyone says I do, except that her hair was less curly than mine, and she was at least four inches shorter."

"She must have been a beautiful woman," Matt stated simply.

"Everyone said she was. She was placed in a skilled nursing facility. The day she left home was the last time I saw her face."

Pulling back, he studied her features. "What about the wake? Weren't you allowed to attend?"

"No," she replied, shaking her head. "My father thought it would be too traumatic for a five-year-old to see her mother for the last time lying in a coffin." Closing her eyes, Eve relived the scene which had haunted her for almost thirty years.

"However, I did attend the funeral and burial services." The timbre of her voice lowered. "It was as if the sun never rose that morning. The sky was gray, and the air was so thick and heavy that everyone kept wiping the moisture from their faces. I complained to my father that the dress I was wearing was too hot for the weather, but he never spoke or looked at me.

"Many of the people who had attended the funeral service did not come to the cemetery, so there was only my father, Uncle Harry, Aunt Dorothy, and, of course, Janice. The sky was so black it could've been midnight in December instead of an early June morning.

"My father picked up a handful of dirt and threw it on the lowered coffin. At the same time I leaned over to throw my white rose onto the coffin, a roll of thunder shook the ground. Then a flash of lightning lit up the entire cemetery. I screamed in fear, tripping over my father's foot and losing my balance. If it hadn't been for the ropes encircling the open grave I would've fallen in it.

"My father yelled at me—probably more in fright than in anger. I blotted out the sound of his voice, seeing what I thought was rage on his face. The service ended, everyone racing back to their cars. I huddled in a corner of a cavernous black limousine while nature vented her fury. I tried climbing onto my father's lap, but he pushed me away. It wasn't until we returned to the house that I realized he'd been crying."

Vertical slashes appeared between Matt's eyes. Floyd Blackwell might have lost his wife, but he hadn't lost his daughter, his only child. The torment of his loss should have been overshadowed by the existence of the child he and his late wife had created; a child who needed his love as well as his protection.

"Now you know," Eve stated resignedly.

"All I know is that you're afraid of thunderstorms."

Pulling back, she stared up at his bemused expression. There were pinpoints of gold in his eyes. "You don't think I'm silly?"

"No. There's nothing silly about being afraid of something." What he didn't say was that he harbored his own fears, fears he refused to acknowledge.

"Whenever there's a storm I close all of the curtains and blinds, turn on all the lights, and get into bed," she admitted.

Matt kissed her forehead for the second time. "Now that I know you don't like thunderstorms I'll try to make certain you won't have to go through them alone. I'll close the drapes and we'll get into bed together."

Eve sat up straighter, staring at the mock sinister grin curving his sensual mouth. "I think you're looking forward to getting me into bed."

"Call it a *perk*. I've never worked with a *partner* as attractive as you."

His eyes darkened to a deep green, sending her pulses racing. *I can't*, she thought. She couldn't permit herself to feel more for Matt than necessary. She wanted only to pretend enough to fool everyone into thinking they were very much in love.

If I keep him at a distance out of the bed, then I'll be able to keep him at a distance when we're in bed.

"You're quite a silver-tongued devil, aren't you?" she drawled, wrinkling her delicate nose.

His eyes widened. "I'm serious, Eve."

"Yeah, yeah." She slipped out of his loose grip, adjusting the front of her robe.

An expression of withdrawal shadowed Matt's features. He'd made a fool of himself. He'd admitted to Eve that he found her attractive *and* looked forward to sharing a bed with her. Again her performance was flawless, while his faltered.

"As soon as *siesta* ends, the salon in the lobby will do

your hair and nails. After that we'll return to Alma's so you can change clothes for the dinner party.''

Her spine stiffened and she bit back the retort on her tongue. It would take Matthew Sterling a long time, if ever, to stop barking his commands.

Her shoulders dropped in surrender. It was useless to argue with him. She would do whatever he told her to do. She was willing to play the game—to win—if it meant getting Chris back.

''Will it bother you if I wear this down to the lobby, Matt?'' she questioned sweetly, lifting the hem of the robe off the carpeted floor.

His face darkened in annoyance. ''You'll have something to wear.''

''Thank you, my darling.'' The words dripped from her tongue like heated honey.

Matt's gaze swept over her smiling mouth, and he knew he couldn't stay angry with her. Eve Blackwell challenged and pushed him to limits he'd never permitted other women, yet he still wanted her.

Rising to his feet, he pulled her up hard against his body, startling her with the speed with which he moved. Lowering his head, his mouth covered hers possessively, not giving her an opportunity to protest.

''You're quite welcome, *Preciosa,*'' he whispered against her moist, parted lips.

Releasing her quickly, he turned on his heel, making his way toward the bedroom. Eve collapsed on the sofa, her legs trembling and every nerve in her body screaming from the overwhelming virility that made Matthew Sterling potent and intoxicating.

Play with fire and you'll get burned.

And that was who Matt was—a fire god descended from ancient African and Zapotec warriors.

* * *

Matt escorted Eve into the courtyard of the sprawling Lopes hacienda, a slight smile touching his generous mouth. He hadn't missed the startled and admiring gazes directed at Eve by those in attendance. There was no denying his own satisfaction of seeing her coiffed and dressed in the silk chiffon, burgundy dress which clung to every curve on her slender frame. The color of his sun-fired eyes darkened to a deep moss green, mirroring the ripple of desire pulsing throughout his body.

His arm tightened around Eve's waist, encompassing more than her body, before he released her and offered his right hand to the man and woman approaching them. He greeted his host and hostess in Spanish, then switched to English as he introduced Eve.

"Diego, Blanca, I'm honored to present my fiancée, Eve Blackwell. Eve, our hosts, Diego and Blanca Lopes."

Eve smiled, extending her hand. She hadn't missed the shocked expressions on the faces of the Lopes's, nor their searching gazes as they peered surreptitiously at the ruby on her left hand.

"My pleasure," she said quietly, her large eyes dark as black satin. "Señora Lopes, the arrangement of flowers in your courtyard is exceptional."

The light from dozens of brightly-lit lanterns hanging throughout the courtyard highlighted the attractive flush creeping up to the hairline of the exquisitely gowned and coiffed Blanca Lopes. Her trim figure and barely silver, pale hair belied her role of grandmother.

Extending her hand to Eve, Blanca smiled attractively. "Let me show you around the gardens before I take you inside," she offered in British-accented English.

Matt watched Blanca lead Eve away, his gaze following until they disappeared. Turning back to his host, he noted the questioning look in Diego Lopes's eyes.

"You mentioned nothing about marrying last week, Mateo."

"That's because I didn't propose until yesterday," he countered with a wide grin.

"Eva—"

"Eve," he corrected quickly.

Diego nodded in apology. "Eve is quite beautiful. Congratulations, Mateo. I hope I'll . . ." He didn't finish his statement, thinking perhaps he'd overstepped the boundary with regard to social protocol.

Matt patted his friend's shoulder. "Eve *is* beautiful. And yes, you and Blanca will be invited to the wedding."

Diego exhaled audibly. *"Gracias,* Mateo."

"Eve and I will marry at the end of April, and hopefully you and I will be able to finalize the sale of El Moro by that time."

Diego Lopes ran a hand over his straight, graying hair. "I'm just waiting for the bank's approval. Did I tell you that two other men have approached me to go in as partners?"

Matt shifted his eyebrows. "Equal partners?"

"Oh, no. I'm prepared to offer them only one-third."

"If you accept, then you won't have to secure bank financing. Think of the interest you'd save."

"I've thought about it, but something bothers me, Mateo."

"What?"

"Why would two *very* successful businessmen from Venezuela and Peru want to invest in a hotel in Mexico City? Why wouldn't they set something up in their own countries?"

Matt shrugged a broad shoulder under his white dinner jacket. "It could be that they have some money they *have* to invest in several foreign markets."

Diego leaned closer to Matt. "Are you suggesting illegal activities?"

"I'm not suggesting anything. It could be that someone told them that you take in dirty laundry."

Blood suffused Diego Lopes's face. "I'm a legitimate businessman, Mateo." There was no mistaking the pride in his voice.

"I know that, Diego, otherwise I'd never offer to sell El Moro to you. Just make certain others know you're legitimate. You've been conservative with your investments. Try to remain that way. If you go in over your head, then you'll be inviting people like these two to help bail you out." Matt's expression hardened. "Remember, Diego, I offered El Moro to you because I trust you."

"And I'd never betray your trust, Mateo."

"Good."

Diego rubbed his palms together. "Now that we've settled that, why don't we go inside?"

Matt's gaze swept around the courtyard, recognizing the faces of several prominent Mexico City residents, searching for Eve.

"I'd like to wait for Eve."

"Mateo. She's not going to run away," Diego teased. "Blanca just wants to show off the new array of exotic plants the landscaper put in last week."

"I'll wait for her," he insisted with obvious impatience. He felt rather than saw Diego walk away.

He'd promised Harry that he would protect his niece, and he couldn't do that if he lost sight of her; and he was certain the word had gotten back to Alejandro Delgado that his ex-wife was in Mexico, and it wouldn't take a genius to uncover why she had come.

Making his way across the courtyard and toward the gardens, Matt's body tensed before relaxing. The involuntary action had heightened all of his sensory reflexes as he registered the distinct sound of Eve's contralto voice, the tapping of heels along the octagonal slate path, and the cloying fragrance of Blanca's prizewinning roses.

The area ringing the garden was lit with soft yellow light, and the shadowy forms of trees, shrubs and bushes took on alien contours; the area on the back of his neck tingled as if cold air had swept across it. His hands formed fists, muscles bunching up along his upper arms, and a cloud of uneasiness tightened his features. A silent voice told him Blanca and Eve weren't the only ones in the garden.

He was annoyed with himself. He never should've permitted Eve to go off with Blanca. "Dammit," he growled under his breath before repeating the word silently, then adding a few more colorful expletives.

A couple headed toward him, and he was able to relax; he recognized the young man and woman as Diego's eldest son and daughter-in-law. Seconds later, Blanca and Eve came into view.

Blanca saw Matt and gasped. "Does Diego need me for something, Mateo?"

His smile did not reach his eyes. "No, *I* came for Eve."

Blanca touched the sleeve of his pristine white jacket. "Forgive me for monopolizing your *novia.*"

He extended both arms. "Ladies."

Eve smiled at Matt, slipping her arm through his. Her smile vanished at the firm set of his lean jaw and the tightness around his mouth. They returned to the large house and she stopped him from following Blanca.

"What's bothering you, Matt?"

"You," he shot back without hesitation. *"Everything* about you bothers me."

As she pulled away from him, her chest rose and fell heavily. Eve was confused by his unexpected response to her query. What was it about her that made him despise her very existence?

Suddenly she felt the need to lash out, to hurt him as much as he'd hurt her. "The feeling is mutual, *Mateo,"* she spat out. Turning her back, she walked into the Lopes house, hiding the humiliation she refused to let him see.

She repulsed Matt the same way she'd repulsed Alex. The only difference was that she'd once loved Alex; with Matt there would be no love.

She realized she had to fight her own battle of resistance.

She would not succumb to Matthew Sterling. Inhaling, she tilted her chin. She had had a lot of experience hiding her feelings, and thirty years of practice had rendered her an expert.

Chapter Nine

Eve made it through the Lopes's dinner party, smiling politely and charming all who congratulated her and Matt on their upcoming nuptials. She'd angled her head close enough to Matt, giving the appearance of hanging onto his every word, smiled up at him, and feathered her fingers over his arm or hand possessively. Her performance was flawless, while Matt had faltered.

He hadn't meant to blurt out that she bothered him. However, it was too late to retract the accusation. Eve did bother him, because she was too damned attractive for him to ignore, too feminine for him not to respond to her as a male, and much too sensual for him to deny he didn't want to make love to her.

How was he going to keep his hands off her? What would happen once they married?

Matt cursed to himself for the second time that evening—raw, ugly curses.

Diego Lopes stood up, clearing his throat and shaking Matt from his reverie. He informed his guests that Isabella had offered to entertain everyone with her last dance performance on Mexican soil before leaving for Spain the following morning.

"While she's changing," Diego continued, "aperitifs will be served in the *sala.*"

Matt pulled back Eve's chair, his strong fingers curving around her upper arm. "Do you mind if I step outside for a few minutes?" he asked close to her ear. He felt safe leaving her with a room filled with more than a dozen people. Her brow creased with concern. "I need a cigar," he explained.

Eve's frown deepened. "Smoking isn't good for you."

You aren't good for me, he thought. "I'll only take a couple of puffs."

"A couple of puffs can kill you," she whispered.

He brushed his mouth over hers. "I hope you're not going to be a nagging wife." Not giving Eve the opportunity to reply, he escorted her to the *sala* before making his way to the courtyard.

Reaching into the breast pocket of his dinner jacket, Matt pulled out a slim gold case. Within seconds he extracted a thin cigar, then flipped the top on a minute lighter; a flame flared around the tip of the imported tobacco, a wisp of fragrant smoke rising and disappearing into the blue-black night.

He'd prided himself on cutting back the habit of smoking a half dozen cigars to one or two a day. There were occasions when the humidor went untouched for days at a time. However, from the first night he'd sat watching Eve Blackwell wait for him he'd begun smoking again.

He took three puffs of the cigar before discarding it, the lingering taste of tobacco sharp and acrid on his tongue. Shaking his head, he snorted derisively. Eve Blackwell had gotten to him. He had *let* her get to him!

All he had to do was marry Eve, reclaim her son, arrange for their return to the States, then annul the marriage; and with the annulment the curtain would come down on the final act of their carefully scripted performance. His smile mirrored confidence about the reminder of his objectivity.

The clear, crisp notes from a guitarist playing a classical composition floated throughout the courtyard. Matt reached for Eve's hand, squeezing it gently. She gave him a warm smile before turning her attention to the young woman who swept dramatically onto a portable stage, her slender, graceful arms poised above her head. The clicking of castanets, the rustle of red and black silk, the passionate strumming of the guitar, and the rhythmic tapping of sturdy shoe heels filled the courtyard.

Eve's breath quickened as she watched Blanca's daughter seduce the assembled. The slight turn of a wrist, the tilt of her chin, or a shrug of a shoulder, every motion was choreographed with an ensuing message of seduction. It was as if Isabella danced for an invisible lover.

Matt stared at Eve instead of Isabella Lopes. Her tightly curled hair framed her delicate face with ebony ringlets, while her expertly applied makeup complemented the burgundy dress. His gaze lowered to her legs and feet. Sheer black hose covered her slender legs, and her feet were encased in a pair of stunning, black, silk, sling strap heels with tiny jeweled buckles.

Eve felt the heat of Matt's gaze on her, refusing to acknowledge him as her pulse fluttered erratically. She had to erect a wall of resistance around her. She had to remind herself that Matt was the conduit through which she would reclaim her son.

Isabella's dance ended and she bowed gracefully to her applauding audience. Her accompanist took his bows, smiling and also applauding the genius of the young woman who was certain to make a name as a gifted flamenco dancer.

Matt tapped the crystal of his watch and Eve nodded. He saw that she'd been unable to stifle several yawns during the meal. It would take some time before she got used to eating dinner after 8:00 P.M. They said good-byes to their hosts and began the drive back to Alma's.

"It was a lovely dinner party," Eve stated simply as she reclined against the leather seat.

"You were lovely," Matt countered, his voice soft and coaxing.

"I thought I was a *bother*."

He gave her a quick glance, smiling. "I didn't mean for it to sound that way."

Eve returned his smile. "Are you apologizing, Matt?"

"I am."

Settling deeper into the seat, Eve closed her eyes. She hadn't expected him to apologize.

"Well, Eve?"

"Well what?" she asked lazily.

A muscle in Matt's jaw twitched. "Aren't you going to accept my apology?" he practically growled. The silence that ensued became almost unbearable. What did she want him to do? Grovel?

"Matt, I don't understand what you want from me," Eve replied, her voice quivering with uncertainty. "You want me to be affectionate, obedient, and passionate. Now you ask that I also humble myself?"

Matt threw back his head and roared with laughter. "Please don't do that, *Preciosa*. I don't need to be bored that much."

Somehow Eve knew Matt enjoyed the gentle sparring as much as she did. "I can be many things, but never boring," she replied confidently.

"*That* is an understatement."

"Don't press your luck, Señor Arroyo."

"Believe me I won't, Ms. Blackwell." His sudden grin was irresistible, and Eve returned it with one of her own.

The light mood continued long after Matt saw Eve to the door of her bedroom and he returned to El Moro, reflecting on what had passed between them.

He'd learned she could purr like a kitten yet show her claws within seconds, and that even though she feared thunderstorms she would not permit herself to be intimidated.

Matt puffed on a cigar, blowing out rings of smoke. He chuckled. She was quite a woman!

A month had come and gone quickly. Alma and Carlos had hosted an official engagement party a week after the announcement of Matt and Eve's upcoming nuptials appeared in all of the local newspapers, initiating a month filled with an endless round of social obligations.

The month had also changed Eve and Matt. They'd become so attuned to each other that they sometimes even fooled themselves with their staged affection.

Alma tutored her constantly in Spanish, and the time had come when Eve began thinking in the language. She understood most of what was being said, but realized it would take a lot more time before she became fluent.

She stood at the window in her bedroom, staring at the distant mountains. Today was her wedding day, and later that afternoon she and Matt would leave Mexico City for their honeymoon. Matt said he would use the honeymoon as a guise—to search for her son.

She sucked in her breath, holding it until her lungs burned. "Chris," she whispered softly. Her son was always in her thoughts. Even when she smiled, a part of her cried for her child.

Turning away from the window, she looked at the dress she had selected for the ceremony. The garment was a street-length, eggshell white silk kimono with an obi in jade green. Her shoes were matching jade silk pumps.

The clock on the dresser chimed the half-hour and Eve knew she had to ready herself for the ceremony, which was scheduled for eleven.

Alma walked into the bedroom, smiling broadly. She

wore a loose-fitting, green silk shift artfully designed for her pregnancy. "Are you ready for your big day?"

Eve returned the smile. "I've been ready ever since Matt proposed to me," she admitted.

Alma sat down on a rocker, raising her feet to an ottoman. "I envy you, Eve. It took me forever to accept Carlos's marriage proposal. I—"

"But you two seem so happy," Eve interrupted.

"We are. But before I married Carlos I had my doubts. I had no inkling that he was interested in me until the father of one my students let it slip that Carlos wanted to see me socially. I thought he was charming and sophisticated, but I wanted nothing to do with a man old enough to be my father."

Eve sat on the side of the bed, stunned. In the month she'd lived with the Navarros, she saw only love and respect between Alma and Carlos.

"What made you change your mind?"

A mysterious smile played at the corners of Alma's mouth. "Kindness. I agreed to have dinner with him, and from the first date I was smitten. Within minutes I forgot that he was twenty years older than I."

"Had he ever been married?"

Alma shook her head. "No. He was the consummate bachelor. And he was also the perfect gentleman. He was so unlike the other men I had dated or had been involved with that it frightened me. This fear carried over when he asked me to be his wife. He talked about having a child, and I called a travel agent to book a flight back to the States. How could I marry a man, give him a child, then raise it alone because its father would never live to see its majority?"

"But you're pregnant."

Alma cradled her burgeoning middle with both hands. "I changed my mind when I met Carlos's grandfather."

"His grandfather is still alive?" There was no mistaking the note of incredulity in Eve's voice.

Alma laughed. "Alive and raising much hell at a hundred and two. Carlos's father just celebrated his eightieth birthday in January."

"Which means Carlos will more than likely see his own grandchildren."

"His child," Alma corrected. "Let's begin with this child first."

Eve saw movement at the corner of her eye and turned. Matt filled the doorway. He wore an expertly tailored, navy blue suit.

Glancing at his watch, he shifted his expressive eyebrows. "Have you changed your mind, *Preciosa?*" he teased with a wide grin.

She stood up, tightening the sash of her robe around her waist. "Of course not, Darling." She crossed the space separating them, her gaze fixed on his sensual mouth. "Give me ten minutes and I'll be down."

Matt's smile vanished. Just for an instant he wished they were not playing a game. He wanted this day to be real, not an act.

He hadn't known when it happened, but his feelings for Eve had changed. The need to protect her was uncontrollable. This tall, slender woman with the exotic face had bewitched him until he didn't know what was real or imaginary. He dared not think he'd fallen in love with her, because that would change everything.

Matt grasped her hand, placing a small velvet bag in her palm. "Please accept this as my wedding gift." He released her hand and walked away.

Alma rose slowly to her feet and made her way to Eve's side. "What is it?"

Eve opened the tiny sack, shaking out its contents. The brilliant sparkle of diamonds stared back at her as she examined his wedding gift.

"Oh mercy!" Alma whispered.

Eve nodded, speechless. Matt had given her a pair of

platinum and diamond earrings in an antique design. The glittering blue white stones hung from levered backs.

"Eve."

She raised her head and stared at Alma. "Yes." Her voice was a breathless whisper.

Alma's chest rose and fell as she tried bringing her runaway emotions under control. "Do you know the significance of these earrings?" Eve shook her head. "The eldest son usually gives them to his wife after the birth of their first son. If there are no sons, then the eldest daughter will pass them on to their first grandson," she explained quietly.

"But . . . but I haven't given Matt a son. I'm not even pregnant," she protested.

Alma touched her arm. "Wear them anyway, Eve. Matthew must have his own reason for breaking the tradition."

Eve couldn't fathom what had made Matt give her a gift meant for the mother of his son. However, she didn't want to insult him or have Alma suspect their subterfuge by refusing to wear them.

"Help me put them in, Alma."

Alma inserted the earrings into Eve's pierced lobes. "They're exquisite on you."

Eve peered into a mirror, turning her head at an angle. They truly were exquisite, and she couldn't wait to ask Matt why he had given them to her. There wasn't enough time to go after him and still dress for the ceremony, so she had to wait until after they were married.

Chapter Ten

Alma knocked on the door, informing Eve that their guests had arrived and Carlos was ready to begin the ceremony.

Eve took one last glance around the room where she'd spent the last month, and walked out. The curtain was going up on the second act. She followed Alma down the staircase and into the cool, spacious living room, stopping short as she met Matt's hypnotic, topaz-yellow, green-flecked eyes.

Matt crossed the room, meeting her. He stared down at Eve, unable to believe she could look so innocent and wanton at the same time. The kimono-style dress was not one of the outfits he had purchased for her. However, the tailoring and design were tasteful and appropriate for the occasion. He smiled. The heirloom earrings hanging from her lobes were made for her.

"Are you ready, Darling?"

"I'm ready, Mateo," she whispered softly.

"I'll introduce you to everyone after the ceremony," he said as her large black eyes noted several strangers among the small group of people staring at her. "But I do think you should meet our witness." A tall, redhaired man stood apart from the others. "This is Cordero Birmingham. Cord, Eve."

Inclining his head slightly, Cordero gave Eve a light kiss on her cheek. He was even with the six-foot mark, and rawboned. His smooth golden skin was taut over high cheekbones, a perfect foil for a thick mane of dark hair in an odd shade of burnished copper. His startling topaz blue eyes under dark eyebrows captured her attention until he smiled. He claimed a perfect set of white teeth, and Eve wondered if he'd ever been approached for toothpaste ads for television or magazines.

"Mr. Birmingham," she said, still dazed by his youthful attractiveness.

Cordero patted her hand. "Cord, please. Mateo's my friend, and I hope you'll also become my friend." His drawling tone revealed that, like Matt, he was also from the American Southwest.

"Of course," she replied quickly.

"Can we begin, please?" Matt snapped, observing the presumptuous interchange between his bride and witness.

Eve responded in a monotone as she repeated her vows, Carlos conducting the ceremony in Spanish and English, and in spite of the warmth from Matt's large body she felt cold. She was reliving the ceremony between her and Alex as vividly as if it had occurred minutes before.

Matt slipped a wedding band of channel-set diamonds on her finger and she raised her head. An expression of supreme satisfaction brightened his features, and she felt her breath falter. Closing her eyes, she inhaled deeply, trying to force air into her constricted lungs.

"Eve?"

Cordero had said her name, handing her a heavy gold band. She blinked numbly at it, then realized she was to place it on Matt's finger. Her hand shook uncontrollably. Matt reached out and steadied it, assisting her as she placed the ring on his left hand. She never heard Carlos telling Matt he could kiss his wife. Matt's mouth closed over hers, and then she knew it was over. She was now Eve Arroyo, having been in Mexico for a little more than a month.

Matt released Eve and she sagged weakly against him. Suddenly she felt warm. Objects blurred and swayed wildly as her eyelids fluttered. Her fingers tightened on Matt's hand, biting into the flesh.

He caught her limp body with one arm while taking the glass of water thrust at him. He mumbled a thanks to Cordero as he held the glass to her lips. She managed several sips. "It's over, *Preciosa,*" he crooned quietly against her moist cheek.

Opening her eyes, Eve pushed against his chest. "I'm sorry, she apologized breathlessly. "I felt so warm and weak."

Matt gave her a tender smile. "No harm done, because you're a beautiful bride, Señora Arroyo." She nodded, permitting him to escort her into the dining room.

Introductions were put off until everyone was seated at the long banquet table. Eve was seated at the opposite end of the table from Matt, and she smiled when he winked at her.

A profusion of white roses in twin crystal vases served as a centerpiece for the table set with an antique white lace tablecloth, translucent white china trimmed with a gold border, and gleaming silver.

Listening to the Spanish spoken by the invited guests, Eve realized that her son probably now spoke it fluently. At Alex's insistence, they had employed a Spanish-speaking housekeeper and nanny, and the little boy had attained enough of a bilingual vocabulary to communicate with his mother and father in their native tongues.

She spread her left hand out atop the table. It was as if she saw the precious stones on her third finger for the first time. The large ruby shimmered like rich, red blood, and the diamonds like sparkling stars under the overhead chandeliers.

She wondered what it was Matt owed her uncle to have him spend so much money on her. Had Harry Blackwell given him the okay to spend the money, only to reimburse him once she and Chris were back in the States?

Eve pushed the nagging question out of her mind as she dined on a consommé. The *bacalo y picadillo a la cirolla,* a dish of smoked codfish and chopped beef, was prepared creole style. She sampled a small portion of fried green bananas and a savory white rice. The spicy food triggered an uncommon thirst, and she drank more champagne than she normally would.

"May I have everyone's attention?" Cordero asked loudly. He raised his champagne glass. "I'd like to propose a toast to the new couple." His bright blue eyes competed with the sparkle of his straight white teeth. "May your marriage be a long and loving one, and may you be blessed with many strong, healthy, and handsome children."

Matt winked as Eve gave him a shy glance. "Thank you, Cord." He poured a small amount of champagne into his empty glass, raising it. "To my wife," he began in a soft voice filled with heavy emotion, "and her beauty and passion, and her happiness for all of the good things for her future."

All eyes were trained on Eve, and she tried composing her thoughts. They expected her to return the toast. Smiling, she raised her glass.

"To my husband, Matthew. Thank you for allowing me a chance to discover real happiness, and to all we both seek for our futures."

The hidden meaning was lost on the others, but Eve and Matt stared at each other for a long time before they attempted to sip their champagne.

Why couldn't it have been different? she thought, bringing the fluted glass to her lips. But it wasn't different, and when it was over it truly would be over. She would relocate and concentrate on becoming reacquainted with her son.

She never would remarry, or become involved with another man. *Not after Matt,* she mused as her gaze met his across the length of the table.

The meal concluded, Matt and Eve chatted casually with their guests. Blanca Lopes admired Eve's earrings while Matt stared at Cord, capturing his attention.

"¿Me permite una palabra, Cordero?" Matt questioned. Smiling at Eve, he whispered, "Excuse me, *Preciosa.* I need to speak with Cord before he leaves."

She returned his smile, nodding and touching his hand before turning her attention back to Blanca.

Matt escorted Cord through the loggia and out into the courtyard. Cord slipped his hands into the pockets of a pair of light gray trousers. "Why so formal, Mateo?"

Loosening his tie with his left hand, Matt ran his right one over his shortened hair. "Did you get in touch with Nate?" he asked without pausing for preliminaries. "I need to know how I'm supposed to pass myself off as a drug lord without jeopardizing the Arroyo name."

Cord gave him a long, hard stare. "Nate's off this one," he stated flatly.

The hardening of his jaw and the flash of amber and green in Matt's eyes was the only indication of his reaction to Cord's unexpected disclosure. He looked like a large cat ready to pounce on an unsuspecting prey.

"Why? Who's replacing him?"

"Why? Because they suspect someone very close to Nathaniel Webb is a mole."

"Surely no one would suspect the Director of the Drug Enforcement Administration of selling out," Matt said quickly.

Cord shook his head. "This has nothing to do with Nate. The man would turn his mother in if he caught her with a joint." Matt rubbed his fingers over his smooth jaw, nodding in agreement. "And to answer your second question. Joshua Kirkland's heading this maneuver."

"No way," Matt protested. "He's out of it. Joshua retired several years back, and is now living in Jamaica."

Cord shook his head. "Wrong, Mateo. The man's back, and I'm supposed to meet him at the airport tomorrow evening. He'll let me know who to contact for the pickup, and he'll also arrange for the transfer of some of the highest grade marijuana ever produced in Mexico. What you have to do is convince Delgado that you have the connections to move his drugs out of the country without implicating him or yourself."

Matt kicked at a pebble, gritting his teeth. He hated masquerading as a drug smuggler, but he did trust Harry Blackwell enough to protect his name if the mission failed. There were too many people on covert U.S. government payrolls who would look the other way, or deny they ever knew Mateo Arroyo.

"Why didn't you tell me about Nate the other day?" he asked Cord.

Cordero Birmingham's blue eyes narrowed. "I just found out this morning. Your orders have been changed."

"To what?" Matt's voice was barely a whisper, his golden eyes resembling those of a trapped wolf.

"Someone has been tipping off Delgado. Your orders are now to take out the mole and leave Delgado in place."

"Whose directive is this?"

"Joshua Kirkland's."

Matt felt a tightness in his chest. Blackwell's orders were now worthless. They didn't want him to rescue Christopher Delgado or identify the leader of the Costa Rican rebels. All they wanted was some damn mole who was embarrassing the United States. "Did you tell him about my marriage?"

"I mentioned you were to be married, but he didn't say

anything. He just stared through me with those damned cold eyes,'' Cord informed a frowning Matt.

Uneasiness etched on his face, Matt snorted audibly. "He's a human machine who can freeze hell just by willing it,'' he mocked, confirming Cord's assessment of Joshua Kirkland. "Well, there's nothing we can do about it now. He's the best in the business, and I could have worse watching my back,'' he added in a lighter tone.

Cord turned away, not permitting Matt to see the expression of hardness marring his young, arresting good looks. "Why are you doing this, Mateo?''

"Doing what?''

"Operating in Mexico.''

Matt didn't have an answer for Cord. His mind spun with the realization that he'd married Eve for nothing. He'd been reassigned; he wouldn't be able to go after her ex-husband and rescue her son. How was he to tell Eve this after their month-long liaison? Or could he hope that the child was safely back in the U.S.? If the child was, then Harry should've gotten the word to him.

The thought also attacked him that Harry Blackwell knew he would never have operated openly in Mexico if it hadn't been for the abducted child. What he had to find out was whether Christopher Delgado was still missing or back in the United States.

Cord turned back to Matt. "Why don't you take your wife and get out of this stinking business, Mateo? Sell the hotel, move north, and settle down. You're getting too old to continue flirting with death. You don't need the money or the excitement any more.''

A wicked grin lifted the corners of Matt's mobile mouth. "Are you finished with the lecture, Cordero?''

"I'll meet you in Puerto Angel in three weeks,'' Cord replied smoothly. He'd seen the smile enough to know better than to test Mateo Arroyo's temper. "Enjoy your wife.'' *While you're still alive,* he added silently.

Matt waited for Cord to leave before returning to the

coolness of the house by a rear entrance, and made his way to Eve's bedroom. Only her purse on the dresser indicated she'd occupied the space. Everything else belonging to her had been removed, and he wondered how long it would be before she would also become a memory.

Without any warning, Cord had informed him Delgado was no longer his target. And that meant he didn't need Eve. But he did need her—not for his mission, not for her body, but for himself.

She offered something more: a sense of peace he never could seem to grasp. And she needed him, to get her son.

He cursed under his breath, the words ugly and savage. He cursed Harry Blackwell and he cursed Joshua Kirkland. The two men could rot in hell for setting him up. Not only had they set him up, but also Eve.

He sank down slowly to the bed, his hands tightening into fists. The uneasiness he felt before returned, and his chest rose and fell heavily from the naked fear snaking through his body. A vision of his death stabbed his brain.

He'd been close to death before, knowing what it felt like to sink deeper and deeper into darkness where there was no warmth or anything to hold on to.

The bullet had hit inches above his heart, instantly numbing his body with fire and pain. He'd run a hundred yards before he found the courage to look down at his tunic soaked with blood. It had taken three men to hold him down before he was injected with a powerful narcotic. His movements had given away their position.

The men later told him that they didn't know what had unnerved them more—his incredible strength or their possible capture by the guerrillas.

He wondered when he'd last actually relaxed and enjoyed being Matthew Sterling. Shaking his head, he smiled. It had been a long time. In fact, too long. Not since he'd taught at the small, private college in El Paso.

Matt, musing on some private memories, failed to notice Eve's presence until his sensitive nostrils detected the subtle fragrance of her perfume. He glanced up, registering the tender expression on her face. Had she noted the void in his existence that money, danger, and other women had not filled?

He wasn't able to tear his gaze away from hers as she stood only a few feet away, watching him wallow in the poignancy of unfulfilled dreams, while he managed a tentative smile. He was slipping. His instincts and reaction time had slowed. In the past he never would've allowed anyone to come within five feet of him without his internal radar alerting him of their approach.

"Yes, Eve?" He still had not risen from the bed.

Her delicate eyebrows inched up a fraction. "Our guests are preparing to leave," she informed him in a calm voice. Turning on her heel, she walked out of the bedroom.

It took Matt seconds to reach her, his hand going to her waist and pulling her possessively against his body. He couldn't leave her. He *wouldn't* leave her or send her back—*not now*.

He cradled her face between his palms, a callused thumb caressing the smooth flesh over her cheekbone. "Well, Señora Arroyo, are you ready?"

"I only have to get my purse," Eve replied softly. She returned to the bedroom to retrieve the small, white, ostrich-skin shoulder bag.

Matt never acknowledged that he was disobeying a directive. What the hell did it mean to him, anyway? He was a private citizen, not an employee of a governmental agency, and Eve *was* his wife.

He would uncover the mole for Blackwell and Kirkland *and* get Christopher Delgado for Eve Arroyo.

Matt never was one to play by the rules, and that was why he had been so successful.

Chapter Eleven

"Where are we going?" Eve asked, not opening her eyes. She didn't see the frown creasing Matt's smooth forehead.

He slipped on a pair of sunglasses while he waited for traffic to inch along at an intersection. "Puerto Angel."

The blistering late April sun hurled bolts of fire from the heavens, while the darkening clouds suspended above the smog-filled air hinted of rain. Matt doubted whether they would be able to arrive in Puerto Angel before encountering a tropical thunderstorm. In two days it would be May, the hottest month of the year in Mexico, and the beginning of the rainy season.

"What's there?"

He gritted his teeth in frustration. The traffic and burgeoning population of Mexico City were incredible. The city had become a place of refuge for Mexicans from all over the vast country.

"We'll be living there for the duration of your stay," he explained in a harsh tone which prompted Eve to open her eyes. She stared at his stoic expression. "I have a friend who allows me to use his house whenever he's out of the country," Matt continued. "It makes it very convenient, because the Delgado-Quinteros also reside in the south. I should be able to pick up enough information about your ex without attracting too much suspicion."

"Stop calling him that."

Matt raised his eyebrows behind the dark lenses. "What? Your ex-husband?"

"Yes," she replied quietly.

"I don't see why not, Eve. After this is over, I'll also be your ex-husband."

Eve visually explored Matt's nose and strong chin. He was right—he soon would become her ex-husband. "That's true," she conceded.

He gave her a long, penetrating look. "The only difference is that I won't make love to you or give you my child. Other than that, we're as married as any other couple."

Eve didn't know why but she felt oddly disappointed. She'd married Alex because she thought herself in love with him, and she'd married Matt because she needed him. It was as if she was destined not to marry a man who loved her as much as she loved him.

She'd learned to shield herself against the advances of many of the glib-tongued politicians, aides, and other influential Washingtonians who came into her shop for gifts for their wives or mistresses. One or two proved quite insistent until they heard the name Blackwell. Harry's name and his position with an intelligence branch of the government had insulated her until she met Alejandro Delgado.

Alex was not put off by her cool demeanor, and seemed unaffected by Harry's reputation. He'd waited a year before he asked her to share dinner with him for the first time. She refused, but finally consented to attend a reception with Alex at the White House, in honor of the visiting Mexican president.

Eve found herself swept up in a whirlwind of parties and passionate encounters with the elegant diplomat, and within a month she found herself exchanging vows with a man who had unlocked her heart to love.

It took her less than six months to discover that Alex was unable to give her what she had sought: love. Alex was unable to love her because the only love he was capable of exhibiting was directed inwardly. Alejandro Delgado-Quintero only loved himself.

Once she discovered herself pregnant, Eve overlooked Alex's selfishness and his discreet infidelities. He moved into a spare bedroom and she welcomed the estrangement. All of her love was transferred to her infant son as Alex became bolder, no longer bothering to conceal his affairs when strange women called the house, leaving cryptic messages. It was as if he wanted her to confront him; he wanted her mindless with jealousy and rage.

Eve surprised even herself when she'd returned home after visiting her uncle and his wife and found a pair of lacy underpants on the floor near her bed. Alex had made love to a woman—*in her bed!*

She didn't unpack her luggage, but gathered enough clothes for Chris and checked into a D.C. hotel. She'd had enough of the shouting episodes. Her son was old enough to realize that his mother cried after arguing with his father, and Eve had no intention of raising her child in a volatile environment where there was more acrimony than love.

"Why don't you try to get some sleep?" Matt suggested as Eve closed her eyes. Nodding, she leaned back against the leather seat.

"Where does your family live?" she asked in a drowsy voice after a lengthy silence.

"Puerto Escondido, Veracruz, Cuernavaca, and of course Mexico City." Matt loosened his tie with one hand, and unbuttoned the top button on the shirt. "I have a few stray cousins in the north but most of them still live in the south."

"Why did you give me the earrings?" Opening her eyes, she watched Matt staring at her as if she were a stranger.

"Alma told you?"

"Yes, she did."

His fingers tightened on the steering wheel as he returned his gaze to the taillights of the car in front of his. "I don't know," Matt lied smoothly. "Call it an impulse."

He did know. Not when he had offered the earrings to her, but now. Only now, after exchanging vows with her, did he realize that he'd fallen in love with Eve.

Once she'd become his wife, he wanted everything to be real. He wanted their pretended engagement and marriage to last forever. The month had passed quickly, too quickly, and he hadn't wanted to leave the Mexico City's glittering social arena, knowing that the pretense would also disappear with their departure. There would be no need to exhibit their passion once they closed the door to the house where they would take up residence in Puerto Angel.

Eve had played her part well, so well that Matt had been taken in by her beauty, charm, and passion. There were times when he wanted to strip away her clothes, and lose himself in the silky smoothness of her body. His need to mate with Eve went beyond a burning need to exist.

He'd offered her the earrings because she was his wife—before man and God—and he was committed to having her as his wife until he ceased to exist.

"I'll return them before I leave for the States," she said, breaking into his thoughts.

"Keep them," Matt countered.

"I can't keep them."

He gave her a quick glance. "Then return them to me after you receive the annulment papers."

"Okay," she agreed. Closing her eyes, she tried relaxing.

Once they left the crowded avenues of the city and sped along a modern highway, she felt herself succumbing to the hypnotic motion of the car and the cooling air flowing from the vents. She couldn't fall asleep. She was filled with an unending feeling of hope and peace; she was closer than she'd ever been in the past six months to her son; she was going to get her child back!

Matt shook Eve gently. "Wake up, *Preciosa.*"

Thick lashes fluttered several times before they swept upward, revealing large, velvet black eyes softened with sleep. She had fallen asleep, and it was nightfall.

"What time is it?" She ran her fingers through her curly short hair, then massaged the back of her neck.

"Here, let me do that." Matt's strong fingers circled her stiff neck, massaging the tight muscles. He smiled as she moaned softly. "We'll stay here for the night."

Matt had selected a converted convent for their overnight stay.

"Where are we?" Her voice was a seductive throaty whisper.

"Oaxaca."

Eve raised her head, her eyes narrowing in skepticism. "I thought you wanted to get to Puerto Angel today."

His hand went from her neck to her hair. "I did," he admitted close to her ear. His warm breath made her shiver. "But I doubt if we'll get there tonight. Most people don't drive along Mexican roads at night, especially during the rainy season, when there's always the threat of falling rocks created by the wet conditions, or animals wandering into the path of cars or trucks."

A feather of apprehension whispered through Eve. She was going to have to share a bed with Matt. She undid her seatbelt and stepped out of the car. The air in Oaxaca at night was hotter than in Mexico City because of the latter's higher altitude. Turning, she stared at the rugged mountain ranges of the Sierra Madre del Sur still visible in the waning light. They rose majestically above the deep gorges and hot arid valleys.

After they registered, a young man dressed in a loose-fitting white blouse and matching slacks escorted them to a spacious room with a large bed. Arched windows with shutters opened out to a veranda, and a lantern-lit court-yard below.

Matt spoke to him in rapid Spanish, informing him that he and his wife would dine in their room instead of in the converted convent's dining room. The young man smiled and bowed to Matt after placing their bags on a leather trunk at the foot of the bed.

Matt removed his jacket and tie, hanging them on the back of a chair, and stared at Eve as she walked out to the veranda. It wasn't going to be easy. He'd asked for a room with two beds but the proprietor had apologized profusely, saying none were available. It wasn't that he didn't want to share a bed with Eve. He was just realistic enough to know that making love with his wife was out of the question. He had to get her to want him as much as he wanted her; he wanted Eve to love him.

Eve returned from the veranda and sat down on the bed, her back to Matt. "If it won't bother you, I'm going to bed. You don't mind eating alone, do you?"

He noticed the taut curve of her spine. "No, I don't mind. But may I suggest you drink something? I don't want you to become dehydrated from the heat."

Moving over to the bed, Matt lay on it and pulled Eve down beside him. Molding her gently against his body, he smiled and kissed her forehead. "Don't worry so much, Eve. Everything is going to work out all right."

She snuggled closer to his chest, not seeing a knowing smile lift his mouth. "I don't believe we're doing this."

"Doing what?" he questioned, feigning ignorance.

"Sleeping together."

A soft laugh rumbled in his chest. "I wouldn't call it sleeping together. It's more like sharing a bed."

"And I suppose you've shared a bed with a lot of women."

Matt arched an eyebrow. Could he hope that Eve was jealous of the women in his past? "I did happen to *share* a bed with one woman who pretended to be my wife," he confessed.

"Did you—" Eve broke off suddenly, realizing what she was going to ask Matt.

"*¿Celosa, Preciosa?*"

"I don't understand the word, Matt."

As he lowered his head, his mouth hovered over hers. The warmth of his breath and the solid press of his large body fired explosive currents throughout her celibate body.

"Jealous," he said, watching her face intently. In the month since Eve had walked into his life, Matt had found her more beautiful each day. Her hair had grown enough to curl softly over her forehead and upper ears, she had gained weight and her cheeks had filled out, and her body had ripened with a slim lushness. He'd noticed other men staring at her whenever she walked into or across a room.

Her naturally arching eyebrows lifted as her lush mouth softened in a smile. "You wish," she teased.

Matt sobered quickly. "You're right, Eve. I wish." Rolling over quickly, he stood up and stared down at the shocked expression on her face. "I'd like to shower before eating, but you're welcome to use the bathroom first."

She needed no further prompting. Leaving the bed, she opened her luggage and withdrew a change of clothing. She had to get away from Matt—even if it was only a few feet.

He had verbalized what she didn't want to acknowledge. Some way and somehow, Matthew Sterling had slipped under the barrier she'd erected to keep him at a distance. How long could she keep up the pretense before he realized she lusted after him?

She hadn't known many men, and never had she experienced what she felt whenever she lay in Matt's arms. He summoned desire with only a look, and whenever he touched her she thought she would dissolve in a mass of heated passion.

She had to keep away from him, praying they would find Chris soon, before she was tested further.

"Careful, Matt," she warned quietly. "You're becoming a bit too zealous in this role as my husband." Blowing him a kiss, she made her way to the bathroom and closed the door.

It was another three minutes before Eve was able to bring her emotions under control. She sat on a small stool, her face in her hands, hyperventilating.

"Damn you, Matt," she whispered over and over. Why couldn't he play by the rules? They were only to pretend for other people that, they were in love.

Rising slowly, she made her way over to a mirror and looked at the strange expression of the woman staring back at her. Her eyes appeared unusually large, her delicate nostrils flared, and her full lips parted; all of her seemed to be flushed with a wanting and a waiting.

Turning away, she stared at the minute cracks in the adobe walls. The charade she'd been involved in for the past four weeks had taken its toll; she'd played her part too well.

Matt had projected a virility and power that was impossible to ignore, and there were times when, without warning, she craved his touch and his kiss. They were now husband and wife, and there were no boundaries to keep them from consummating their marriage, except the ones they had imposed on themselves.

Eve showered and changed into a pair of taupe cotton slacks with a matching blouse. She left the bathroom, her face free of makeup, her hair brushed off her forehead. The bedroom was dark, the only illumination coming from the lighted courtyard. Matt's shadowy figure was silhouetted as he leaned against the veranda's wrought-iron railing, smoking. The aromatic smell of tobacco lingered in the air.

He shifted from his lounging position, and she saw that he'd unbuttoned his shirt. The breadth of wide shoulders and a broad back which tapered to a narrow waist were outlined in the wavering light from below.

Making her way across the room, she stood at the floor-to-ceiling window, watching him. *Magnificent* was the only word she could come up with to describe her husband. She closed her eyes briefly, hoping to shut out the awesome sight of his half-naked body.

Her breathing quickened, coming out in a ragged whisper, and he turned quickly. Despite the darkness, Eve registered the gleam of interest in his large, luminous eyes as he stared at her seductively, his gaze traveling slowly from her face to her breasts.

Dropping the half-smoked cigar into a terra-cotta urn, he moved toward her. Eve saw him float to her as quietly as a breath of wind. She was amazed that a man his size could move as silently as a stalking cat. Without warning, the realization of who he was, who she had married, surfaced. The enormity of who she'd been involved with for the past month rocked her to the core. There was no doubt that Matthew Sterling, also known as Mateo Arroyo, was a hired gun, an assassin.

She moved quickly, anxious to escape him, making her way to the other end of the veranda. She was quick, but not quick enough. Matt's arm snaked out, catching her around the waist.

"No, Mateo," she gasped. A sob welled up in her throat as she pounded his bare chest with her fist.

Matt caught her hand, holding it firmly. "What's wrong, Eve?" There was a thread of alarm in his query.

You're wrong, Eve thought. She was unable to conceal the shudder shaking her body. *And I've been wrong,* her runaway thoughts shouted. How could she have desired someone who was a killer? Had she been so desperate to get her son back that she'd agreed to hire *and* marry a killer?

"Are you all right?" Matt asked, gathering Eve closer to his body. She nodded slowly, her cheek pressed against the hardness of his chest. One hand came up and cradled the back of her head.

Matt held her, the thumb of his right hand pressed against the rapid pulse along her neck. He counted the brisk beats until they slowed to a normal rhythm. Eve had lied to him. Something had frightened her, and it took only a second before he realized what it had been.

"Are you afraid of me?" he asked perceptively.

I'm terrified of what you are, she said silently. *And I'm afraid of myself and what I feel for you.* "I don't know," she said, unable to admit the truth.

"I would never hurt you, Eve." His voice was soft and comforting. "I've taken a vow to honor and protect you, Señora Arroyo. I don't ever want you to fear me."

Eve raised her head, the tip of her nose grazing the furred surface of his broad chest. "Matt, I can't ignore what you do for a living."

"Don't ignore it, *Preciosa.* Forget it. What I do for a living has nothing to do with you. Just think about your little boy."

Again Eve nodded. "I'll try," she replied, knowing Chris was all she needed to think about. Managing a tentative smile, she said, "I left some hot water for you," hoping to lighten the strained mood.

Matt stared down at Eve, trying to make out her expression in the muted light. A flash of light from a swaying lantern in the courtyard highlighted the precious stones hanging from her lobes. Leaning over, he pressed a soft kiss on the area below her ear.

"Don't go away," he whispered.

"I won't," she countered quietly, watching as Matt returned to the bedroom.

Eve stood on the veranda listening to the night sounds,

recognizing an occasional feminine laugh and the melodious strains of a lone guitar playing a Mexican folk song.

When she'd stepped off the plane in Mexico City a month before she never would've imagined that her life would have changed so dramatically. She was now Eve Arroyo, the wife of a man who led a double life—depending on which side of the border he resided.

A man she'd found herself inexorably bound to, and a man she desired.

Chapter Twelve

Eve sat at a small, round table with Matt, drinking bottled water and accepting small morsels of a dish he called *pescado al mojo de ajo,* fish in a garlic sauce.

Matt watched her chew a portion from his fork. "I thought you didn't want to eat anything," he teased, pointing to her untouched plate of grilled peppers, black beans, rice, and chicken.

"I'm not hungry. And besides, the chilies are too hot."

Matt speared a pepper from her plate, bit into it, closing his eyes and nodding while chewing slowly. "Wonderful."

Eve wrinkled her nose. "How can you eat something that spicy?"

"Don't you ever put hot sauce on your fried fish, chicken, or pork chops?"

"Yes," she admitted. "But this stuff is liquid fire."

Reaching across the table, Matt captured her right hand. *"Pobrecita,* he crooned softly. "It's too hot."

Eve pulled her hand away. "What we have in the States is nothing like the peppers here, and you know it."

Matt stared at her enchanting face. "That's because

there are more than eighty varieties of chilies, ranging from mild to fiery hot."

Raising her chin, Eve met his gaze. "Did you grow up eating the hot ones?"

"Only the moderately hot ones. Those on your plate are mild."

She snorted delicately and settled back on her chair. "I'll stick with the bottled sauce, thank you."

"Cobarda," he whispered.

"What?"

"Coward," he said in English.

"That's right," she confirmed, smiling.

Matt continued with his meal, occasionally winking at Eve as she picked cautiously at the contents of her plate. He enjoyed sharing meals with her. There was a certain kind of intimacy in the routine of sitting at a table while eating.

It was the only time that he was allowed the privilege of observing her stunning mouth opening and closing in a sensuous rhythm that conjured up sexual images of what he wanted to share with her. His penetrating, luminous gaze devoured the delicate shape of her exotic face with her large, haunting, black eyes staring back at him.

Placing his knife and fork on the table, Matt wiped his chin with a cloth napkin, drawing Eve's gaze to his mouth. "Under a different set of circumstance I would've enjoyed serving as your Mexican guide," he began quietly. "I would've shown you the huge pyramids dedicated to the sun and moon in Teotihuacán near Mexico City, the religious centers here in southern Mexico, and in northern Central America where the Mayans erected beautiful homes, pyramids and temples made of limestone.

"Their civilization recorded important dates and events on stone, and they wrote in what archeologists say is a kind of picture writing. Here in Oaxaca the Zapotec Indians leveled and flattened a mountaintop known as Monte Albán, where they conducted their religious ceremonies."

Eve dabbed her mouth with her own napkin. "I've read about the Mayans and the Aztecs, but not the Zapotex."

"Z-a-p-o-t-e-c," he corrected. "I share the bloodlines of the Zapotec Indians. The great majority of Mexicans are mestizos, persons of mixed European and Indian ancestry, while Africans and Asians are also a significant part of our racial mixture. Our Indian ancestors were living here when the Spanish began their conquest in the early sixteenth century.

"Most Americans think only of the Aztec and Mayan civilization when talking about Indians in Mexico, totally ignoring the other groups. Almost all Indians in Mexico speak Spanish. However, most Mexican Indians speak Spanish in addition to their own ancient language."

Eve was intrigued by this disclosure. "Do you speak Zapotec?"

Matt laughed, shaking his head. "No. I have enough with Spanish and English. Sometimes I think in one language and speak in the other. My grandfather speaks the tongue as easily as he speaks Spanish. His English is limited, but you should be able to communicate with him."

Eve felt uneasy. It was one thing to deceive Matt's cousin and her husband, but she wanted to draw the line when it came to deluding his grandfather.

"I didn't think I'd have to meet your grandfather."

"Grandfather and mother," Matt confirmed. "My grandmother called me after she read about our engagement, and she said she couldn't wait to meet you." Eve grimaced openly. "Don't worry, *Preciosa*, she'll love her new granddaughter."

"You're taking this too far," she mumbled.

Matt's expression grew somber. "Remember, Eve, you're my wife and . . ."

"I'm not your wife in the real sense of the word."

His eyes widened, all traces of gold absent. "Are you asking me to take you as my wife in the biblical sense?"

Her face flamed with heat. "Of course not!"

"Then, what are you implying, *wife?*"

Eve was angry with herself. She felt trapped. "I didn't mean it that way, and you know it."

Matt stared at her petulant lower lip as she sulked. What he wanted to do at that moment was pull her from her chair and take her lower lip between his teeth and suck it gently until she moaned in his arms. He wanted her pliant, and begging him to make love to her in the way a husband and wife shared each other's bodies.

"In case you change your mind, we can always use *that* bed," he stated quietly, motioning with his head toward the bed, "for something other than sleep."

Eve noted his smile. Matt was teasing. "I won't change my mind," she retorted.

"Do want to put some money on that?"

Realization dawned like a cold shower as Eve realized her position as Matt's wife. She was at his mercy. "I don't have any money." Her voice was a breathless whisper. All she possessed was a return ticket to the United States, and all the money she claimed was still in a Virginia bank.

Rising slowly to his feet, Matt circled the table and pulled her to her feet. "It appears as if you're at a distinct disadvantage, Señora Arroyo."

"And knowing this, I suppose you're going to take advantage of me."

He drank in her beauty, fragrance, and the essence of her femininity. His chest rose and fell heavily under a navy blue T-shirt. "Never." The single word conveyed all that he felt for the woman he'd claimed as his wife.

He walked over to a closet and withdrew a billfold from the pocket of his suit jacket. Counting out a dozen bills in large demoninations, he retraced his steps and handed them to her.

"Now you have the advantage," he stated with a smile.

Eve took the money, rose on tiptoe, and kissed his cheek. "Thank you."

* * *

The converted convent was quiet, most of the guests in bed as the night staff worked silently to prepare for the morning's arrivals and departures.

Matt lay in the dark beside Eve, forcing himself not to touch her. He knew by the rhythm of her breathing that she wasn't asleep. Shifting slightly, he cradled his head on folded arms. He had made it easy for her to dress and get into bed when he'd waited on the veranda.

The slight heat emanating from her slender body and the distinctive fragrance of her perfume swept over him like a gentle breeze, and he smiled. It was only the first night wherein they'd shared a bed, but Matt knew he could get accustomed to it—quickly.

He remembered the bathroom after Eve had showered, the smell of her everywhere in the small space. She'd stacked her perfumes and lotions neatly on a small table in one corner, hung her wet towel and cloth on a rack and wiped the basin and tub clean.

"Eve?" He heard her breathing halt, then start up again.

"Yes, Matt."

"What are you thinking about?"

There was a comfortable silence before she spoke. "You."

"What about me?"

"I know nothing about Matthew Sterling."

They were in Mexico, and in Mexico Matthew Sterling did not exist. Only Mateo Arroyo mattered. But Eve was his wife, and she had a right to know about the man she'd married, even if she thought it was transitory.

"What do you want to know?"

Eve turned toward him, her left arm resting on his flat stomach. "What did you do before you began rescuing people?"

Lowering one arm, Matt pulled her to his side. The silk of her nightgown grazed his flesh like static electricity. Out

of deference to her he'd worn a pair of pajama pants
without the top. Normally, he slept nude.

"I taught school."

Pulling out of his loose embrace, she sat up. "You—a
teacher?"

"I *was* a teacher," he said with laughter in his voice.
Rising slightly, he pulled her down beside him. "I went to
the University of Texas at Arlington and joined the ROTC.
After graduating I fulfilled my commitment to the Army.
Being in the military made a man out of me." What he
didn't disclose was the elite branch of the army he'd been
recruited to serve in, or the survival skills he'd been taught.
"After my military tour I taught Political Science for a few
years while earning a graduate degree in International
Relations. Then I began to imagine that the walls of the
classroom were closing in on me, so at the end of one
semester I walked into the office of the dean of faculty
and quit. I bummed around for a few years before deciding
to go into business for myself."

Eve pressed her nose to his hard shoulder, savoring the
scent of his clean flesh. "Who do you work for?" Her
breath was barely a whisper.

Matt tensed, every muscle in his body rigid. "People like
you, Eve," he replied through clenched teeth. "People
who can't wait for governments or agencies to wade
through the red tape."

"Would you have killed Alex if I'd offered you enough
money?"

The silence that ensued was deafening as Matt struggled
valiantly to control his temper. He was angry at himself
for his vulnerability. He'd revealed more about Matthew
Sterling to Eve than he'd ever disclosed to *any* woman.
Not even his mother or his sisters were aware of his double
life.

"I told you before that I don't want your money, Eve.
Your body would be payment enough." She gasped, pulling away from him. "What the hell kind of an answer did

you expect? I want you to get it through your head that I'm not looking for your son for you, but for your uncle," he railed in a half-truth. "After I get your son back it's over for you and me. Once I put you on that plane you're history, lady, *ancient history.*"

His original order had come from her uncle. However, it was rescinded with Cordero Birmingham's revised directive. Eve didn't know that; and she also didn't know that he had no intention of giving her up.

"That suits me just fine," Eve retorted, again pulling out of his embrace. This time he permitted her as she turned her back. There was more she wanted to say but she decided against it, swallowing back the virulent words poised on her tongue. She had to remind herself that she needed Matt. She couldn't afford to alienate him.

"Forgive me, Matt. My question was out of order."

Matt didn't believe she was sorry. Her words dripped honey while he imagined her eyes flashed fire. And even though he was cognizant of her quick temper he wasn't put off by it, because anyone familiar with Mateo Arroyo would say his stunning wife merely complemented his dominating personality.

As it was, she knew too much about him. If she had been anyone other than a relative of Harry Blackwell's he would never have agreed to meet her. He had accepted only one assignment from a woman in the past—a very beautiful and very wealthy woman—and it had almost cost him his life when he'd refused her advances. It was also the first time he had ever been set up.

But somehow he hoped it would be different with Eve. He knew she would strike a deal with the devil if that would reunite her with her son. He knew that the moment she agreed to the *matrimonio de conveniencia.*

He lay motionless, listening to the soft sound of her breathing. His own breathing deepened and within minutes sleep overtook the both of them.

Chapter Thirteen

Eve stepped out of the car, staring out at the blue-gray haze rising above the dense jungle in the distance. A few dark clouds hovered overhead, signaling the approach of another tropical downpour.

Turning, she glanced up the hill, steep and unpaved, where Matt had disappeared. He claimed there was a house at its summit. She moaned, noting the soft black earth seeping into her impractical footwear. How was she to pretend elegance in the jungle?

She and Matt had spent two nights in Oaxaca. Torrential rains had flooded the southern region, forcing them to seek an additional night's refuge in the converted convent.

Matt inched his way down the path and to Eve, where she leaned against the bumper of his car. The two day delay in Oaxaca did little to improve his disposition. He was falling more in love with Eve and that created a problem for him. Her presence reminded him of what he had become, and how he had come to abhor what he did for a living.

He moved closer, studying her delicate profile. The tropical dampness had curled her hair tightly against her scalp, and droplets of moisture dotted her velvety, dark brown forehead. His gaze moved down to the soft curve of her breasts under a cotton blouse.

"What do you think of it?" he asked.

Eve crossed her arms over her chest. Her obsidian gaze followed a large bird as it settled on the upper branches of a tree, its wings outstretched in majestic, colorful splendor. "It's beautiful, but it frightens me, Matt," she admitted. Turning, she noted his strange expression.

"What frightens you?" The tenderness in his eyes vanished quickly, replaced by wariness.

"The jungle, this mountain, and the house not visible from the road below. I thought the house would be closer to the water, not up here where it resembles some sort of hideout." Eve missed the tension tightening Matt's mouth and the wild, animal-like glow of the gold in his eyes as she noticed the mud on her leather sandals.

"My friend had his reasons for building a house up here," he answered in a strained tone.

Her head came up quickly. "Does he also kill people for a living?"

The fire in Matt's eyes glowed like an inferno. He wanted to shake Eve until she was breathless. He slipped his hands into the pockets of his slacks instead. "You seem to have a problem with your memory, Señora Arroyo. I've told you everything I feel you should know about me, and that means *everything*. I don't like to repeat—"

"You've made your point, Mateo," Eve snapped, cutting him off.

"I don't think I have!" he shouted.

"I told you before not to yell at me!"

Matt's lower lip curved downward as he glared at her from his superior height. "I have very little patience with stubborn, mule-headed women who refuse to follow orders. How the hell do you expect to raise a child properly when you're still a child yourself?"

"If I don't know what I'm being drawn into, I won't live

to raise my son.'' She slammed her fist against the hood of the car, her body shaking with rage. "I didn't want to come here. I don't want to be with you." Her eyes filled with tears. "You asked me if I was afraid of you, and I told you I didn't know. Well, the truth is, *I am.* You're a human killing machine, a weapon. Your existence is filled with death, and that makes me susceptible. I grew up without my mother. I don't want the same for my son."

Matt reached out, capturing her shoulders, and stared down at the tears in her eyes. Her fear was real. It wasn't for herself, but for her child. He knew he should never have brought her with him. He should've put her on the first plane back to the States and left Harry Blackwell with the responsibility of getting the boy back. She was afraid of him and probably hated him. She saw him as a messenger of death.

"Do you want your son?" She nodded, her face wet with tears. He pulled her to his chest. "Can you let go of your fear and hatred long enough for me to try to find your child?"

He didn't know what else to say to comfort Eve as she cried silently, her body trembling uncontrollably. Matt had never played comforter before.

"Eve, Eve," he crooned softly.

She wound her arms around his waist, immersing herself in his strength and warmth. She'd weakened. As much as she tried, she couldn't shake off the feeling of danger. It swept over her as she lay in bed trying to fall asleep at night, and in the early hours when she waited for the sun to rise. Whenever she was alone, it attacked. She was embarking on a journey of death, and she didn't know whether it was for herself or for Matt. Or for both of them.

"I don't want you to fear me, Darling. Not now, not ever," he whispered against her ear. His lips caressed her soft, fragrant hair, then moved over her closed eyelids, his tongue tasting the salty tears on her cheeks. A rush of air from her parted lips mingled with his. Her breathing was slower, even. "That's it, Baby. Everything is going to be okay."

Eve swallowed her fear and threw herself into settling into the house. Matt had carried the luggage up to the second-story bedrooms while she inspected the structure designed with spaces instead of rooms.

The Spanish-style house was created with a sense of openness. A spacious entry was filled with towering cacti, and provided a pivotal stage for viewing a living and dining area situated several steps below the raised kitchen before a curving stairway led to the upper level and the private bedrooms. The kitchen was equipped with a large, walkin freezer, stocked with packaged and labeled meat, poultry, fish, fruits, and vegetables.

Stucco and brick walls kept the coolness in and the heat at bay. The dark brown, leather-covered furniture and earth tones of rust and tan on the first floor were predominant throughout most of the masculine dwelling.

The second-story loft contained two large bedrooms and a bathroom with a dressing suite. There, everything was either black or white. Large blocks of white tile were repeated throughout the bedrooms and bath. A black marble vanity, sunken tub and shower stall, and frosted glass walls overlooking the ocean made her feel like a libertine in a tiled temple.

She grimaced when she spotted the muddy footprints she was leaving on the pristine floor. A roll of thunder shook the heavens and the surrounding jungle, and she flinched, wrapping her arms around her body.

"Eve?" Matt's voice echoed from one of the bedrooms.

Slipping out of her shoes, Eve left them in a corner of the bathroom and made her way to the bedroom nearest the staircase. Piles of clothing covered the bed as Matt searched through a stack of T-shirts. He had changed into a pair of jeans.

His back was to her and she gaped at the dark, sun-browned skin over his broad back. She had twice shared a bed with him and not once had she seen his bare back. A long, pale, jagged scar ran from his right kidney up to his left shoulder. The unscarred right shoulder blade was tattooed with the design of a bird in flight, rising from fiery flames. Closing her eyes, she bit down hard on her lower lip at the same time Matt turned around.

"What's the matter? Are you all right?"

His hoarse whisper prompted Eve to open her eyes. She wiped her moist palms down the sides of her slacks, nodding. He thought the impending storm had frightened her. "Your back," she mumbled weakly.

Matt's mouth curved into a wide grin. "Oh, that," he replied glibly. "My father had a bull that wouldn't allow anyone to ride him. I bet some of the men who worked for my father I could."

"Did you?" Her gaze was fixed on his chest covered with thick, curling black hair. The masculine beauty she'd only had glimpses of over the past two days was blatantly displayed; and for the first time she noticed several medals suspended on a thick gold chain that was nearly hidden in the furred darkness. He hadn't worn them before.

"I managed to stay on for a record time of ten seconds before he threw me and ripped open my back. His horns just missed my kidney. He was the best damned stud bull we owned, but my mother threatened to shoot him if my father didn't sell him."

Eve had to smile. "Did he?"

"Damn right," he drawled. "A dead bull isn't worth a dime. And knowing my mother, Clayton Sterling had it on the market before the end of the week." Turning back to the pile of clothes, Matt picked up a black T-shirt.

"When did you get the tattoo?"

Matt pulled the T-shirt over his head, tucking the hem into the waistband of his jeans. "I had it done on a lark," he explained noncommittally. What he didn't tell her was that it was a constant reminder of his brush with death in El Salvador.

Eve cocked her head at an angle. "It's a phoenix, isn't it?"

His gaze met hers. "Yes, Eve, it's a phoenix. I'm going out," he continued smoothly. "Will it frighten you to be here by yourself if it begins raining?"

She shook her head. "I'll be okay."

Matt smiled. "Good. I should return within a few hours. I'll put my clothes away later."

"What would you like for dinner?" Eve asked. She registered his amused expression. "I managed to get an A in Home Economics."

Matt walked over to her and cradled her face between his hands, his thumbs tracing the curve of her eyebrows. "Surprise me," he whispered, leaning over and brushing his lips against hers.

Eve curved her fingers around his strong wrists, unable to tear her gaze from his bold features. "Be careful, Matt."

"I will be more than careful, *Preciosa,* because I want to come back to my beautiful wife."

Eve heard the words, felt his warmth and then his loss as he released her. She stared at the doorway, long after Matt disappeared through it, and listened for the car's engine. The rumbling sound of thunder drowned out everything, and soon the only sound she heard was the staccato tapping of the driving sheets of rain against the windows.

She went into her own bedroom and began unpacking. *How convenient,* she thought. How orderly everything was that had been set up for them. An unoccupied, furnished house hidden away on the top of a mountain, with a freezer stocked with food.

Who were these invisible people Matt worked for? How far did his network reach? Would this mission be added to his list of successful and completed, or would he fail? She whispered a prayer that he would succeed. To fail meant there would be more than one loser. Counting herself, there would also be her son.

Matt whistled to himself as he maneuvered the Range Rover down the rain-soaked mountain. He silently thanked Horst for leaving the rugged four-wheel vehicle. He knew Horst preferred driving back to Mexico City to piloting his Cessna.

Horst Van Holt complained bitterly whenever he had to put his aircraft down on the narrow strip of land beyond the house. The rising fog always made his descent and landing difficult, but each time Matt had flown with him he was amazed by his ability to bring the plane in for a smooth, bump-free landing.

The flat stretch of land had been the reason Horst built the house high up on the mountain instead of near the beach. Like Matt, Horst valued his privacy, and living in Puerto Angel allowed him to mingle comfortably among the natives who knew him as a wealthy European who preferred Mexico to his native Holland.

Matt liked Puerto Angel. It was even more laid-back than its nearest neighbor Puerto Escondido. It remained unchanged, unlike Acapulco and Puerto Vallarta, and he never tired of returning to enjoy the unhurried solitude it offered.

He slowed the Range Rover, parking in a narrow alley next to a small grocery store. Sprinting from the car, he jumped several puddles and landed heavily on the wooden boards under a faded awning.

"Took you long enough to get here," came a muffled voice from under a battered straw hat.

Matt glanced down at the extended legs and feet of the man slouched in a rickety chair. "Couldn't be helped. The rain held us up in Oaxaca City."

"Us?"

Matt leaned against a post, doubting whether it could support his full weight. "My wife—"

"Wife?" The man jumped up and knocked over his chair in a loud clatter. He stared up at Matt, shock and surprise on his face.

"*Sí*, Jorge," Matt replied, smiling.

"Where is she?"

Matt laid an arm over Jorge Martín's shoulder. "She's up at the house. You'll get to meet her later. Right now you and I have to discuss a few things. Business my wife knows nothing about," he added with a firmness Jorge had no difficulty interpreting.

Jorge put a sign on the door indicating he was closed and led Matt inside. "I haven't made more than twenty pesos all day. It's a good thing I don't depend on these people for my livelihood or I would starve to death, and so would my wife and children." He chuckled.

Matt followed Jorge through a sparsely stocked store to a back room. He waited until Jorge turned on a small lamp, illuminating the dark space. "How many children do you have now?

"Two," Jorge announced in a proud voice. He removed two bottles of beer from a freezer, handing one to Matt.

Matt straddled a low stool and took a deep swallow of the cold beer. He shook his head in amazement. "Damn, man, give the woman a break. Two children in three years of marriage."

Jorge shrugged his shoulders. "She likes babies and I like making them." He winked at Matt, then put the bottle of Carta Blanca to his lips, not stopping until it was empty. "Good beer, a good woman, and strong children. What else could a man want?"

Matt ran a forefinger down the moist bottle. "How about seeing this job finished so you can go back to Texas?"

Jorge Martín ran a hand over his face and through coal black hair. Large, equally black eyes stared blankly into space. "I want to go home so much that I sometimes think

I'm going to lose my mind. Every time Lilian has another baby I freak out.''

Matt knew the man was under a great deal of pressure when he began slipping into English. His amber-green eyes searched the chiseled features of his friend. "It's almost over, Jorge," he said in English. "I'm here to wrap it all up."

Jorge blinked several times, his mouth working furiously before he was able to speak. "Nate's using you?"

"Kirkland's now in charge. Cord told me Nate is off this one."

"Well, I'll be double damned." Jorge sighed, smiling. "I knew *El Halcón* couldn't keep his hands clean by passing himself off as a Jamaican entrepreneur."

"Falcon is the best man for this operation, and we both know it," Matt murmured under his breath.

"When is all of this going down?" Jorge asked, his dark eyes bright with excitement and anticipation.

Matt accepted another bottle of beer from his grinning friend. "Cord will be here in less than three weeks. He'll have the dates and positions on everything and everyone. I'm going over to Puerto Escondido in a few days to visit my grandparents. While I'm there I'll see what I can pick up on my own."

"When it hits, Mateo, all Mexico is going to feel it."

He nodded in agreement. "Just be sure you're far enough away from here when it does happen." He stared down at the scarred table top. Talking about getting out of Mexico reminded him of Eve and her son. He had to find the little boy before Joshua Kirkland and his men began their campaign.

"I'm sending Lilian and the kids up north to her sister in Nueva Casas Grandes," Jorge said softly. "From there I'll have the American authorities get them back to the States." Jorge's eyes narrowed as he peered closely at Matt. "What about you, Mateo? Do you have any idea of what you're risking by throwing in with the rest of us? Mexico is your home. You still have family here. What are they going to think about you once everything is out in the open? The Arroyo name will be worth less than donkey dung.''

Matt propped his feet up on a chair and leaned back against a wall. ''I've thought about it. I'm hoping I can remain far enough away from the center of activity so I won't be implicated or named when the authorities come around asking questions.''

''How about your wife? Does she know about you? Does she know that her husband will be up to his ears in Mexican drug trafficking?''

''Eve knows nothing,'' he mumbled harshly.

Jorge leaned closer. ''She's American?''

Matt searched for a cigar, then remembered he'd left them back at the house. Jorge pushed a pack of cigarettes across the table. They were a Turkish brand.

He shook his head, refusing the cigarettes. ''Yes, she's an American,'' Matt confirmed, staring at his contact. Jorge Martín was more than a contact. He was a boyhood friend from Texas. They ran together as teenagers, dated the same girls and joined the military together. After they were discharged, they lost contact with each other until Matt was reunited with the undercover DEA agent less than a year ago. Now, again, they had to watch each other's backs.

Jorge leaned back on his chair, frowning. ''What the hell are you doing bringing her down here?'' he hissed.

''I'm trying to locate her son.''

''Here in Mexico?''

Matt decided to be direct. ''Her ex-husband kidnapped the boy.'' His jaw hardened noticeably. ''She was married to Alejandro Delgado-Quintero.''

Jorge stared at Matt in disbelief. ''What are you going to do to Delgado?'' he asked as a savage expression distorted Matt's features, an expression that he was familiar with. It meant trouble. Serious trouble for Delgado.

''Nothing until I get the child back. Then I'm going to

cut him into little pieces for shark bait." He drained his bottle of beer. "How about you and Lilian come up for dinner one night? Bring the kids if you can't get someone to watch them."

"I think she'd like that." Jorge gave Matt a weak smile. "In fact, both of us would like that."

The rain had stopped and the emerging sun revealed its tropical brilliance in the late afternoon shadows. Eve ignored the wetness seeping through the canvas covering of her jogging shoes as she inched her way down the slope. The raucous cries of birds and other forms of wildlife filled the humid air, and the redolent aroma of wet earth rose sharply in her nostrils. Water from rustling activity in a tree rained on her.

The hill leveled off until it flattened to a dirt-packed plateau. Recalling what Matt had told her about Indian ceremonial places of worship, she wondered if this hill had been flattened for that purpose hundreds of years before. Shielding her eyes with her hand, she stared out at the stretch of beach near the ocean, and turning east she saw the density of the jungle and what she assumed was the country of Guatemala.

She continued her tour, gasping loudly when she discovered a waterfall spilling over into a large pool of clear, cold water. Lying flat on her belly, she looked down into the pool, trying to determine its depth. All around her, vines, wild flowers in every hue, and large fronds from towering trees created a curtain that tempted her to partake of the natural splendor of the exotic boudoir.

Eve took off her shoes and trailed her feet in the water. She'd managed to repress her impulsiveness. Leaning back on her hands, she closed her eyes. For the first time in her life she felt free from ridicule and rigid restrictions.

Whenever she came home from school during a recess, she had made certain to do and say what was proper so that her father and stepmother wouldn't think about sending her back. It was always "Thank you" and "Yes, Ma'am" and "Please," and of course, "Thank you very much."

All of her good manners and demure smiles went completely unnoticed. She'd always been sent back to school.

She punished her teachers and her classmates instead of her parents. She broke curfew, wore makeup, and chewed gum. Floyd and Janice Blackwell were unable to believe the reports they received from the headmistress, and promptly re-registered her for another year, praying she would become the model daughter they sought.

The sun shifted position, filtering light through the trees, and Eve moved over to a sunny spot to take advantage of the strong rays. Moisture formed quickly on her flesh as she tied the hem of her blouse under her breasts in a tight knot. Resting her back against a massive tree trunk, she closed her eyes.

Eve had to sort out her feelings. She kept telling herself that she was afraid of Matt, but the more she thought about it the more she realized that he didn't frighten her—what he did for a living did. With this, she felt guilty. She'd come to him for help, then become guilt-ridden whenever snatches of morality crept into her consciousness. Even after she dismissed how Matthew Sterling earned his living, he continued to haunt her. Her needing him went beyond needing; she now wanted him.

She hadn't thought she would ever want a man the way she wanted Matt. Total surrender and possession. That was what she was ready to offer him.

It was those feelings that made her tongue as sharp as a rapier in order to keep him at a safe distance. She would not permit herself to get close. There was no way she could make it back this time from the heartache and disappointment.

Chapter Fourteen

Matt stood watching Eve as she sucked in her lower lip. She was engrossed in dicing onions and didn't see him as he crept silently into the kitchen. Her hair had been neatly brushed off her forehead and over her ears. He smiled. She wore one of his T-shirts over a pair of shorts. The sleeves ended below her elbows, and the hem inches above her cuffed shorts. Her firm breasts moved gently under the cotton shirt as she reached up for a platter from an overhead cabinet.

Being drawn into this scene of domesticity was like a punch in the gut; he'd missed so much. Now he knew how Carlos felt when he'd talked about wasting so many years playing the perennial bachelor before he married Alma. Walking into the house filled with mouthwatering smells and seeing Eve casually dressed and concentrating on preparing a meal he would share with her grabbed him and stirred emotions he hadn't realized he possessed.

He had only known her for a month, and already he'd grown used to her shy smiles and seductive glances. There were times she was so at ease with him that he couldn't help responding to her. He'd say something to make her smile, and she would lower her chin and glance up at him through thick, black lashes.

It had shocked him once he realized he was falling in love with her; he made love to her in his mind because he was honest enough with himself to know that once he claimed her soft, fragrant body he would never let her go. There was the realization that every woman he'd ever met became meaningless when he thought of the woman he'd claimed as his wife.

He knew what she looked like with his eyes closed, what she smelled like—even if he had to pick her out in a dark room with ten other women—and when they were apart his mind always drifted back to the satin blackness of her eyes that teased, seduced, and went through him.

"What's on the menu, *Preciosa?*"

Eve spun around, giving him an open smile. "French onion soup, salad, veal cutlets sauteed with herbs, and a peach mousse."

Matt strolled into the kitchen and examined the table covered with bunches of fresh herbs. "I see you discovered Horst's herb garden behind the house."

Eve brushed past Matt. She separated several leaves of thyme from parsley. "I discovered his garden and his delightful waterfall." His hands circled her waist, stopping her as she turned back to the sink.

She went limp when he lowered his head and pressed his mouth to the nape of her neck. Closing her eyes, she couldn't stop the soft groan escaping her parted lips. "Matt, no."

"Why not, Eve?"

"I . . . I have to finish dinner," she mumbled ineffectively.

"I'd rather have you for dinner," he teased. "Think of me as the Big Bad Wolf who has his hungry eyes on Goldilocks. And this time there's no woodcutter to save you."

Eve giggled. "Wrong story, Matt. It was Goldilocks with the Three Bears, and Red Riding Hood with the Wolf."

Matt's hand searched under the red T-shirt. "You're wearing red, so I'm not entirely wrong." His fingers brushed the velvet flesh over her ribs until they grazed a ripe breast.

The gesture shocked Matt as much as Eve. They both froze. Her breath was coming quickly as her breast filled his large hand.

His hand fell away, the red shirt floating back into place around her thighs. "I'm sorry."

All she could do was nod as he turned on his heel and walked out of the kitchen. She clenched her teeth tightly, her fingers shredding the pungent herbs as they floated to the floor. He was sorry, and she was a mass of screaming nerve endings.

"Damn you, Mateo," she mumbled. Damn him for being so attractive. And damn him for teasing her.

Matt watched Eve take a sip of wine. "How do you like it?"

Eve rolled the wine around on her tongue, then swallowed it. "Excellent."

"Châtenauneuf-du-Pape, nineteen seventy-eight," Matt stated. He took another swallow of the vintage red wine. "I must remember to leave a note for Horst, thanking him for replenishing his wine stock." He raised his glass. "And I thank you for a delicious meal."

Eve flashed him a slow smile. "I thank you for not leaving leftovers. I don't like to eat the same thing the next day." Matt bowed to her from across the table.

He drained his glass of wine. "I'll keep that in mind. But if you continue to prepare meals like you just did you'll never have any leftovers."

Preparing tasteful and eye-appealing meals was an art she had perfected once she had moved to Washington.

And as a diplomat's wife she had earned a reputation by hosting some of the most elegant and extravagant dinner parties in the capitol city.

"Are you ready for dessert?"

Matt didn't answer, preferring instead to stare at Eve. She was the most feminine woman he'd ever met. Being femine was as inherent to her as taking her next breath, and he found her delicate beauty startling.

The curve of her eyebrows, the slant of the large black eyes, the straight nose and wide generous mouth that he had discovered was made to be tasted all held him spellbound. She was like an oasis in the desert where he'd become a wanderer seeking her life-giving fruit.

"You'd better think about putting some protection on your face before you decide to sunbathe again," he suggested. The end of her nose and her cheekbones were darker than the rest of face. "And on any other area you've manage to expose," he added in a teasing tone.

"You've got a dirty mind, Matt," she retorted softly.

"Didn't you go skinny-dipping?"

Eve shrugged a shoulder. "I thought about it, but changed my mind," she confessed. She couldn't believe he was that perceptive. Maybe she was that easy to read.

Lines deepened around the golden eyes which had spent too many years squinting in the hot sun. "Why is it that men have to have dirty minds? Just once I'd like to know what you *innocent* women talk about when you get together for a bridal shower. It can't be too chaste if men aren't allowed to participate."

Eve stood up and began clearing the table. "What about your bachelor parties?" she threw over her shoulder as she made her way from the dining room up the three steps to the kitchen.

Matt followed, his hands filled with stacked dishes and cutlery. "Oh, that's where you're wrong, Señora Arroyo. We have women at our bachelor parties."

"Sure you do. Topless bimbettes and strippers."

He arched an eyebrow. "They're still women, *Preciosa.*" He glanced at Eve and she stuck her tongue at him.

Eve watched as Matt rinsed dishes and stacked them in the dishwasher. He seemed quite comfortable in the kitchen. Alex had never entered their kitchen, saying it wasn't the place for a man.

"You guys don't take it too well when women go to clubs to see male dancers, do you?" she challenged.

Matt sobered quickly. "Male strip joints," he snarled in disgust.

"Exotic dance clubs," she insisted.

"We won't argue about semantics, Eve," he stated firmly, crossing his muscular arms over his chest. "Those places are set up to cater to frustrated women who fantasize about something they're not getting at home." His machismo wouldn't allow him to admit to her that there were frustrated men at home as well.

Eve went rigid. She thought about Alex and his affairs. What hadn't she given him, to make him stray? "And just what is that?" she asked. The atmosphere had become tense and strained.

Matt reached out, drawing her close to his body. His eyes lingered on her frowning face. "Sex."

She met his unwavering stare. "I don't think they need sex as much as they need love."

"Wrong, Eve." The amber and green lights in his eyes sparkled like precious gems. "Love and sex are not inseparable. When a man loves a woman he's able to express that love through the very intimate act of sexual intercourse. He discovers what pleases her, and each time she offers her body he makes certain that she's satisfied before he takes his own pleasure. However, some men are selfish. They're only concerned with their fulfillment, leaving women to search elsewhere for gratification. Whether it's *exotic male dancers,* books, porno flicks, or another man, they usually aren't to blame. That is, if they are normal women."

Eve stared up at him in astonishment. She was unable

to believe he was that sensitive. "You seem to know a great deal about women and their needs."

His hands dropped and she took a step backward. "I've known a lot of women," he stated in a solemn tone, "and I'm also a good listener."

She lowered her chin, peering up at him through her lashes. "With other mens' wives?"

He snorted softly. "I only *listen* to their wives, *Preciosa*. I wouldn't like to be a cuckold, therefore I wouldn't put some other man on the receiving end of my philandering."

How unlike Alex, she thought, her smooth forehead wrinkling. Alex thought all women were his for the taking— married or single. Somehow no woman was immune to his charm.

"Eve?"

Matt's voice brought her back to the present. "Yes."

His forefinger touched her lower lip. Leaning down, he replaced it with his firm mouth. "Don't look so worried, Darling. For as long as we're married I'll remain faithful to you."

"It wouldn't bother me if you weren't," Eve replied, turning away. "After all, we both know this so-called marriage isn't a real one." She didn't want to believe what she was saying. How she wished she had married Matt first.

Matt fingers circled her waist, drawing her back against his length. "That's where you're wrong. We are married, and we'll remain married until I let you know it's over." He loosened his grip, turning her around until she faced him. "When are you going to get it into your brain that this is not a game we're playing? Alex Delgado isn't your common peon from a coffee plantation. He's a member of a privileged family; a very wealthy and influential family. He was an official representative from this country, and still has all of the connections. You don't need me to remind you of that."

"What makes you think you can penetrate this wall of protection Alex has set up around him?"

Matt wanted to tell her of his plan, but couldn't. To tell her would make her too aware of the danger he would be drawn into. He would have to protect her—with his own life if necessary.

"I'll get to Delgado because I don't play by the rules, Eve. I'll meet with him, get the information I want regarding your child, and make the appropriate arrangements to get both of you out of Mexico." He exhaled heavily, trying to relieve the tightness in his chest. "You've got to trust me, Darling. If you don't trust me, then we might as well call it quits right now. What's it going to be?"

Eve melted against his body. She needed him. Who else did she have? "You win, Matt. No more questions. No more doubts."

"How about our marriage?"

She smiled. Her left hand grazed his chest before her fingers caught the fabric of his black T-shirt. The overhead light caught the fiery sparkle of the diamonds nestled between blood-red rubies. "What about it, Mateo? I'm Eve Arroyo. Who did you think I was?" she crooned.

Matt lowered his chin to the top of her head, trying not to laugh. Eve was like an addiction. She was bad for him, but he wasn't ready to give her up. Not yet.

A bright, rising sun in a still clear sky was all Eve needed to convince her to seek out the waterfall she'd discovered the day before. The house was quiet and the door to Matt's bedroom was closed as she made her way down the staircase and out of the house.

She had surprised herself when she slept soundly through the night in the strange bed. She hadn't heard Matt climb the stairs hours after she had bid him goodnight.

He'd sat smoking, giving her a nod when she told him she felt fatigued. The golden eyes said what he refused to say—*stay here with me.* She was going to change her mind, but decided against it. She didn't want to become too used to him. Sleeping under the same roof and sharing meals and chores was enough. She didn't want to compound their temporary liaison by establishing a routine of talking about their pasts and what they wanted for their futures.

The tropical sun had begun to harden the dirt-packed road, and she found it easier to navigate the path to the pool. The day was alive with shrill noises and rustling movements from the tall trees reaching upward above the jungle floor.

Trailing vines with tiny flowers wound themselves around massive branches. Eve stopped to watch a minute green lizard become a part of a large leaf before its darting tongue flicked out, catching a fat, unsuspecting, hairy insect. The lizard had its breakfast.

She wanted to get in a swim before she returned to the house to prepare her own breakfast. A canopy of leaves graced her tropical boudoir as she sat down on the grass. Moisture had already formed on her skin by the time she pulled her T-shirt up over her head, kicked off her muddied jogging shoes, and slipped out of her jeans.

She judged the pool to be about eight feet wide and at least six feet in depth. A gentle rush of water over smooth rocks drowned out the cries of monkeys and large-billed birds. Adjusting the straps of her black maillot, she eased her feet and legs into the icy-cold water.

Eve had put on the one-piece swimsuit when she remembered Matt's comment about her skinny-dipping. The sun filtering through the trees warmed her quickly as she slipped into the pool and floated on her back, then on her face. She lost track of time as she frolicked like a child.

The sun had shifted position by the time she swam over to the edge of the pool; holding onto the smooth rocks, she hoisted herself up and out of the water. She slipped back, sputtering and gulping a mouthful of water as strong fingers gripped her wrist.

"What's the matter, Señora?"

Eve blinked furiously and glared up at a smiling Matt. Treading water, she floated back into the middle of the pool. "What are you trying to do? Give me a heart attack by sneaking up on me?"

He stood up, hands folded at his waist. The heat in her face had nothing to do with surprise, but with the shock of observing Matt wearing nothing more than a brief pair of black swim trunks that could hardly be called decent. They rode low on his trim hips, leaving nothing to her imagination as to his obvious maleness. The sparse triangle of fabric teased more than concealed. The thick, black hair covering his chest, arms and long muscled legs made his golden-brown skin appear darker.

Matt watched Eve retreat as he slid down into the pool, seeing her eyes widen as he came closer. His toes touched the silt-covered bottom. "I waited as long as I could, Darling." Her hands adjusted the top of her swimsuit and he smiled. "I heard you leave the house almost an hour ago, but when my stomach began growling I decided to come look for you."

"You don't need me to prepare your breakfast."

He gave her a forlorn expression. "But I can't cook, Darling."

Eve retreated until she felt the rocks against her back. "I'll teach you," she gasped breathlessly, seconds before he reached for her.

Matt's fingers curved around her narrow waist, the water adding to her buoyancy as he pressed her breasts to his bare chest. She felt his body's heat through her swimsuit. His fingers became steel bands, holding her captive. The heat from their bodies was enough to make the frigid water boil.

The gold and green eyes seemed to strip away her suit to photograph what lay beneath the black spandex. What did he want? What was he waiting for?

Eve tried, but she couldn't pull her gaze away from his mouth. The fire spreading from his massive body warmed her quivering flesh. How she wanted him. She wanted him to protect her, make her laugh and make her feel safe.

She needed him to give her the security her father had failed to give her, and she needed him to make her feel desirable again.

"I just might need some extra tutoring," Matt teased, before he released her and floated on his back. Eve swam quickly to the edge and climbed out of the water. "Aren't you going to share the pool with me, Eve?" he shouted.

I don't want to share the pool with you, screamed in her head. *I want to share your life with you.* A life away from the killings and secret missions; a life where she could feel like a woman loved by her child and desired by her husband.

Trembling hands reached for the towel atop her discarded clothing. There was no way she was going to swim with him. Seeing him fully clothed was tempting; seeing him with nothing more than swim trunks was torture.

"I'm going back to the house to prepare *your* breakfast."

"Forget about breakfast," he ordered sharply.

Sitting down on the ground she slipped into her jeans. "You can't ask me to prepare breakfast for you, then change your mind in the same breath. I've offered to do the cooking because I happen to like it. Not because you deem it my duty."

"This has nothing to do with cooking. What the hell are you frightened of, Eve?" he taunted. "I told you before that I'm not going to touch you." Frowning, he waded closer to the edge. "I'm not going to lie and say I don't find you attractive, because I do. You're a beautiful, sexy woman, and I don't think I'll ever forget you. But we happen to be actors in a play where we'll have to give the performances of our lives, and when the curtain comes down it will be over. For both of us."

Eve shoved her feet into her jogging shoes, stopping only to tie the laces. She had to get away from Matt. His words were branded into her brain. They were bound together, but were destined to live their separate lives.

And as much as she believed she was beginning to love him, she wanted it to be over. She didn't want to spend another day living a lie. The pretense was beginning to wear on her nerves, and she doubted whether she would be able to pull it off.

And while under the guise of wearing haute couture, attending high society parties, and living in luxurious surroundings, she had had feelings of guilt creep into her being. Matt claimed all of it was necessary to obtain information about her son, but there were times when she thought his stratagy too laid-back. She had been in Mexico more than a month, and she was no closer to regaining possession of her child than she had been when she first arrived.

Walking back to the house, she prayed for strength; she needed it if she wanted to reclaim her son.

Chapter Fifteen

Eve raised questioning eyebrows as Matt sat down at the kitchen table. It looked as if he had waged a personal war with his razor, as evidenced by the many dots of drying blood on his cheeks and chin.

She removed a plate filled with warm rolls from the oven, leaning over his shoulder and placing them on the table. "I think you'd better *retire* that blade before it decides to slip from your chin to your throat," she teased mercilessly close to his ear.

"That's not funny," he growled.

"I think it's very funny." She had recovered from their encounter at the pool, but apparently her refusal to swim with Matt had left him in a foul mood.

He'd returned to the house shortly after she did, and waited for her to shower before he stalked into the bathroom, slamming the door violently. He'd said over and over that their marriage was legal publicly and a sham privately. However, his display of affection had shifted to their private world, and when she didn't respond he was annoyed.

Sitting down, she flashed him an open smile. The short, wet, black hair clinging to his scalp resembled a seal's coat with its weight and sleekness.

Reaching for a roll, Eve missed the tightening of Matt's jaw and the imperceptible movement of his broad shoulders. She was barely given the opportunity to cry out before he sprang from his chair and brought her up hard against his body and tickled her. His hands swept up her rib cage as she collapsed, unable to catch her breath, in hysterical laughter.

"Apologize," Matt demanded. He held her firmly, not hurting her but not permitting her to escape him.

"No-o-o," Eve gasped. She wasn't going to give in that easily. Besides, there was nothing for her to apologize for.

"Give in, Darling. You can't win."

"Never." She wiggled sensually, her breasts brushing against his chest.

"Stop wiggling."

Eve shifted, unintentionally pressing her pelvis to his groin. "Let me go."

"I . . . I warned you," Matt said between clenched teeth.

He was going to release her even if she didn't apologize, but it was too late. The involuntary tremors of arousal began, bringing with it an explosive reaction in his loins.

Eve raised her chin and saw the unbridled passion in Matt's eyes before he lowered his head. His mouth took hers, the heat rising so quickly she weakened immediately.

She was only aware of his tongue forcing her lips apart and the solid hardness in his groin searching through the layers of fabric concealing their nakedness.

His tongue made a sweeping motion over her mouth, plunging in and out frantically and devouring the honeyed sweetness making him drunk with passion.

Matt's motions were jerky as he pulled his shirt from the waistband of his jeans. "Touch me," he demanded, his fiery breath on her face. Eve collapsed in his embrace and he supported her limp body with one arm. His right

hand was busy guiding her left under his shirt to his fevered
flesh.

"Matt," she groaned, her own breath coming in a staccato hiccuping. She couldn't think with his tongue explor-
ing the moistness of her mouth, then moving to the
runaway throbbing pulse in her throat.

"Yes, darling. Yes-s," he urged, his voice heavy and quivering with the passion Eve elicited as her fingers swept
over his belly and chest.

Eve needed no further urging. Her fingers charted a
course along the long scar on his back and traveled around
to the thick, coarse hair on his chest. She pressed her face
to a muscled shoulder, inhaling the scent of his skin. She'd
become a sculptor, tracing the planes of his beautifully
symmetrical male body: the broad shoulders she was
unable to put her arms around, the thick, deep chest and
the hard, flat belly.

Matt's hands were as busy as Eve's. His fingers swept over
her velvet-smooth flesh, leaving her gasping and trembling.
High, full breasts swelled against his palms, and he buried
his face against her neck.

"No more—please," she pleaded. Matt's harsh, uneven
breathing echoed in her ears while her own blood coursed
through her body like a heated, rushing stream.

As quickly as it had begun, it ended. Matt released her,
turned on his heel, walked out of the kitchen and up the
staircase.

What was happening to him? He had initiated an act
which could prove costly to both of them because he had
come close, much too close, to making love to Eve right
on the kitchen table.

Making his way down the hallway and into the bedroom
he'd selected, he lay across the bed, his mind a torment
of jumbled thoughts. He could rationalize and blame his
behavior on Eve's acid tongue. He'd told her over and
over that he wouldn't make love to her, yet he'd come
within seconds of doing just that. He'd spent the past

month lying to Eve and lying to himself. Mateo Arroyo needed Eve Blackwell-Arroyo. He needed the peace only she could give him, her warmth and passion, her pure light that eradicated the darker side of Mateo Arroyo, and he needed her to love him.

"I love her," he whispered to the silent room. Having said it aloud filled him with a sense of fulfillment, and the confidence he sought to see his mission to a successful conclusion.

He would give Eve back her son, give Joshua Kirkland his mole, and he would win the love of a woman he'd claimed as his wife.

Eve put away the remains of breakfast once she realized Matt was not going to return. She swept the floor, wiped the table, and adjusted the chairs' seat cushions, until she realized that she was about to plump up and straighten the same cushion for the third time.

She'd tried banishing the memory of what had occurred between her and Matt by keeping busy, but failed.

Walking out of the house and into the sultry morning, she recalled the erotic scene, frame by frame. Closing her eyes, she relived the taste and feel of Matt's mouth on hers, the warmth and strength of his hands on her bare breasts, and the clean, masculine scent of him in her nostrils and on her skin. Pleasure, pure and explosive, ripped through her body, resulting in a startling wetness between her thighs.

Breathing in deep, soul-drenching drafts, Eve savored the aftermath of her traitorous body. A smile softened her full lips. She'd enjoyed her husband's seduction; she wanted him to love her, and she wanted their marriage to last—forever.

Opening her eyes, Eve inched her way down the hill and headed through the thick underbrush until she came to the clearing with the waterfall. She sat on a half-rotting tree trunk, staring at the gentle rush of water flowing over pale rocks, trying to recall her mother's face. The shadowy image was replaced with that of her son.

Christopher Blackwell Delgado. Eve smiled, remembering the child who had inherited the best of his parents' genes and personalities. He was her love child who never complained when he was put to bed and always woke up smiling, and, like Alex, he adored the opposite sex. If she wore a new dress or gown or changed her hairstyle, Chris always responded effusively with compliments, and she'd prayed that he would not adopt his father's proclivity for infidelity. Chris sometimes displayed a quick temper and a streak of stubbornness she recognized as a characteristic of her own personality.

A shower of water rained down on Eve's head and shoulders, and she quickly vacated the downed limb. Shading her eyes with a hand, she peered upward, hoping to see what had startled the tree dwellers. The treetop activity increased, and seconds later large, fat drops splattered the leaves of massive trees before finding their way to the dark, heavy earth of the jungle floor.

A rumble of thunder reverberated over the mountains, followed by a crash and flash of lightning, chilling Eve before the rain soaked her skin.

Fear closed around her like a shroud, and she took a deep breath. *Don't panic; don't panic;* the refrain played over and over in her head; if she didn't panic, she would be able to make it back to the house, and safety.

The rain-soaked earth under her feet became a quagmire. Her shoes were sucked deeper into the morass with her every step.

Using a prolific, yielding banana tree as her landmark, Eve headed in the direction of the house situated at the top of the steep hill. She took a few steps, then fell forward, trying desperately to reach for something to break her headlong fall. Her right hand caught a thick, trailing vine as her heart pounded loudly in her ears. A shield of rain

and a rising fog distorted her vision, making it difficult to
see more than a half foot in front of her face. She couldn't
believe how quickly many pools of water formed around
her feet as she groped through the forested area.

A curtain of rain fell in a vertical pattern and Eve
stopped, holding onto a branch. A shriek of pure panic
escaped her lips when she felt movement under her hand.
Her fingers were locked around a slithering reptile which
had wrapped its length around the branch under an
umbrella-like leaf. She pulled her hand away, bringing it
close to her face and counting quickly to see if she had
all of her fingers.

She moved on, fan-like wet leaves slapping at her face
with each step. The effort to lift her legs as she struggled
with the thick mud became a tortuous exercise, and she
failed to notice the large, jutting root as she fell a second
time on the forest floor.

The violent rumble of thunder and the pelting sound
of rain against the bedroom windows propelled Matt from
the bed in a smooth motion. Making his way to the windows, he peered out. The downpour obliterated the outside.

Remembering Eve's reaction to the storm the day they'd
shopped in the *Zona Rosa,* he waited for her to come to
him.

He waited.

She did not come.

Quickly, silently, Matt searched every room, unable to
believe that Eve would be out in the storm.

He slowed his breathing as he inhaled deeply with the
realization that Eve was not in the house. There was only
one place he knew she would go, and he headed in that
direction.

He half-ran and half-slipped down the hill, golden eyes
searching through the thick screen of rain and fog. Mateo

Arroyo had become the hunter. He searched the wet ground for Eve's footprints. He became the big cat, seeking his prey, moving silently and swiftly. His stealth, coupled with a total absence of fear, made him a natural hunter.

As an adolescent he'd hunted snakes and cougars with his friends on a dare. Whatever they dared—he did. Whether it was catching a rattler with his bare hands before the fangs sank deep into his exposed flesh or facing a large cat armed only with a knife, he had lived on the edge.

He'd always won the wagers which prepared him for the rescue missions he led many times for the United States military.

There were times when he'd been close enough to his "target" for him to smell the perspiration clinging to their flesh, and still he had gone undetected. He'd stood motionless, slowing down his heart rate until a pulse was almost nonexistent.

He had become a weapons expert, knives his specialty. He found them silent and as lethal as a handgun. Many times his hands were his only weapons, causing unconsciousness within seconds with a blow to a vital area.

His work frightened Eve; his work and the dark world he occasionally ventured into. Harry Blackwell had told her about him, and her knowledge of his double life would keep her from trusting or loving him.

And Eve was the first woman Matt cared enough about to make her reaction to him matter.

Matt found Eve. She was motionless, facedown on the ground. Her clothes and hair were stained with mud and leaves. Turning her over, he cradled her to his chest, using his T-shirt to clear her nose and mouth of mud. His pulse quickened as he spied a thin ribbon of red along her hairline, over her left ear. His fingers grazed her scalp quickly and he discovered a small lump above the ear.

The driving rain washed away the traces of blood and dirt on her face as Eve's head fell back over his arm. Matt picked her up and rose to his feet in one continuous motion. She groaned once, not opening her eyes.

"Matt?" Her voice was weak and trembling.

"It's me, *Preciosa*. You hit your head, but you're going to be all right."

She mumbled as Matt cradled her protectively to his wet body. She counted silently with every step back to the house, temporarily forgetting about the band of pain enveloping her temples.

Matt expected resistance as he began stripping the muddied clothing from Eve's body. However, she lay rigid on her bed, her gaze fixed on the ceiling.

He removed her blouse, then raised her hips and pulled off her soggy slacks. A delicate scrap of silk and lace concealed her most private part from him, and that was also removed, leaving him to admire the perfection of her slim body.

His gaze lingered on her narrow waist and rounded hips. They shifted upward to her firm, dark-brown crested breasts, then moved downward again.

Sweet heaven! She was beautiful, Matt mused, transfixed by the flawlessness of Eve's body. His own body reacted with a rush of heaviness in his groin. This woman was his wife! He could claim her as his own! Pride and possession filled him as he leaned over and gathered her from the bed.

Whenever he went undercover in the past, he'd been grateful that he hadn't married. He hadn't wanted a woman to worry about him whenever he disappeared for months, or if he returned with a serious wound or new scar. He also hadn't wanted to have to explain where he'd been, or what he'd been doing, during his absence.

Only when he thought about relocating to New Mexico to breed horses did he think about a wife and children, and with his own family, he would be able to lead a normal life wherein he'd look forward to coming home each night. He also wanted to father his own children—he wanted Eve to have his children.

Eve pushed weakly against his chest. "Don't shake me, please. My head feels as if it's going to fall off."

Matt slowed his step, seemingly floating toward the bathroom. "I have to give you a bath, Eve. I want to make certain a parasite hasn't decided to use your body as a host for procreation." He lowered her to the bathtub he had filled with warm water.

Moaning softly, Eve closed her eyes and languished in the strength of Matt's fingers as he lathered her hair and body with a medicial-smelling liquid. His touch was impersonal as his hands grazed her breasts, and again when he drew a cloth between her thighs.

He drained the tub, refilled it, and washed and rinsed Eve a second time, confident that he'd cleansed her thoroughly. He'd witnessed what some of the tiny little tropical insects did to the human body—internally and externally.

"I'm going to give you something for the pain," he said quietly against her ear.

Eve nodded slightly, smiling. "Thank you."

Matt wrapped her in a large bathsheet and carried her to his bedroom. Placing her on the bed, he pulled one of his T-shirts over her naked body and eased her gently between the sheets. Minutes later, he held a glass of water to her lips as she swallowed a tiny pill.

All of Eve's senses were dulled within twenty minutes. The pill had taken effect, and she slept in Matt's bed and in Matt's arms until the sun rose in the sky, verifying the beginning of a new day.

Chapter Sixteen

Eve woke to a dull, throbbing pain over her left ear and a ribbon of waning daylight threading across the embroidered sheet. Her mouth felt as if it had been filled with dry, fluffy cotton. A faint odor of tobacco hung in the air, reminding her that Matt was not far away. Her fingers grazed the small lump along her hairline, and she winced and remembered falling. Closing her eyes, she recalled what had followed.

Matt was there, then he wasn't. He was there again, his hands moving gently over her body. He'd been warm and comforting. He'd whispered calming words, soothing away her panic and fears, and she hadn't protested when he undressed her and bathed her.

Whatever embarrassment she'd felt once he observed her nakedness dissipated quickly. Matt's large hands massaged her sore muscles with the impersonal touch of a physician. He'd applied an antiseptic cream to the scratches on her palms before cradling her to his chest, where she finally succumbed to the drugging effects of the pain reliever.

"Do you want me to fix you something to eat?" His disembodied voice came from somewhere in the bedroom.

Eve turned her head slowly, searching for him in the darkened space. "I thought you couldn't cook," she teased. Her voice was still heavy from sleep.

Matt moved from the chair in a corner and made his way across the room. He stared down at Eve, then sat down beside her. "I'm sure I can find something in the freezer."

She nodded, swallowing several times to moisten her throat. The freezer contained a cornucopia of containers with prepared and frozen soups, sauces and desserts.

"I'd like that, thank you." She didn't see his eyes soften with his acknowledged love for her.

Leaning over, Matt press his lips to her silken cheek, his nose nuzzling her ear as he inhaled her sweet, feminine fragrance. "Eve. My wife," he whispered, his voice filled with awe. "You are beautiful—all over. And one day I'm going to taste all of your ripe fruit even if it means that I'll burn in hell for breaking my vow that I'll never consummate this marriage."

A soft gasp escaped Eve and her heart pounded wildly as she watched Matt rise and walk out of the bedroom. A new and unexpected warmth flooded her body. Could she hope that there would be no annulment? That he was willing to share his future with her?

She loved Matt, but could she afford to take a chance on discovering happiness with him, then have it snatched away whenever he decided to embark on one of his "secret missions" and risk losing his life?

Maybe, just maybe, she could take the chance and the time given to her—to them.

Matt handed Eve a tray and settled down beside her on the bed, supporting his back against the mound of pillows along the headboard.

"It looks delicious," Eve said, examining the tray filled

with a bowl of beef stew, a saucer of sliced cheese and crackers, and two glasses of milk. "Where did you get the milk?"

"It's powdered." Picking up a glass of milk, the heavy gold ring on the third finger of his left hand glinting in the glow of the bedside lamps, Matt quickly drained the glass. He noticed Eve staring strangely at the remaining glass on the tray. "It's not half bad."

She wrinkled her nose. Powdered milk reminded her of boarding school. If it wasn't powdered milk, it was powdered eggs, potatoes, or dehydrated vegetables.

She took a sip of the milk, her eyebrows shifting in surprise. It was delicious. "What's in it?"

"It's a secret recipe." Matt's luminous eyes glittered mysteriously as he stared at her beneath lowered lids.

Eve felt her breath halt in her chest. Once again she found herself caught in Matt's smoldering, sultry, male magnetism. She felt the power in his muscled shoulder pressing against hers and the potent masculine scent of his cologne. His lean, sun-browned face was shadowed with the stubble of a beard as black as the thick hair covering his scalp. The long lashes framing his eyes highlighted their brilliant topaz and emerald colors. His sensual mouth curved into an unconscious smile, and she wondered if he knew how much she desired him.

"What are you looking at, Eve?" he questioned softly.

"You." Her chin came up slightly in a challenging gesture.

Matt came closer without moving. "What about me?"

She smiled and wiped away the residue of milk ringing his upper lip with her finger, but Matt's hand moved with incredible speed, capturing her wrist. He stared at her hand, then drew her forefinger into his mouth, sucking the tip of it in an agonizing slowness that fired her body like molten lava. His straight teeth tightened, not hurting her, but not allowing her escape.

Eve felt the heat from his mouth all over her body.

Matt continued the sucking, his tongue flicking across the sensitive tip while her womb contracted with the erotic rhythm. Her eyes widened until Matt saw into their black depths. He quickened the motion, increasing the jolts of passion rocking her body.

Her breathing was short and raspy. Matt released her finger, and she escaped from his rapacious tongue; he'd begun to fulfill his promise to taste her, and she would not permit herself to imagine what his mouth would claim next.

She managed to eat the beef stew without spilling it. Each time she raised and lowered the spoon, her hand shook as she fought the powerful virility Matt exuded.

"I love to watch you eat," he said, taking the tray from her lap and placing it on a side table.

Eve stared up at him in surprise. "Say what?"

Matt gathered her tightly, pulling her over his chest. She could feel the steady pumping of his heart against her breasts. The sheet twisted around her waist and served as a barrier between her naked thighs and his denim-covered legs and hips.

"You have a sweet little mouth, Eve," he crooned in her mussed hair.

For once, Eve did not have a comeback. She lay in Matt's arms, refusing to think about anything else except that for the first time in her life she truly felt protected.

She wanted what she had with Matt, at that moment, to last—forever, if that was possible.

"After this is over I'm leaving Mexico, Eve," he informed her. "I have a buyer for the hotel, and I'll be returning to the States as soon as the sale is finalized."

"What will happen to Mateo Arroyo?" she questioned, her warm, moist breath feathering over his throat.

"He will cease to exist, *Preciosa.*"

Raising her head, she looked down at Matt. "What will happen to Eve Arroyo?"

He stared up at her for a long time. "She will also cease to exist," he stated firmly.

She was numbed by his statement. *Fool*, she thought. What did she expect? She'd hoped and prayed for what was beyond her grasp. Matthew Sterling would not be a part of her future. As smoothly as she could, she eased herself from his embrace.

"Where are you going?" he demanded.

"I need to brush my teeth." She also wanted to put on more clothing, and put some distance between herself and the man she had married.

"I'll bring you what you need to brush your teeth."

"What I *have to do* in the bathroom you can't help me with," she said over her shoulder.

"I have quite a reputation for being versatile," he said teasingly at her departing figure. Eve hadn't turned around, but he was certain she was smiling.

Amusement flickered in his own eyes, and he felt relaxed for the first time since he found Eve facedown in the mud the day before.

Reclining on the bed, he folded his arms under his head and closed his eyes. His confession to Eve washed over him *. . . I'll burn in hell for breaking my vow that I'll never consummate this marriage.* He knew he'd shocked Eve when she'd gasped. However, it was time for him to stop lying to himself *and* to her. She deserved to know how he felt about their liaison, and now that she knew all Matt had to do was wait for her to come to him.

Eve left the bathroom, her fingers trailing along the wall for support. A wave of dizziness had hit without warning, and her knees buckled.

"Matt." Her voice was weightless as a mist.

Within seconds he was at her side, swinging her up into his strong arms. His black eyebrows nearly met in a furious scowl. "I told you to let me help you."

She covered her forehead with the back of one hand. "You couldn't help me with—"

"I could," he interrupted savagely. "You forget that I've seen and touched everything you claim as private, Señora Arroyo."

"Don't be vulgar, Matt," she admonished through her pain.

He cursed under his breath, implying what she could do with his vulgarity. Her eyes widened in surprise. "There are times when I have to be vulgar, cruel, and immoral, if it means staying alive. That's what I become whenever I accept a job from your uncle. And I'll be whatever I choose to be until all of this is over."

Another wave of dizziness shook Eve, bringing with it a film of moisture, and she moaned. "Matt . . . I'm going to be sick."

"You're going to be just fine," he reassured her. He placed her gently on the bed, pulling a sheet up over her trembling body. "I'm going to give you one more pill."

Closing her eyes tightly, she shook her head. "No more. You're turning me into a junkie."

"Don't be ridiculous, Eve. Two pills won't turn you into an addict."

Eve continued to protest, but Matt would not relent. She swallowed the pill, and half an hour later she lay slumped over his chest. "I hate you, Mateo Arroyo," she slurred.

Matt kissed the top of her head. "Sure you do, *Preciosa*. If this is the way you hate, I want to see how you love."

She struggled, unable to keep her eyes open. "You're taking advantage of me. You fill me with drugs, then threaten me. Just wait . . . wait until . . ."

"Until what, baby?" he whispered to a now sleeping Eve. *Until you come to love me as much as I love you*, he added silently.

All he wanted from Eve was her love, while he was willing to give her financial security, a father for her son, and the passion he had always withheld from any woman he'd ever known.

Eve woke up ten hours later, blinking and trying to orient herself. The first sight she saw was Matt's bared, broad back, her gaze fixed on the colorful tattoo of the red bird soaring above crimson-tinged gold flames. She also examined the path of the long scar, a symbol of an incident which had almost cost Matt his life, or a serious disability.

"How do you feel?"

Matt's voice, soft and quiet, startled Eve. "How did you know I was awake?" She had opened her eyes while not moving.

Matt shifted, turning to face her and pulling her into his embrace. Pressing his lips to her forehead, he whispered, "Your breathing changed."

Her slumberous gaze swept over his features, missing nothing. She examined the deep hue of his skin and realized that his dark coloring wasn't entirely from the hot Mexican sun; his coloring was a luminous contrast to the brilliant gold and green of his eyes, eyes that studied her and analyzed her reaction to him.

"How do you feel?" he repeated.

Eve managed a slight smile. "Wonderful."

He shifted a black eyebrow. "No pain?"

"No pain," she confirmed softly.

"Does that mean you can take care of yourself now?"

She ran a forefinger down the middle of his chest, leaving a thin path in the thick mat of hair. "Exactly. Now can you get me a robe so that I don't have to continue to model your T-shirt. I'm beginning to feel like Eve in the garden before the Fall."

Matt's arm curved around her waist, pulling her half-naked body flush against his. "There shouldn't be any modesty between a wife and her husband."

"There's a difference between modesty and brazenness," Eve said against his shoulder.

"I'll show you brazenness," Matt challenged. He cradled her to his chest, sat up, and swung his silk-covered pajama legs over the side of the bed. "It's time you began acting like a wife." He took purposeful strides that took him from the bedroom to the bathroom.

"What's that supposed to mean?" Her heart pounded uncontrollably.

"You'll see," he stated mysteriously. "We're going to share a shower. You're going to wash my back and I'll wash your back, then . . ."

Eve stared up at his smooth cheek rather than his broad, bared chest. It was obvious that he'd shaved while she slept. "Then what?"

Matt lowered Eve to her feet. His hooded gaze caressed her face. "Then anything you want to happen will happen," he answered cryptically.

Her breasts rose and fell in a shuddering tremor, bringing Matt's gaze to the full, firm globes of flesh under his T-shirt. "We can't, Mateo." Her voice was barely a whisper.

"Why not, Eve? There's nothing and no one to stop us."

"It will complicate everything."

He hesitated, trying to form the words to tell Eve that sleeping together would be the least complicated aspect of their liaison. How would she react when she discovered that he was masquerading as a drug trafficker? When she discovered that he had no intention of terminating their marriage?

"It will only become complicated if you want it to be," he argued as he pulled her to his chest.

"Matt, I—I've never been one for gratuitous sex." She found it difficult to remain coherent.

His mouth searched for hers, finding it and drawing

the last bit of resistance from her. "We're married," he reminded her.

"I know," she murmured between the light, nibbling kisses he brushed across her lips. "But—"

"But nothing, *Preciosa*. I want you. I want you the way a husband wants and needs his wife," Matt continued. "I've promised to honor you, protect you, and love you."

Eve was caught off guard by the passion in his voice as she registered what he'd just confessed, and through the roar of her pounding heart in her ears she focused on a single word.

"Do you, Matt?"

He laid his palm against her cheek, savoring the feel of her silken skin, one finger toying with the brilliant diamond hanging from her lobe. "Are you asking if I love you?" She nodded slowly.

A smile parted his sensual lips and passion darkened his eyes to green. "I fell in love with you the moment I saw you."

Eve's heart danced with excitement. He loved her and she loved him. "I—"

"Don't," Matt said, placing his thumb over her lips and cutting off her words. "Don't," he repeated, "say anything, my darling. If you feel only half of what I feel for you— show me."

Rising on tiptoe, she buried her face against his hot throat. "I love you, Mateo." She disobeyed him. She'd confessed to Matt that she loved him.

A surging wave of love and passion flowed between them as they clung together, savoring the emotion that made them one.

Eve could feel his uneven breathing against her cheek as he lowered his head and pulled her closer. They stood together, embracing, until their passions cooled.

She inhaled deeply, then let out her breath slowly. The magnificent man in her arms loved her as much as she loved him. "Come, *Precioso,*"she urged quietly, "you promised to wash my back."

Matt released Eve, stepping back and staring at her face. His hands went to his waist and seconds later his black silk pajama pants lay on the bathroom floor. She stared straight ahead, her gaze locked with his. It was a full minute before her gaze inched downward.

Her heart lurched, her lids fluttered, and Eve shivered from the wave of desire warming her limbs. Matt hadn't lied. He wanted her; he was aroused, his sex full, straining, and throbbing with desire.

Chapter Seventeen

Eve's trembling hands grasped the hem of her T-shirt, pulled it up, and drew it over her head. It, too, settled onto the bathroom floor with Matt's pajama pants.

He extended his arms and she walked into his embrace. Both of their hearts were pounding in a runaway rhythm as desires, repressed for hours, days, and weeks hovered close to the edge, threatening to erupt with every breath.

Swinging Eve up into his arms, Matt headed toward the oversized shower stall. She had wantonly, wilfully, and silently given approval to consummating their marriage. Fastening his mouth to hers, he opened the door to the stall and molded her shoulders to the tiled wall.

Matt's tongue swept over her lips and teeth before plunging deeply into her mouth. His breathing was slow, controlled, masking the throbbing hardness searching against her groin.

"Oh," Eve whispered, pulling back to catch her breath.

"Open your mouth," Matt ordered. She complied and he crooned, "That's it, Baby." Her arms went around his neck, bringing him closer. Her tongue dueled with his before her teeth sank gently into his lower lip and drew it into her mouth, while her hands swept up and down his body from his chest to his flat belly.

He couldn't believe Eve could be so sweet, enticing. His hands were just as busy—threading through the soft curls of her hair and grazing the velvet smoothness of her sweet-smelling flesh.

Matt's body was out of control, but his mind was methodical. He forced himself to slow down, wanting to erase the memory of Alejandro Delgado from Eve's mind. He wanted to be the only man in her life and in her memory. She was his and his alone, and he meant to brand his image on her brain.

Reaching out, his right hand searched for the cold water faucet and he turned it on. He turned on the hot, alternately adjusting the temperature until it was lukewarm. The water spilled down their naked bodies, the wetness glistening on their flesh.

They were transported back to their private waterfall and pool, but this time there were no scraps of spandex to conceal their desire for each other.

Matt cradled her breasts in his hands, examining their shape and weight. He lowered his head and drew his tongue around her large dark areolae and erect nipples while soft moans escaped her thoroughly-kissed, swollen mouth.

The pleasure was so exquisite Eve thought she was going to faint. Why was he torturing her? Why didn't he just take her?

His hold on her body eased, and her head dipped in slow motion. Her mouth claimed his breast and she suckled him as he had done her.

"Eve!" Her name was ripped from his throat the moment her hand slipped between his thighs.

At one time Matt had begged her to touch him, but now he didn't want her to touch him—not yet. He captured her hands and held them tightly as he guided her down to the tiled floor and buried his face in the tight curls in the valley of her thighs. Eve arched, but she couldn't free herself.

"No, Darling. Please don't fight me."

Eve felt her face flame with embarrassment. His mouth and breath were burning her. "Not there," she pleaded.

He released her hands and slid up over her body. The falling water beaded up on her flesh like shimmering jewels. "Why not there, Baby? You are as beautiful there as you are everywhere else."

Eve closed her eyes against his flaming gaze. "It's not right," she whispered.

"When two people love each other everything's right, Eve." Matt's voice was soft, coaxing. "There's nothing wrong or ugly between a husband and wife. Let me show you how much I love you," he implored softly. "Let me taste you, my love. It will be good; so good for both of us." Her eyelids fluttered open and she gave him a shy smile. They closed again, long, thick, black lashes resting on high cheekbones. "Do you trust me?" he whispered.

"Yes. I trust you." She sighed.

"Do you love me?"

She blinked up at him, a slight frown marring her smooth forehead. "Of course I love you."

His brooding lower lip widened with a smile. "Make me happy, Eve. Let me taste you." She nodded tentatively, consenting.

He touched his lips to hers and increased the pressure until he felt her respond. He didn't want to frighten her, but to bring her maximum pleasure, and that meant unleashing her inhibitions and releasing her fears.

Eve clutched Matt's shoulders tightly and caught her lower lip between her teeth as he began his exploration. She tried but couldn't stop her little whimpers and breathless moans when his mouth staked its claim on the soft, wet folds of her sex. She arched as his tongue swept over the tiny bud of flesh in a flicking motion. The motion sent explosions throughout her body, rocking her womb.

She couldn't control her trembling legs as Matt pulled them up and over his shoulders. Her composure slipped and her head thrashed wildly. What began as small waves increased and rocked her womb until she cried out loudly with the magical force which took over her body, lifting her higher and higher until she was thrust beyond reality. He gathered her to his chest, and she couldn't talk or move. Her heart raced uncontrollably as she clung to him.

"Still afraid, Darling?"

Her fingers searched his chest, discovering more scars hidden under the furred thickness. "No," she gasped. "It was wonderful."

Matt smiled. "Thank you for sharing with me."

Eve returned his smile, oblivious to the water falling on their prone bodies. "I should be thanking you. You've made me feel like a woman for the first time in a very long time."

He kissed the tip of her nose. "And I'm hoping it won't be the last."

"It'd better not be," she teased.

He shifted, rising to his feet and pulling her up with him. "I promised you that I'd wash your back." He reached for a bath sponge and squeezed out a glob of shower gel from a plastic bottle hanging from the shower head.

He washed her hair and body, and Eve returned the favor. She lingered between his thighs and he moaned in frustration. Kissing him deeply, she tasted herself on his lips. Her tongue traced the outline of his mouth and she shivered when he growled deep in his throat. Her hands and mouth charted every inch of his flesh, discovering several more scars on his large, hard body.

Their roles changed. Eve realized the power she wielded as Matt slumped against the glass doors, groaning under her touch. That all ended when he reversed their positions, lifted her effortlessly, and entered her newly awakened body.

Her soft gasp of pleasure made the blood pound in his head, and he forgot everything. There was no mission, no outside world. There was only Eve.

He felt her tight flesh stretch to accommodate his swollen appendage before her body closed tightly around his manhood. Her body was made for his, and he marveled at the perfect fit.

Her desire rose again, matching the fury of his as flames of love consumed them, leaving behind floating cinders of shattered ecstasy.

Matt slid to the floor, taking Eve with him. He had no way of knowing that the moisture streaming down her cheeks was not water, but tears of awakened passion.

"Te amo," he whispered against her ear. *And thank you, Harry,* he added silently, gathering his wife's limp body from the floor.

Eve pushed back the sheet and slipped from the bed, hoping not to wake Matt, but found her wrist caught between his strong fingers.

"Where are you going?"

Leaning over, she pressed her cheek to his solid shoulder. "I don't know about you, lover, but I need food."

Matt's grip moved up her arm and he flipped her over his chest. He kissed her passionately. "I need you."

"Later," she mumbled between the soft, moist kisses. The weak light streaming in through the windows indicated the dawn of another day. "Only one of us can cook, so I suggest you'd better let me go while I still have the strength to prepare something palatable."

Matt kissed her hard, then fell back and stared up at her radiant face. After sharing the shower they had spent the night discovering each other's bodies, and he was overwhelmed by Eve's passionate response to his demanding lovemaking once she'd overcome her initial inhibitions.

He picked out the short curls pressed to the sides of her head, rubbing the soft strands between his fingertips. He visually examined the woman who'd been thrust upon him—the woman he'd married and fallen in love with.

Her large dark eyes watched him watching her, and for a brief second he detected a look of sadness passing over her delicate features.

"What's bothering you, Darling?"

Eve's brow wrinkled and she closed her eyes. "I don't know how to explain it, but right now I feel so guilty because I'm so happy."

Matt pulled her down to lie beside him, and shifted to face her. "There's nothing wrong with feeling happy."

She opened her eyes and stared at her husband. "How can I be happy and not have Chris?"

"You will have your son, *Preciosa.* I've promised you that I'll get him back." He brushed a gentle kiss across her forehead. "You belong to me, Eve, and Chris will also belong to me, because he is a part of you."

Lowering her head, Eve buried her face against his chest; the medals suspended from the thick, gold chain around his neck pressed against her cheek. "You picked the wrong time of the month to make love to me." They'd made love several times without the benefit of protection.

Matt was enchanted with her display of shyness. "It's never the wrong time, Baby. Nothing would please me more than for you to have our children."

She kissed his breast. "I suppose you'd want a son to carry on the Sterling name."

He anchored a finger under her chin and raised her face to his. "I already have a son, Eve. Your son will be my son." He gave her a sensuous smile. "I think I'd like to have a daughter. A little girl with her mother's perfect face and body and—"

"And her father's golden eyes," Eve interrupted softly.

Smiling, Matt pressed his lips to her hair. "Now that I think about it, I don't know if I want a daughter."

"Why?"

It was his turn to frown. "When I think of what I used to do with other men's daughters, I don't think I'd survive watching her grow up into a woman. And I don't think she'd appreciate her father meeting her dates at the door with a gun or knife in his hand."

Eve pulled out of his embrace, sitting up. "You wouldn't!"

Matt shifted his eyebrows, trying not to laugh. Eve thought he was serious. "Of course not. I plan to teach her to ride and shoot. And I'll dry her tears whenever she falls or when some guy stands her up on a date. Then, I'll go looking for him and break both of his legs."

Eve shook her head, laughing. "You're impossible, Matthew Sterling."

He gathered her to his chest. "And you're incredible, Mrs. Sterling. I'm exhausted and starving, but I still want to make love to you."

"Later," she whispered, pushing against his firm hold.

He released her and watched as she slipped out of the bed. He had come to know every facet of her delightful body: the length and strength of her long slender legs, the shape of her well-groomed hands and feet, the full firmness of her perfectly shaped breasts that were perched high above her narrow rib cage, and the velvet smoothness of her skin, whose color and texture reminded him of a luxurious sable pelt.

Folding his arms behind his head, Matt closed his eyes. One phase of his mission had proven successful. Now all he had to do was uncover Joshua Kirkland's mole and find the child he had come to think of as his stepson.

"Get out of the kitchen and leave me alone!" Eve shouted at Matt, her voice drowning out the melodious sound of taped music coming from the stereo player on a countertop.

He retreated a few steps. "Are you certain you don't need my help?"

She poked a long-handled, wooden spoon in the middle of his broad chest. "Go. Why don't you shave? You look scruffy."

Matt rubbed a hand over his whiskered cheeks, glaring at Eve from under lowered eyebrows. "You're kind of ornery today, aren't you?"

"I'm not ornery, as you put it, Mateo. It's just that I can't put together a dinner for guests if you continue to sample everything I put out on the table."

In a motion too quick for the eye to follow, Matt captured the spoon, threw it to the floor and pulled Eve into his arms. "Loosen up, Darling," he crooned in her ear as he led her into a smooth dance step, keeping perfect rhythm with the Spanish love song.

How could she loosen up when he couldn't keep his hands off her body? He'd disappeared from the house for several hours earlier that morning, then returned with the news that he'd invited a friend and his wife for dinner.

She'd panicked, wondering how she was going to plan a dinner with only hours notice. However, Horst Van Holt's magic freezer had provided the ingredients for a paella: chicken and chorizo. She'd ordered Matt to the fish market to bring back the seafood: clams and shrimp. She had taken advantage of his absence to clean the house and defrost the chicken and sausage.

Eve relaxed against Matt's body, giving in to the hauntingly sensual voice of the vocalist and the pulsating Latin music. "Where did you learn to dance?" she questioned.

Matt lowered his chin to the top of her head. "It's an old story, Sweetheart."

"Tell me about it."

"It's about a girl I once had a crush on."

"I want to hear about it, anyway," Eve insisted. She

wanted to know everything she could about the man she'd married.

"Abigail Carson was the daughter of the wealthiest black man in Lubbock, and every boy in the whole county thought himself in love with her. And I was no exception. Abby wore fancy clothes and drove an expensive car, while I was lucky if I got the pickup on weekends. She was a few years older than me, but she invited me to one of her parties because I looked older than sixteen.

"Her mother served fancy food to her daughter's fancy guests, and I couldn't pronounce half of what I'd eaten. After dinner came the dancing, and Abby asked me to dance with her." He pulled back and stared down at Eve's amused expression.

"And you danced all over her fancy shoes," she said perceptively.

He nodded, grinning. "All over her feet, legs, and knees. She screamed at me in front of everyone, calling me uncouth. I was so mad that I grabbed her and kissed her right in front of her mother and guests. Then I stormed out and drove my pickup back home.

"Her father came to see me the next day, threatening to have me arrested for assaulting his daughter. At sixteen I was well over six feet, and weighed close to one eighty-five. My father came into the barn when he heard us arguing, but didn't interfere. I told Mr. Carson exactly what I thought of his stuck-up daughter, and he nearly fainted when I told him that his daughter was a tramp. I don't believe he knew she was sleeping around. He saw my father, and asked him if he was going to allow me to defame his daughter's reputation.

"Dad smiled and said very calmly, 'You're lucky I don't let him loose to beat the crap out of you. Now get the hell out of my barn, Carson. You're stinking it up.'"

Matt's eyes crinkled in amusement as Eve laughed. "My folks sent me to a dance studio, and after that I never stepped on another woman's foot."

She'd insisted on hearing the story and he had told her, but she felt jealous of the women in his past. Her arms curved around his waist as she pressed her cheek to his chest. "One more dance, then I'll have to finish dinner."

His arms tightened on her body. "Let's enjoy ourselves tonight, Eve. Tomorrow morning we leave for Puerto Escondido." He felt her stiffen in his embrace. The time had come when he had to encounter Alejandro Delgado-Quintero.

Eve closed her eyes, nodding slowly. What she'd shared with Matt in the house high atop the mountain would end, and her journey to confront her ex-husband was about to begin.

Chapter Eighteen

Eve dipped a small, rounded brush into a jar of styling gel, then brushed her hair until the sides were straight and smooth. She left just a hint of curl at the crown of her head.

She smiled at Matt's reflection in the mirror over the bedroom's triple dresser as he entered the room. "Simple enough, Darling?"

He walked over to her and placed his hands on her shoulders. His black hair glistened with moisture from his recent shower. His gaze met hers in the glass. "You'll never look plain or simple, Eve." The compliment brought a wave of heat to her cheeks. She'd selected a yellow linen sheath dress with a pair of low-heeled, black, patent leather pumps. His hands moved down her arms, encircling her waist, and she leaned back against his body. "You're ravishing," he whispered.

Turning around to face him, Eve stared up at Matt. She cradled his lean, dark-skinned face between her slender hands. "Thank you, my love."

He leaned down and kissed her cheek. "Let's go downstairs, *Preciosa*. Jorge and Lilian will be arriving at any moment."

"You've gotten yourself quite a prize, Mateo," Jorge said softly, staring at Eve's profile as she smiled at the photographs Lilian proudly showed her of their children.

Matt merely nodded. He sat at the dining room table, puffing in a leisurely way on his cigar. He hadn't liked the way Jorge continued to stare at Eve throughout dinner, and also hadn't liked the way he held her hand a bit too long for convention.

Eve had been the perfect hostess, making their guests comfortable. She had made an attempt to communicate in Spanish with Lilian, who patiently helped her when she did not remember the Spanish equivalents for several words.

"I'm leaving tomorrow morning," Matt said very quietly. "I'll remain in Escondido until I get my orders from Cordero."

Jorge stared at a growing ash on the end of his cigar. "I can't believe it's almost over. Five long, hard, dirty years in this grubby hellhole."

Matt stared at dark-haired, dark-eyed, petite Lilian Martín. "You found a lovely wife and you have two beautiful children, so I don't think you've been too bored."

A quick smile deepened the lines around Jorge's obsidian eyes. "I suppose you're right. It was either Mexico or Colombia. Right now I think Mexico is safer for a DEA agent than Cali or Bogotá."

Matt smiled through the rising smoke. "I'll attest to that. I almost didn't make it out last year. I wonder if Barranda upped the bounty on my ears."

"Rumor has it that he wants you real b-a-d, Mateo."

"He can keep wanting, because I'm never going back."

"You don't have to go back for them to take you out, *amigo*. Look what happened to Moreno. He got whacked while sitting in his car waiting for the light to change at the height of the Miami rush hour.''

Matt stared at Jorge, raising his eyebrows. "Moreno was sloppy *and* greedy. The money he was paid wasn't enough. He wanted more, and in the end he lost his life.''

Jorge took a final drag from his cigar and crushed it in an ashtray. "Well, *amigo,* I'd better get back to the house. I'm suppose to meet someone tonight who'll have word on a Chihuahua operation. He claims there's a multimillion-dollar marijuana cultivation and processing complex in the desert.''

Matt and Jorge returned to the kitchen and their wives. Eve glanced up, her eyes widening in surprise.

"Are you leaving?''

Jorge's ebony gaze swept appreciatively over her body. "The babysitter has to be home by ten.'' Lilian nodded in agreement. "When you and Mateo come back, please come down and meet the rest of the family.''

Eve stared at Matt, and he bowed his head. She hugged Lilian, thanking her for coming. Jorge stepped forward, but Matt stopped him from reaching Eve when he grabbed his hand and pumped it.

"Thanks for visiting. Eve and I will contact you the moment we return.''

Eve gave Matt a strange look as he ushered the Martín couple to the door and out into the sultry night. "Why did you do that?'' she questioned after the door closed behind them.

"Do what?'' Matt asked, feigning innocence.

She folded her hands on her hips. "Throw them out.''

Matt leaned against the door and slipped his hands into the pockets of his slacks. "I didn't throw them out. It was time for them to get back to their children.''

"You were rude, Mateo Arroyo.''

He straightened from his leaning position, his body rigid. "Jorge was the rude one, Eve. He has a wife, yet he couldn't keep his eyes off *my* wife. So don't talk to me about being rude. He's lucky I didn't knock his teeth out."

"Why pick on the man's teeth? It's his eyes you had a beef with," Eve retorted angrily.

Matt muttered a curse under his breath and opened the door, only to slam it violently after he'd stepped out into the black heat of the night.

He was losing it! Being in love was turning him into a maniac. He wanted to beat up his friend because he had stared at Eve. He didn't want to think of what he would've done if Jorge had touched her!

Eve felt Matt's presence before he entered the bedroom, even though her back was to the door. "Are you coming to apologize?"

He sat down on the side of the bed and removed his clothes. "No. There's nothing to apologize for."

She sat up, the sheet falling down to her waist and giving Matt a view of her breasts through the lace of an ice-blue silk nightgown. "Are you telling me that every time we have someone for dinner that you're going to rush them out of the house before they're ready to leave?"

He reached for her, but she was too quick and scooted off the bed. "Only if they're men," he stated, also moving off the bed and stalking her.

"Mateo," she wailed.

"I know that I have a jealous streak a mile wide, Eve."

She retreated until her back hit a wall. "I guess Jorge can consider himself a lucky man that he escaped unharmed."

Matt reached out and swung her up in his arms. "I'm the lucky man, Darling." He buried his face against her neck. "You're so good for me. You make me feel things I never felt before. I'm a son, a brother, and an uncle, but I never felt truly alive until you came into my life." He lowered her to the bed, his body following. "It was as if I had to challenge death to see who would come up the winner.''

"Oh, Matt,'' Eve whispered against his mouth.

"I've traveled all over the world,'' he continued, "not knowing what I was searching for. Now I know I was looking and waiting for someone like you. You've made it all so very worthwhile, Baby.''

Eve didn't know why, but she felt like crying. His confession meant more than a declaration of love.

She cradled his head to her breasts. "You're home, Matt.''

He turned her and pulled her to his chest, her buttocks pressed to his belly and groin. "Tell me all about yourself, Eve. Any and everything you can remember.''

Eve walked out of the house the following morning and saw Matt leaning against the bumper of his car. He was clothed entirely in black: shirt, slacks, and shoes.

She walked several feet beyond him in the driveway. The Range Rover was parked behind the house and Matt's Lincoln was readied for the trip to Puerto Escondido.

She was going to miss the blazing orange and pink sunsets, the colorful birds and exotic butterflies and the creeping, trailing vines and wildflowers surrounding their private waterfall and pool.

Matt moved over and stood behind her and she settled back against his chest as if she had been doing it for years. Somewhere, somehow, they had settled into the routine, and neither of them consciously had given it a second thought. Without realizing it they had become a couple.

Eve closed her eyes. His fingers tightened on her waist. She found Matt's presence, his touch, comforting. They had spent the night talking and laughing over incidents from their pasts, becoming friends as well as lovers.

"I'm going to miss this place,'' she whispered hoarsely.

"We'll come back, *Preciosa*,'' Matt stated in a quiet tone.

"We'll make certain to come back before we leave Mexico."

Antonio and Pilar Arroyo greeted their grandson and his wife with a mixture of tears and passionate embraces. Eve and Matt were not given an opportunity to protest as they were led through an open courtyard and garden at the rear of the large house to partake of some liquid refreshment before retiring to their bedroom for the *siesta*.

Matt moved quickly to seat his grandmother, but Antonio waved him away. "Seat your own wife, Mateo. I'll take care of mine," he snapped, ignoring the flush darkening the younger man's face. "I'm not so old that I can't take care of what belongs to me," he continued, leaning over and kissing the dry, paper-thin cheek of Pilar.

Matt successfully concealed his scowl as he offered Eve a cushioned chair. He doubted whether she understood his grandfather's scathing reprimand.

Antonio's light brown eyes were still bright even though he had recently celebrated his eighty-fourth birthday. The hot sun had darkened and creased his skin until it resembled soft, worn leather. A fringe of white hair covered his tanned pate, and he ran a thin, heavily-veined hand over his face in a weary gesture.

He flashed a tired smile at his grandson's wife. "Are you trying to learn Spanish, *nieta?*" he questioned in English, his firm mouth tightening in a manner which reminded Eve of Matt's. "My son-in-law has been married to my daughter for more than forty years, and somehow he never got around to learning more than a few words."

"I can assure you that I've learned more than a few words," Eve said in halting Spanish.

Antonio sat up straighter in his chair. "Very good." He motioned to a young woman who had approached silently with a pitcher and glasses on a large tray.

Pilar Arroyo spoke quietly with the woman after she'd

placed the glasses on the table, instructing her to make certain a bedroom had been readied for her grandson and his wife's *siesta*.

Pilar was a tiny, white-haired, shy woman who spoke very little English. On their journey to Puerto Escondido, Matt had revealed that Pilar had allowed Antonio to make all of the decisions in their sixty-five years of marriage. Antonio loved her as passionately now as he had when he first met her, and there were times when he exhibited fierce displays of jealousy.

Like grandfather, like grandson, she thought.

Matt had also related that the Spanish-style hacienda was more than a hundred years old, and its grace and beauty had remained undaunted throughout the many generations of Arroyos who had lived there. The hacienda was situated in a valley at the foot of the mountains, and the coolness of the ocean winds and the higher elevation of nearby mountain ranges sweeping over the coffee fields yielded an abundant, flavorful crop year after year.

"You must be very special to have lured my grandson away from his other women," Antonio remarked in English, his expression deadpan.

"I'd like to think of myself as lucky to have met and married your grandson, *Abuelo,*" Eve replied, also in English.

Antonio smiled openly for the first time, a network of lines crisscrossing his weathered face. *"Bueno.* You are a wise woman, *nieta.* You know what to say to make a man feel like a man. Mateo is the lucky one, I think."

Matt gave Antonio a direct stare. "You doubt whether I'll be a good husband to Eve?"

Antonio reached over and covered Pilar's hand. "No, I don't. Arroyo men make good husbands and good fathers. They're loyal to their women and their families."

Pilar touched Matt's arm and he leaned over to hear her soft words. A tender, loving expression lit his eyes as he stared at his grandmother's face. He shifted and glanced at Eve, his gaze narrowing when he saw her eyes look through him. There were times when he felt as if she knew exactly what he was thinking or feeling.

"My grandmother says you're very beautiful, and that if we decide to have children they will also be beautiful."

Eve couldn't look at Matt. There was the possibility that she was carrying his child within her body at that very moment.

"Having Mateo's children would make me very happy," she confessed.

Antonio shook his head. "You young people wait until you could be grandfathers and grandmothers to marry and have children. I married my Pilar when I was nineteen and she sixteen, and she gave me all of my children before I was thirty. Mateo will be almost forty, practically *un viejo,* before you make him a father, *nieta.*"

Eve gave Matt a look of confusion when she heard the chastising words from the older man, and he winked at her. "You have enough great-grandchildren to brag about, *Abuelo,*" he reminded Antonio gently. "Allow me to enjoy my wife for a while before we settle down to raising a family."

"Her having children should not stop you from enjoying her body, Mateo," Antonio countered.

Eve didn't understand Antonio's last retort because it was spoken in rapid Spanish, but she knew it hadn't pleased Matt because his lower lip mirrored his annoyance.

Antonio filled each glass with chilled mixture of fruit juices and offered a glass to his wife, then Eve and his grandson.

Pilar shook her head, then took a sip of her drink. The conversation was one she'd heard many times before. Antonio hadn't understood why his favorite grandson hadn't married, and now that Mateo had, he couldn't understand why Eve wasn't already pregnant. *Men and their obsession with fathering children,* she thought. They seemed to equate their maleness with the ability to make a woman's belly swell with their seed. Her husband's way of thinking was dying out in Mexico, and there were times when she felt that hadn't come soon enough.

Matt watched Eve take meager sips of her drink, his mind filled with what he had been ordered to do. Jorge had informed him that planned raids on targeted sites by both the Mexican police and U.S. DEA agents was in its final planning stage. Jorge had gathered enough information in the five years he'd been undercover to stem the flow of cocaine and marijuana into the United States for years to come.

And in less than ten days Matt was to meet Cordero Birmingham and give him the name of the person who was passing U.S. military and DEA secrets to Alejandro Delgado and the rebels.

Rising to his feet, he extended a hand to Eve. "Come, *Preciosa,* it's time we took our *siesta. Buenas tardes, Abuelo y Abuela.*"

Eve smiled at Matt's grandparents and followed him into the house. Their suite of rooms was on the second floor of the southern wing of the large house. A breathtaking view from the veranda revealed the calm, blue waters of the Pacific Ocean.

Matt unbuttoned his shirt and shrugged out of it while Eve strolled around the bedroom, examining pieces of sculpture on several tables and on the mantel over the fireplace.

"I hope you won't let my grandfather intimidate or frighten you," he said quietly.

She spun around, a secret smile curving her lips. "I think he knows that I don't frighten that easily."

"And you don't," Matt agreed, coming toward her. "I can honestly say that, because I've tried bullying you enough."

His hands went to her blouse and he unbuttoned it. Inhaling deeply, he stared at the perfection of her firm breasts. He withdrew the silk garment from her body and buried his face against her neck.

"Why are you torturing me, Eve?" he gasped.

Closing her eyes, Eve melted against his bare chest. "How?"

"I can't keep my hands off you. I crave you even in my sleep."

Eve did not want to tell Matt that he'd echoed her feelings. He'd awakened her mind and body to a rushing, heated passion that intensified with every moment she was in his presence. Each time he touched her a delicious shudder rippled through her body, bringing with it a welling desire to surrender all she had to him.

She clung to him, his touch warm and comforting. "I love you, Matt." Pulling back slightly, he stared down at her upturned face. His gaze widened and Eve was trapped in the depths of the savage hunger radiating from the force field he had created around them.

"You will never love me the way I love you," he stated in a challenging tone.

Her arms dropped and she took a backward step. "Why would you say that?"

"Because it's true," Matt insisted. He folded his hands on his hips.

Eve was puzzled by his abrupt change in mood. "You have no right to make that kind of determination."

"I can say that because I know that I'd give up my life for you. Would you do the same for me?"

She stared wordlessly at him, her heart pounding uncontrollably. Why was Matt testing her? What did he hope to prove?

"I—I don't—"

"There's no need to say anything, Darling," he interrupted. "You hesitated too long."

"You can't test love," she countered.

"I just need to know how far you'll go for me, Eve."

"I thought being obedient, affectionate, and passionate was enough."

"That was before I married you."

She laughed, hoping to lighten the dark mood. "You're taking all of this so seriously, Matt."

His eyebrows nearly met in a frown. "I am serious. Because after all of this is over there's not going to be an annulment or a divorce. I'm in this marriage for keeps."

Eve nodded slowly, blinking with bewilderment. She opened her mouth, but no sound came out. Her eyes filled with tears, and she blinked them back before they fell.

He held out his arms and she collapsed in his embrace. The medals on his chest bit into her tender breasts, but she barely registered the pain as he crushed her to his body.

"Darling, my darling," she whispered over and over as he swung her up in his arms and walked to the bed.

Matt undressed her, then undressed himself. Within minutes he came into her outstretched arms, parted her legs with his knee and entered her body with a force strong enough to rob them both of their breath.

He wanted it to be slow, leisurely, but his body would not listen to his brain. He established a pounding rhythm with powerful thrusts, communicating his need to possess her totally.

Eve's passion rose like the hottest fire, spreading from her to Matt, and he moaned aloud in erotic pleasure. Her body writhed sensuously beneath his, and she told him what she wanted to do to him.

"I can't, Eve," he panted. There was no way he could withdraw from her hot flesh—not now. "The next time," he promised breathlessly through clenched teeth.

Neither of them thought of a next time as each wrung the vestiges of passion from the other where they lay together in a tangle of limbs, gasping for breath.

Eve fell asleep in her husband's arms while he lay awake staring at the ceiling, trying unsuccessfully to sort out all that had happened since Eve had walked into his life. Each time he made love to her he had not used any form of contraception, and it wasn't until now that he realized why he hadn't.

There was always the possibility that he would not leave Mexico alive, and he wanted to make certain he continued to exist; that was only possible if he got Eve pregnant. He wanted her to have more than just the memories of their time together.

Chapter Nineteen

Matt came around the car and opened the door for Eve. She placed her hand in his and stepped out into the warm May night. The setting sun fired the pristine whiteness of his dinner jacket and her matching white, ribbon-silk dress. She turned her face into the cooling breeze blowing off the Pacific Ocean before slipping her arm through Matt's.

"Do you think Alejandro will be here?" she asked quietly.

"I was told that he was invited," he replied softly, smiling as they approached their hostess.

His own invitation had arrived at his grandparents' hacienda weeks before. Magda Castillo always hosted a party to celebrate the end of Acapulco's bullfight season. Matt suspected Magda's soirée was a fête of thanksgiving that her matador husband's life had been spared for another season at the Plaza de Toros.

Magda Castillo floated toward Matt, her gaze fixed on the tall, slender woman at his side. It had taken only a glance to realize that Mateo Arroyo was lost to the women who had openly lusted after him for years. There was a time when she'd been counted among those women.

Before she'd married Enrique Castillo she had thought that perhaps she had a chance to seduce the dangerously attractive owner of El Moro and get him to propose to her. After seeing the woman he'd chosen as his wife, Magda knew she never would've been a likely candidate to become Señora Mateo Arroyo.

"Congratulations, Mateo," she crooned, tilting her face for his kiss. Matt disappointed her when he pressed his mouth to her cheek instead of her lips.

"Thank you, Magda" he returned graciously. "I'd like you to meet my wife. Eve, Magda Castillo."

Eve gave the beautifully coiffed and attired woman a warm smile, and was rewarded with a forced one that didn't quite reach Magda's dark eyes.

She quickly examined the woman whom she suspected might have had more than a passing interest in Mateo Arroyo. Magda's glossy black hair was swept up in a mass of curls and secured with diamond clips which blazed brilliantly in the light coming from lanterns ringing the perimeter of the courtyard. Her hair was a startling contrast to the paleness of her skin, and Eve wondered if the woman ever exposed herself to the sun.

"If Mateo can bear to part with you for a few minutes, I'd like to introduce you to my husband."

Matt's arm curved around Eve's waist in a protective gesture. There was no way he was going to let her out of his sight until he found out whether Alejandro Delgado was present.

"Later."

Magda registered the finality in the single word and shrugged her bare shoulders, her generous breasts threatening to spill from the revealing décolletage of her body-hugging black dress.

"Eve and I would like to circulate first," Matt offered as an apology.

"Thanks, Darling," Eve said under her breath after Magda walked away.

"Don't mention it, Darling." Matt smiled at her and tightened his hold around her waist.

It took less than twenty minutes for him to uncover that Alejandro Delgado had declined the Castillo invitation. After that he was able to relax.

Eve accepted Magda's invitation to see the interior of the large white stucco structure she and her husband had recently redecorated. She was monosyllabic as Magda proudly stressed that the house was designed in an almost pure Spanish Colonial Revival style.

She was definitely not interested in the ornate furnishings which the Castillos seemed quite taken with. Eve was disappointed because she would not get to see Alex and question him about Chris.

Suddenly she was annoyed with Matt. He had retreated to the grand salon with a group of men and had left her with the boring, chatty Magda.

Eve escaped her hostess when Magda flitted off to see if her kitchen help needed instructions or chastising. Making her way to the courtyard, she accepted a glass from a passing waiter and took a sip of the cooling liquid. The drink slipped smoothly down her throat. She recognized the cocktail as a tequila sour.

I just might acquire a taste for tequila, she thought, smiling and recalling the first time Matt had offered her the drink. So much had happened in the short time since she'd come to Mexico.

"Eve."

She turned at the sound of her name. Cordero Birmingham headed in her direction.

"Cord," she returned, relieved to see a familiar face. She had had enough of what Matt had referred to as the Mexican elite.

A wave of dark red hair fell over Cord's forehead as he reached for her hand. "Where's Mateo?"

The muted lights strung along the galleria failed to highlight the intensity in Cord's bright blue eyes. However, Eve recognized the tension in his voice. "He said he would be in the grand salon."

"Don't move from here," Cord ordered before turning and running toward the house.

Eve felt a rush of weakness and leaned against a stone statue to steady her shaking legs. She did what she hadn't done in a long time—she prayed. Without having to be told she knew Cordero Birmingham and Matt were in the same business. She should've realized that when the two of them disappeared on the day of her wedding.

A savage grip on her arm jerked her into awareness. "Let's get out of here, Eve."

The strength in Matt's fingers impeded the circulation in her upper arm. "Where are we going?" she asked breathlessly as he pulled her along at a furious pace.

Her heels slowed her down and Matt swept her up in his arms, the flowing silk of her dress draping over the sleeve of his dinner jacket and his black dress trousers.

He shoved her into his car and appeared to start and put it into gear all in one motion. "I'm taking you back to Puerto Angel."

"Why?" Matt didn't answer. He stared straight ahead, concentrating on the road. "What's going on?"

"Nothing," he retorted, his jaw tightening.

"Don't lie to me, Matt. I—"

"Enough, Eve!" he snarled. "I have enough to think about without you asking me questions I won't answer."

Her jaw snapped loudly and she slouched down on the seat and tried cooling her temper. She was too busy calling him every dirty name she could think of to notice the needle on the speedometer inching closer to the automobile's maximum speed.

Matt was barely aware of Eve as he recalled the information Cord had given him. The man was seven days early and his message carried death: The Falcon was snared, and was lying close to death in a tiny hospital in a town so small it barely made the map.

He stopped long enough to inform his grandparents that he and Eve were returning to Puerto Angel, then threw their luggage into the trunk of the Lincoln and began the journey back along the Pacific side of Mexico.

Matt parked his car along the narrow alley bordering Jorge's store. Even though he'd removed his dinner jacket and turned the Lincoln's air-conditioning to the maximum, the fabric of his dress shirt was pasted to his back and chest.

Jorge was out on the porch before Matt could exit from the car. The light coming through the store's front windows revealed an expression on Matt's face he hadn't seen since they were teenagers in Lubbock. He knew without asking that Matt was upset.

"What's up?" he asked in Spanish.

"Take care of Eve, Jorge."

Jorge nodded. It was apparent Matt wasn't going to elaborate. "When will you be back?"

Matt stared at Eve as she stepped out of the car and came toward him. Her eyes were wide with fear, and never had he wished more that he was out of this business.

"I don't know," he answered slowly, his gaze locked with that of his wife. He removed her luggage from the trunk of the car and handed it to Jorge.

Eve stared at the bag in Jorge's hand before she looked at Matt. He was leaving her. He was going away—maybe even to lose his life—and leaving her with a man who was practically a stranger.

Matt extended his right hand. "Eve." His voice was hoarse with heavy emotion.

"Go, Matt," she whispered. His hand dropped. "Please," she whispered as she turned and walked to the front door of the grocery store. She opened and closed the door, shutting him out of her vision and her life.

Matt followed the directions Cord had given him, hoping he would make it to the tiny town of San Miguel without mishap. Cord had left Joshua's bedside long enough to give him the news of the attempt at murder, then returned to await his arrival.

He arrived at San Miguel at ten o'clock and encountered silence. The town claimed a single main street with a hotel, café, and a general store which operated as a grocery-post-office-pharmacy and service-station-auto-repair establishment. A handpainted sign, nailed to a wooden post, indicated the direction of the hospital, which was housed in what had one time been an old mission.

Matt rang a large bell attached to a massive wooden door and was admitted by the nurse, whom he later discovered was the doctor's wife. She led him down a corridor and to one of the small, clean rooms at the far end.

Joshua Kirkland's bloodless face blended with the stark whiteness of the pillowcase cradling his sun-bleached hair. His breathing was shallow, barely detectable.

A doctor sat next to the bed, holding a stethoscope to Joshua's bandaged chest. Matt nodded to Cord, sitting in a corner, then waited for the doctor to finish examining Joshua before he introduced himself.

"He's lost a great deal of blood, Señor Arroyo, but fortunately none of his vital organs were damaged."

Matt did not take his gaze from the motionless figure. He knew Joshua would survive only because if he wasn't he would've died before he was brought into the hospital. On the other hand, he knew Joshua's chances for survival diminished alarmingly with every second he remained in Mexico, because whoever attacked him would probably try again.

"He's very strong," the doctor continued, registering the look of concern on Matt's face.

"Is he in a coma?"

"No. I've been practicing medicine for a long time," the elderly surgeon confessed, "but I've never seen anything like this. It's as if he's willed his brain to shut down so that he won't have to acknowledge his pain or weakness."

Matt smiled for the first time. The doctor had unknowingly analyzed Joshua Kirkland. Those who knew Joshua joked about him being a human computer. This comment was never made aloud because no one dared to let Joshua know how he'd been categorized.

"How soon can he be moved?" Matt questioned.

"No, no, Señor Arroyo. He cannot be moved. He's holding his own, but I can't guarantee that he'll live if you try—"

"Nothing is guaranteed, Señor Médico," Matt interrupted. *"Nothing."*

The doctor shrugged and spread out his hands in a futile gesture. "He's your responsibility. I'll sign the discharge papers, and you can take him whenever you're ready."

"You know damn well we can't move him, Mateo," Cordero Birmingham argued softly after the doctor left the room.

Matt turned and stared at Cord. "What do you suggest we do? Neither one of us can stay here and watch him."

Cord ran long fingers through his already mussed hair. "How are we going to get him out?"

"I'll have his family make the arrangements."

Cord went still. "I thought he didn't have anyone."

"He has family," Matt confirmed.

"I'll stay here with him while you contact his family," Cord suggested.

Matt nodded and left the coolness of the mission-turned-hospital and stepped out into the arid heat. The shadowy figure of an emaciated dog wandered slowly across the darkened landscape.

He removed the cellular phone from the car and punched in the area code for Florida. The telephone on the other end buzzed several times before it was picked up.

"Martin Cole, please," Matt said into the receiver after a woman had announced he'd reached the Cole residence.

"I'm sorry, sir, but Mr. Cole is not at home at the present time."

"Where can he be reached?" Matt snapped impatiently.

"Mr. Cole is unavailable, sir."

He clenched his teeth in frustration. The drawling Floridian accent reminded him of how far he was from home. "Look, Ma'am," he continued in a softer tone. "I don't have much time, but it is important that you get a message to Mr. Cole. This is an emergency."

The woman on the other end registered the urgency in his voice for the first time. "Give me the information, sir, and I'll have Mr. Cole contact you."

Matt sat in the car, the door open, his feet planted on the dusty ground, waiting for the return call. He only had to wait three minutes. He swooped up the phone after the first ring.

"Martin?"

"What the hell is going on down there?"

He decided not to mince words. "I need you to arrange to get Joshua out of Mexico. Your brother's belly met with the blade of someone's knife, and I'm afraid if you don't get him out they'll try again."

The raw expletive coming through the receiver raised Matt's eyebrows. All traces of Martin Cole's normally velvet tone were absent.

"I'm at the hospital," Martin informed him. "Parris is in labor, and it's been tough going for her." There was a pause. "I can't leave her, but David's in your backyard. In fact, he should be touching down in San José in about an hour. Tell me where you are, and I'll have him make the arrangements to get Josh back here."

Matt completed the call, then returned to the hospital. "It's set," he informed Cord as he slipped quietly back into the room. "I'll stay with him."

Cord rose from the chair beside the bed. "He hasn't stirred at all. Not even when the nurse changed the intravenous feeding."

Matt gave him a reassuring smile. "He'll be all right." This was Cord's first international mission and he knew the younger man was uneasy about risks he and Joshua had experienced many, many times in the past.

Cordero Birmingham turned toward the door, then hesitated. "I'll be back in three days for Eve Blackwell. I've been ordered to see that she gets back to her uncle. Three days and no more, or you're on your own."

Sudden rage lit up Matt's golden eyes. "You son of—"

"Orders are orders, Mateo!" Cord ranted, spinning around on his heel.

Matt quickly brought his temper under control. "She's now Eve Arroyo."

Cord registered the shift in Matt's mood immediately. "Why didn't you tell me she was Blackwell's niece when I told you Delgado was no longer your target?"

"You didn't ask."

"That's because I didn't know." He moved closer to Matt, analyzing his expression. "You're in love with her, aren't you? Blackwell sets you up with his niece and you fall in love with the woman." His bubbling laughter bounced off the walls of the small room.

Matt removed his bow tie and the onyx stud under his pleated shirt's wing collar. "What the hell is so funny?"

"You, Mateo. You're getting soft, old man." He took a glance at Matt's scowling face and sobered quickly. "You have impeccable taste. Eve Blackwell Arroyo is exquisite."

Matt had to agree. "That she is, Cordero," he confirmed, the vibrancy in his tone revealing the depth of affection he had for the woman he'd claimed for his wife. "You'd better get back before someone realizes you're missing.'' He held out his hand. ''I'll see you in three days. Eve will be ready.''

Cord took the proffered hand. ''Thanks for making it easy for me. By the way, I've had a chance to talk to Delgado. It looks as if he's willing to meet with you.''

Matt didn't take the chair Cord had vacated once he left the room. He was too wound up to sit. He had only three days with Eve, and in another seven it all would be over. Joshua Kirkland had set up and mobilized the operation which had been given the code name MESA before someone sought to eliminate him.

David Cole walked into the hospital room and Matt rose slowly from the chair beside Joshua's bed. His once shoulder-length, wavy black hair was cut close to his scalp, the diamond stud in his left ear was gone, and his perennial black attire had been replaced by an expertly tailored, lightweight, dark gray suit.

Eyes as black as pitch were fixed on the motionless figure on the narrow hospital bed. ''How is he?''

Matt ran a large hand over the stubble on his chin, then massaged the tight muscles in his neck. He'd waited patiently for David Cole's arrival from Costa Rica.

''He's lost a lot of blood.''

''How is he?'' David repeated, tension quivering in his voice.

''The doctor thinks he has a good chance of making it.''

David leaned over and placed a brown hand on Joshua's forehead. His skin was moist, but cool. ''Help me get him out of this cesspool.''

Joshua's inert body was covered with a sheet as Matt and David carried him on a stretcher from the hospital to an awaiting converted ambulance.

David extended his hand. ''Thanks again. It seems as if the Coles owe you another one, Matt.''

Matt managed a tired smile. "Think nothing of it. Joshua and I go back a long way. I owe him my life."

"And we owe you. Joshua and I aren't as close as he and Martin, but we're still brothers. I think it's time we became better acquainted."

"How are you getting him back?"

David tugged at his left ear. "I have a medical team standing by with a helicopter at Ejutala. From there we'll fly into Oaxaca. The company jet will take us home."

Matt patted David's broad shoulder. "Good luck. Send Martin and Parris my best for the new baby, and let Regina know that I asked about her."

"Why don't you come for a visit? Regina has grown into quite a beauty."

"I'll take you up on the invitation one of these days. Right now I'm anxious to get back to my wife."

Matt watched David climb into the back of the ambulance and close the door. He was able to draw a normal breath for the first time in more than twelve hours. He waited until the vehicle disappeared in a cloud of red dirt before he turned to where he had parked his car.

Eve. He was going back to her, and he did not want to think of the time when he would have to hand her over to Cord, to be escorted back to the United States and safety.

He glanced up at the brilliant, cloudless sky. At least he was given a three day reprieve.

Chapter Twenty

Lilian Martín opened her door to a weary Mateo Arroyo. "Eve has not slept all night, Mateo. She's been waiting up for you." He followed Lilian into the kitchen and she handed him a cup of steaming black coffee. "She helped me put the babies to bed, but wouldn't go herself."

"She'll sleep after I take her home," Matt replied, giving Lilian a tired smile. "She has trouble falling asleep in a strange—"

He couldn't finish his sentence as Eve walked into the kitchen. She saw him and her eyes widened, a trembling hand going to her mouth. She moaned his name and Matt was beside her, catching her sagging body to his chest while placing tiny kisses on her closed lids.

"Eve. My precious, Eve," Matt whispered against her ear.

Eve thought she had dreamt him up. All night she had sat waiting for him, and when the sky brightened with the beginning of a new day she had almost given up hope. Waiting and praying; praying and waiting. For the past six months she'd prayed and waited enough for Chris to last her a lifetime. Now she'd added Matt to her prayer list. She felt his warmth and his strength. Pressing closer, Eve wanted to fuse herself with Matt, become a part of him.

"Matt, my darling," she half-laughed and cried, inhaling his familiar masculine scent. She wanted to touch him all over, love him until she fainted from the ecstasy he wrung from her.

Eve gave a small cry of protest as he pulled away. "It's all right, Baby. I'm going to take you home where I'm going to show you just how much I've missed you," he whispered.

She stared up at her husband, not seeing the strain and fatigue ringing his generous mouth. All she knew was that she loved him, and he would give her back her child.

"Let's go home, Matt."

Eve had drifted off to sleep by the time Matt slipped into bed beside her. She'd promised to wait for him while he shaved and showered, but couldn't. He, on the other hand, was wide awake and operating on reserved adrenalin. His mind craved sleep but he knew that wasn't possible until he made love to his wife.

Matt reached out for her, his fingers grazing bare flesh, and he smiled. Eve had left off her nightgown. The feel of her velvety skin snapped whatever control he had on his dammed passions.

Eve moaned in her sleep and settled back against Matt's body. His hand moved from the curve of her hip, up over her ribs and to a full, firm, silken breast. As he fondled it gently, the nipple hardened against his palm.

She rolled over, the motion bringing her chest to his. His head dipped, and a jolt of erotic pleasure shocked Eve awake.

"Matt . . . oh, Matt," she said, his name rolling off her tongue while he sucked her breasts in a drugging, agonizing, slow motion.

His breathing was slow, deep, and controlled, masking the throbbing hardness pressing against her belly. The fingers of one hand skimmed her abdomen, then her thigh.

Eve's thighs parted involuntarily as a rush of moisture bathed her core. Her desire dampened his fingers, signaling she was ready, and Matt moved over her and she welcomed him into her body.

She felt the heat of his body course down the length of hers, and her whole being was scorched with a desire she hadn't known she was capable of feeling.

She gripped his buttocks, pulling him closer. The rhythm he set changed, quickening. She followed his pace, arching as he drove into her, the thick blood-engorged length plunging in and out with longer and deeper strokes.

Matt buried his face against Eve's neck, straining valiantly to prolong the ecstasy. Reaching down between their bodies, he spread the folds hiding her moist sex and exposed the tiny bud of flesh at the apex of her femininity. Angling his body slightly, he rubbed his member sensuously up and down against the distended nub, and he achieved the reaction he sought from Eve as she stiffened, screaming out his name, then convulsed as her body opened and closed around his rigid flesh. The thrust of his powerful hips forced her thighs open wider and he exploded, filling her body with his hot seed.

He collapsed heavily on her, his chest heaving in exertion. *Sweet heaven,* how could he send her back? Did he have the strength to let her go?

Reversing their positions, Matt held Eve to his chest until they both fell asleep.

Matt sat watching Eve's animated face, not touching his dinner.

"Matt," she scolded in a gentle voice. "You haven't heard a word I've been saying."

He twisted several strands of spaghetti around his fork, then gave up the pretense all together. Covering his face with one hand, he exhaled slowly.

"I'm sorry, Eve," he apologized through his fingers.

"I'm sorry, Matt. I've been clucking like a barnyard hen while you're falling asleep—"

"I'm not tired," he cut in sharply. Pushing back his chair, he rose to his feet. "Excuse me," he mumbled before walking out of the dining room.

It had finally hit him. The fairy tale was over and it was back to reality. Ugly, dirty, reality and the job he had been paid to do.

He wanted to admit that he'd forgotten the reason he was operating in Mexico. He wanted to forget that he was to uncover the person or persons responsible for leaking information about how the American and Mexican governments were cooperating to eradicate the flow of drugs from Mexico into the United States.

In the past some Mexico officials had proved infuriatingly evasive, looking the other way or denying a Mexican-American, marijuana, cocaine and heroin connection; now that the Mexican government had offered their full support, someone in the States wanted to sabotage the campaign.

Even with the removal of DEA Director Nathaniel Webb the leak had not been stopped. The attempt on Joshua Kirkland's life meant that the mole knew exactly who he was. Only a half dozen people were privy to Joshua's function within the U.S. military.

Matt walked out of the house and lit up a cigar. He drew deeply on the fragrant tobacco and stared up at the darkened sky littered with millions of twinkling stars. The heavens were clear, indicating there would be no rain this night.

He inhaled deeply, taking in the fragrance of blooming night flowers, damp earth, and rotting vegetation over the odor of cigar smoke. The nearby forest was quiet, except for night predators preying on the weak and unsuspecting.

Focusing on a wall of black, he tried vainly to see through it. His concentration was slipping. He had to identify which one of the people involved in Operation MESA knew that Joshua was the mastermind, people he had worked with before on other covert missions. He mentally eliminated the three who had on one or more occasion shielded him from certain death: Manuel Rivera, Lupe Morales, and Rene Izquierdo; that left two: Cordero Birmingham and Jorge Martín.

He wanted to believe that Cordero wasn't suspect, because it was Cord who had taken Joshua to the hospital. If he'd wanted Kirkland dead he would've finished the job.

Matt exhaled a stream of smoke, shaking his head. No, it couldn't have been Cord. There would've been no way Cord would've been able to pull a knife on Joshua without being wounded or killed himself. Joshua's hands and feet were as lethal as any gun, and Matt knew there had to have been more than one attacker.

That left one other person—Jorge Martín! Jorge was the agency's senior drug law-enforcement agent in North America. It had become a personal vendetta for Jorge to lure and snare drug traffickers, after his youngest brother had been shot and crippled as he stood in a schoolyard during a lunch break. Several teenage dealers had gotten into an argument over territorial boundaries and begun shooting randomly, hitting the young boy in his spine.

Matt shrugged off the possibility that the mole could be Jorge. He couldn't afford to become emotionally involved. If it was Jorge, then he'd report it to Harry and turn his back on the whole affair.

And he still had to find Christopher Delgado. Was the child still in Mexico? If he was, where?

He also wondered if Jorge had told Delgado that Mateo Arroyo secretly directed a heroin and cocaine enterprise which had proven to be quite lucrative because he was able to travel between the United States and Mexico with relative ease.

Dammit to hell, he was tired of it! Why couldn't he just walk away and say the hell with it? When had he developed a conscience? He wanted to say that Eve was responsible, but he had had enough of it before Blackwell had come to see him.

He crushed out the cigar and leaned against the side of the house. It was only one more job, one more with a bonus—Eve Sterling Arroyo. Somehow she would make all of it worthwhile.

Eve lay beside Matt, staring up at a void. She counted his measured, even breaths in the darkened room, and she knew he wasn't asleep. She was amazed at how much she had learned about the man by sleeping with him.

She knew if he was tense or relaxed, awake or asleep, or if their coming together was an act of passion or one of desperation; and when Matt had returned to the house and joined her in bed, he came to her with a savage need which took her breath away.

He withdrew from her almost immediately and turned away. Without seeing, she knew the convulsions shaking his body were not from passion but from internal forces which would not allow him peace.

"If you want to talk about it, I'll listen. But if you don't, I'll understand," she stated gently.

Matt shifted, cradling her to his side. His right arm pillowed his head. The tension in his body eased slightly and she turned and slipped her leg over his. He inhaled deeply, then let out his breath slowly.

"I have to send you back." The six words sounded like a sentence of death. "Cord's going to come for you in two days."

"Why?" she asked. The single word sounded like a sob.

"Harry Blackwell wants you home."

Eve blinked back tears in the darkness of the bedroom. "Why, Matt? Why?" she repeated.

"You can't remain here. It's too dangerous."

His words didn't frighten her as much as the way he'd said them—in a lifeless monotone.

"What about Chris?" She couldn't stop the tears forming behind her eyelids.

"I'll find him, Eve," Matt said, trying to reassure her.

She nodded, brushing her fingers over her eyes and cheeks. She turned her face into his shoulder. "I believe you. I trust you."

"I want you to love me," he demanded. "If you love me I'll make it," he continued in an almost pleading tone.

Eve tried swallowing the lump which had formed in her throat. Realization dawned. Matt was afraid. Not for her, but for himself.

Pulling away from him, she sat up. "You're involved in something which has nothing to do with my son, aren't you?"

Matt also sat up. "You don't know what you're talking about."

She rose to her knees. "If I don't know what I'm talking about, then why don't you answer my question? What are you involved in?"

"It doesn't concern you, Eve."

She was too incensed to register the warning in his voice. "Tell me, Mateo." Leaning over, she turned on the bedside lamp, flooding the room with light.

Matt reached out and pulled her across his body. "No," he shouted, his hot breath searing her face.

"Does it have anything to do with Alex?"

His fingers sank painfully into the delicate flesh of her upper arms. "Listen, Eve, and listen good. Don't—"

"Don't!" Eve screamed back at him. "It's always 'don't ask me anything.' Do you know what I think, Matt? I think you've used me. You have your own hidden agenda where you play your dirty little games, but with me you get an added bonus. You marry me, pretend that you love me, then get free use of my body. Now I know why you wouldn't accept any money from me. I pay you every time I lie down with you, Mateo Arroyo. And I don't come cheap. I've *pleasured* you at least a dozen times since I became Señora Mateo Arroyo, so consider yourself *paid in full* for services rendered!''

Matt's hands fell away, the blood draining from his face as rage hardened his features. His expression was a mask of stone. "You don't know you're saying," he ground out through his teeth.

Freed, she slipped off the bed and backpedaled to the door. "I know exactly what I'm saying."

Turning, she ran out of the bedroom and into the one she'd occupied when they first arrived in Puerto Angel, locking the door. She braced her back against the door, trembling. How could she have believed him? The tender words of love, the passion, and her response to his love-making?

She'd fallen in love with him, shared her body with him, and could possibly be carrying his child. The cold lump forming in the pit of her stomach spread, chilling her until she shook uncontrollably.

"Not again," she whispered in a maelstrom of anguish and pain. First Alex, and now Matt. Was she destined to always pick the wrong husband?

A thud hit the door, followed by Matt shouting, "Open the door!"

Eve closed her eyes and pressed her fists against the solid wood. "Go away and leave me alone."

"Open the damn door or I'll break it down," he threatened.

Naked and trembling she turned and faced the door. Matt's duplicity dulled the pain and blinded her with rage. "I hope they kill you, and leave your body for the vultures."

There was complete silence before a heavy thud hit the

door, then another, and with each thud Eve moved further away from the door until she stood beside the bed. There was a crash and the wood splintered, leaving the door hanging crazily by one hinge.

Tilting her chin, Eve stared across the room at Matt standing in the doorway, praying her shaking legs would support her body, refusing to exhibit her fear. He had bullied her for the last time. She placed her hands on her hips and watched him walk slowly toward her.

Eve's eyes narrowed into slits as she measured each step Matt took, and she was certain that if she hadn't been so incensed she would've been turned on by the man, who looked like a large stalking jungle cat. Tall, large, dark, and naked, Matt was a magnificent male predator.

She took in the breadth of his shoulders, the bunched muscles in his upper arms, the power in his large hands, and the strength of his long, muscled legs, and she thought perhaps she'd pushed Matt too far. Her uncle hadn't elaborately detailed Matthew Sterling's exploits, but he had told her there were times when Matt did not need a weapon to subdue an opponent.

Did he now see her as an opponent? Would he kill her to keep her from revealing that he was also Matthew Sterling? Would he stop and consider that maybe she was carrying his child?

She swallowed hard, trying not to show her fear. Raising her hands, she beckoned, saying, "Come on, Mateo. You want trouble, you'll get trouble. I know you want a piece of me," she continued tauntingly.

Matt halted, completely surprised by the unpredictable woman he'd pledged to love and protect. He was six-four and weighed a solid two hundred and eighteen pounds, and five-feet-seven-inch, one hundred eighteen pound Eve Arroyo-Sterling was challenging him. Men who matched his height and weight usually did not challenge Matthew Sterling.

The pain of her wishing him dead eased, admiration

and pride taking its place. "I should tie you to the bed and spend the next forty-eight hours making love to you," he threatened quietly.

"You'd never survive," Eve countered. "You . . ." She never completed her statement as her breath was snatched from her lungs when he swept her off her feet.

"At least I'd die happy."

Eve struggled in his unyielding grip. "You've proven your point, Mateo. You're stronger than me."

He couldn't believe it. He'd subdued her yet the naked she-cat was still spitting and clawing. What had he married?

"Count yourself among the lucky ones, *Preciosa.*"

She stared at his scowling features. "Why? Because you married me?"

Matt's expression softened, a small smile inching up the corners of his mouth. "No," he said softly, "because I love you."

Without warning, just as he'd captured her, he released her, crossed the room and disappeared through the splintered door.

Tears welled up in her eyes and overflowed. What had she said? How could she have wished him dead? She loved him; she loved him so much that she was as afraid for him as she was for her own child.

Chapter Twenty-One

Eve made it to the bed on trembling legs and sat down, tears distorting her vision. She felt more alone than she ever had in her life. Forty-eight hours. That was all she and Matt had left, and she was pushing him away from her.

She didn't want him to die; she didn't want to leave him; all she wanted was to love Matt, love him until time ceased to exist for the both of them.

Wiping her wet cheeks with the back of her hand, Eve choked back a sob. How could she have gotten so used to Matt in less than two weeks of marriage? She had to swallow her pride and apologize to him.

Slipping off the bed, Eve made her way across the room before she could change her mind. She took two steps outside the bedroom and she saw him.

Matt sat on the floor, eyes closed and his back pressed to the wall. He had put on a pair of jeans but left his chest bare. Shifting slightly, he opened his eyes and stared up at her.

Eve's heart halted, then pounded relentlessly. She recognized his pain and longing, feeling it as her own. His left hand came up slowly as he averted his face, and she knew that if she was going to reject him he didn't want to see it.

"Matt," she cried, the sob coming from the back of her throat. She grasped his hand and he pulled her down to his lap.

"Forty-eight hours, *Preciosa*. That's all we have left," he whispered near her ear.

Turning on his lap, Eve pressed her mouth to his throat. "I love you, Matt. I love you so much."

He smiled down at her. "Thank you, Mrs. Sterling, because I love you, too."

"I'm sorry I said what I did about wishing you dead."

"Shh-hh, Baby. It's all right. I can understand your frustration. I want to tell you what I'm involved in, but I can't. If you know too much it might put you in jeopardy."

Eve moved closer, one arm curving around his neck. "There's no way I can stay here with you?"

"No way, Eve. If I could keep you here and protect you I would."

"Not even if I throw a tantrum?"

Matt forced a smile. "Not even a tantrum will make me change my mind." Slipping an arm under her legs, he lifted her and rose to his feet. "If I defy your uncle I'll lose whatever protection I'll need to return to the States safely."

She refused to think of the possibilities if Matt wasn't able to return to her. "I'll be waiting for you," she promised in a low, trembling voice.

Matt carried her to their bed, flicked off the lamp on the bedside table, slipped out of his jeans and lay down beside her. Slowly and deliberately, he pulled her to his body. His punishing grip would not allow Eve to move, and she suffered the closeness because she knew they would have only two more nights together before her interminable waiting began.

* * *

Eve became like a zombie. She ate because she knew she had to in order to maintain her strength, and she went to bed, but sleep was elusive. Even after Matt made love to her she lay awake, staring into space. And instead of slowing, the hours seemed to speed by, taking with them her promise to herself that she would remain stoic.

She stared at the flickering candles on the end tables in the living room. She felt listless, bereft, and alone, even though Matt sat less than five feet from her.

"*Una mariposa,*" he said, smiling at her.

"What?"

Matt moved over to her, brushing his mouth over her ear. "A butterfly. A fragile, exquisite, beautiful butterfly," he explained, punctuating each adjective with a light kiss on her cheek.

Eve smiled a sad smile. "*Mariposa.* A beautiful word for a delicate creature."

Matt's large hands gently cradled her head. Supporting her body, he eased her down to the woven Indian rug. "And that's what you are, my darling. A beautiful, delicate creature."

Her lids fluttered wildly as she fought back tears. What was wrong with her? She'd cried more in the past two days than she had in all of her life.

"Mateo—"

His mouth stopped her words. "Don't, Baby," he whispered, his gaze filled with an emptiness he refused to verbalize. "Didn't we promise each other that we would enjoy the time we have left?" She nodded and pressed her face to his shoulder. "Let's continue to make this last night special, Eve."

She tried making it special by preparing his favorite dish: *arroz con pollo.* She'd found a box of scented tapers and placed them throughout the living and dining rooms, surprising Matt when he came down the stairs.

"Make love to me," she pleaded softly.

"No, Darling. We both decided that—"

"I've changed my mind," Eve interrupted. Her fingers tightened on his shirt. "Please, Matt. Please don't make me beg you."

He heard the desperation in her voice and knew he couldn't deny her or himself of this last opportunity to share the deep feelings which had made them one.

Most of the tapers were hissing and burning out by the time Matt carried Eve up the staircase to their bedroom for the last time.

He placed her on the bed, his body following and covering hers. Her fingers were busy undoing the buttons on his shirt before they went to the waistband of his slacks.

Matt reached for the lamp, but Eve's hand caught his. "Don't turn off the light."

He obeyed. Each time they'd made love he had come to her, but this night was to be hers.

He lay down, closing his eyes and permitting his senses to take over. He heard her quickened breath against his ear as she leaned over and removed his shirt. He could smell the floral scent of her shampoo and the sensual blend of jasmine, rose, orange blossom and amber spices that made up another of her perfumes.

Raising his hips, Matt aided Eve as she removed his slacks and briefs. He folded his arms under his head, listening to the whisper of fabric graze her silken flesh as she shed her clothes. All movement ceased and he opened his eyes.

Eve's onyx gaze met that of Matt's citrine and emerald. Her gaze inched down to the thick, roped muscles under the dark-brown arms glistening in the diffused lamp light. The underside of his arms were a paler, palomino gold where the hot sun had not darkened them. Tufts of straight, black hair grew out from his armpits, unlike the crisp, curling strands covering his chest that tapered down to a narrow line and spread out in a triangle to coarser, tighter curls at his loins.

They had promised each other that they would not make love again until they were reunited in Virginia, but she had weakened. Eve couldn't control or quell the spiraling compulsion to try to persuade Matt to disobey her uncle's orders once she realized she would risk her own life to remain with him. Some unknown fear taunted her that if she lost Matt then Chris would also be lost to her—forever.

She moved over his prone body, straddling his thighs while bracing her hands on the headboard above his head. Matt pulled himself up into a sitting position, his hands circling her waist. A rush of air was expelled from his lungs as she pressed her breasts to his chest.

Lowering her head, Eve lightly touched her lips to Matt's before devouring his mouth. Her tongue then moved slowly and traced the outline of his full, sensuous, lower lip. Her fingers bit into his scalp, and he couldn't stop his deep moans of passion when she wouldn't permit him to escape her marauding mouth. Using his superior strength, he jerked his mouth from hers and lowered his head while searching for a ripe breast. His teeth fastened around a bursting nipple. The gentle tugging elicited a keening cry from Eve.

Only Matt's incredible strength allowed him to maneuver Eve's slender body with one arm, lifting her high enough to guide his sex into her and filling her with the fire which threatened to consume him. She tried pulling away but he held her fast.

"No, Baby."

Eve closed her eyes and gritted her teeth. She wanted it to last. Her heated blood raced through her veins like molten lava. She had fantasized about an even more intense ecstasy with Matt, and now that she was experiencing it she was frightened.

"I can't, Mateo," she pleaded.

Matt did not slow his powerful thrusts in his attempt to touch her womb. "I belong to you, *Preciosa*. I'm yours, Eve. Take all of me," he crooned in singsong, clenching his teeth and praying he would not explode. She was so moist, so tight, that he doubted whether he could hold back long enough for Eve to achieve her own fulfillment.

In the past, Matt had always been able to hold off fulfillment if he lay on his back. This time he knew it wasn't possible. "Let it go, Darling," he begged. Everything within him threatened to soar beyond his control. "Let it go. Please." It no longer mattered if Eve knew she controlled him.

Eve folded her arms under his and grasped his shoulders. She buried her face against his throat, her hot breath coming quickly in his ear. His fingers tightened on her waist, setting the pace and guiding her sleek body each time she rose and fell over his manhood.

The nectar flowing from Eve mingled with the perspiration coating their bodies. The sensitive nipples of her breasts grazed Matt's damp chest hair, sending more shocks throughout her lower body. Her fingernails sank deep into the tight muscles of his shoulders, and she tried suppressing the uncontrollable screams bubbling from her parted lips.

Matt's hoarse breathing resounded in her head and she issued a little cry of surprise when he reversed their positions. She welcomed his weight and arched, receiving his frenzied thrusts as his hands cradled her buttocks, pulling her closer.

She was too caught up with the emotions Matt had summoned from the part of her where sanity and insanity merged to realize the primal forces that had taken over her mind and body; raw, savage screams exploded from her throat just before satisfaction consumed her in the hottest fire of oblivion.

Matt's growl of sexual triumph echoed Eve's as he quickened his movements and buried his flesh deep within her soft, throbbing warmth. He lay heavily on her slight frame, eyes closed.

It had only taken the last seconds of his waning passion

to realize that they had made a mistake. This act of love was not love, but an act of torture and desperation. They had said good-bye for the last time.

Eve's hands moved slowly over Matt's back to his waist and down to his hips. "I've just discovered something, Matt."

Resting his chin on the top of her head, he let out his breath slowly. "What is that, Darling?"

She pulled back and looked up at him with a teasing smile curving her mouth. The rising sun turned Matt's face and black attire into a statue of gold and onyx. She caught the intensity in his startling eyes and her smile faded. His agony sucked the breath from her lungs. She'd managed to sleep throughout the night, unaware that Matt had lain awake with the uncharacteristic emotion of fear attacking him relentlessly.

"Your buns are a lot better than the ones I've seen at a Sunday afternoon football game. You're blushing, Matt," she teased as a flush darkened his face.

Matt gathered her close to his chest, one hand ruffling her curly hair. "You're a wicked tease, Mrs. Sterling. A teasing, sexy, exciting witch who manages to fire my body and blood until all I think about is taking you to bed."

Eve leaned back against his chest, her hands clasping his around her waist. She closed her eyes against the brilliant rays of the rising sun. "We can't spend all of our time in bed."

"We can damn sure try," he whispered in her ear. His eyes narrowed in concentration when he spotted movement from the road below. Without glancing at his watch, Matt knew it would take Cord less than five minutes to reach the house, and he swallowed back his apprehension.

"Do you think you could adjust to living on a horse farm, Eve?"

She stiffened in his embrace. "I thought you would go back to teaching."

Matt turned her around to face him. The wild, savage fire was back in his eyes. "Tell me *now!*"

Eve winced as his fingers bit into the tender flesh over her shoulders. She was certain his grip would leave bruises. "Yes," she said quietly. "I'd live in hell with you, Matthew Sterling."

He cradled her face between his callused palms, his eyes examining her features and committing them to memory. "What a precious gift you are," he murmured. His head dipped, and he kissed her with a hungry tenderness that left them both trembling for more; much more.

He released Eve, taking a step back while reaching up and removing the heavy gold chain from his neck. The sunlight caught and flamed the dull yellow of the twin medals. He slipped the chain over her head and concealed the medals under her loose-fitting blouse. "Return them when I come for you."

Eve clutched the medals to her breasts. They were still warm from Matt's body. She stared at the broad expanse of his back as he turned and walked into the house. The door closed quietly and her fingers tightened on the lumps of gold through the fabric of her blouse.

Return them when I come for you. It was his way of saying good-bye.

The man she had married was still shrouded in mystery. He hadn't given her a hint that he was superstitious, yet he'd given her what she knew were his good luck pieces.

She didn't need the luck. He did. She was returning to the States, to safety, while he still had a mission to complete in a land where her uncle's influence and protection was tenuous when negotiating with Mexican government officials.

"Good luck, my darling," she whispered into the air.

Chapter Twenty-Two

Eve did not return Cordero Birmingham's sober greeting before he stacked her bags in the back of an old, battered, four-wheel drive pickup truck. He hadn't bothered to ask for Matt, and she didn't volunteer to tell him. A denim shirt, jeans, and boots replaced his usual tailored suits and imported footwear, while a black baseball cap concealed his recognizable dark red hair.

She sat in the truck beside Cord, watching him put the ancient vehicle into gear. As they moved slowly down the steep, rutted hill Cord squinted behind the lenses of his sunglasses.

"Don't worry about Mateo," he said, not glancing over at his silent passenger. "He loves you too much to get careless." Eve's head spun around. "He has told you that he loves you, hasn't he?"

Eve stared at Cord's well-defined profile with his thin, hawklike nose and high cheekbones. Seeing him like this allowed her to see another side of Matt's friend. There was an aura of hardness layered beneath his youthful appearance; hardness and ruthlessness.

"Yes, he has," she finally answered. "As many times as I've told him that I love him," she added, this eliciting a smile from Cord.

He shifted his dark eyebrows. "If that's the case, then why the long face?"

She returned her gaze to the mud-dotted windshield. "Have you ever been in love?"

Frowning, he shook his head. "No. At least I don't believe or think I have. But what does that have to do with it?"

"Everything." Her eyes were filled with the love she found difficult to conceal. "When you find that special someone, you'll discover the emptiness only a separation can bring."

Cord chuckled. "I'll keep that in mind when I think about taking off and leaving a woman behind," he said flippantly. "If I feel as if my heart is being ripped out, then I'll know *she's* the one."

Eve's sulky mood lifted. "You sound like a real heart-breaker, Cordero Birmingham."

Cord grinned broadly. "There's nothing wrong with love them and leave them." Shifting into a lower gear, he steered off the road to a jungle foot trail. "I'll drop you off in another kilometer," he informed her, changing the subject. "From there you'll be transported to an airstrip where a prop job will pick you up to take you to Mexico City. Once there, you'll travel first-class back to Washington."

Eve closed her eyes, clutching the medals nestled between her breasts. How was she going to make it through *two* flights without dissolving into hysterics? She hadn't completely overcome her fear of flying.

Cord slowed the pickup, searching for the almost nonexistent trail to the shack where a man waited to transport Eve Blackwell-Arroyo to the next relay sector.

"There he is," he murmured under his breath.

"You're right on time, Cordero," said a slight, dark-

skinned man. He stepped from the cover of massive, towering trees and approached the driver's side of the truck.

"Make certain you get her to Manny on time," Cord
ordered in Spanish. He motioned with his head toward
Eve. "If anything happens to her, none of us will be able
to stop the carnage."

The man nodded. "I read you."

Within minutes, Eve was transferred from the truck to
a dilapidated Volkswagen. Wrinkling her nose, she dared
not guess what or who had been the previous passengers.

Her driver did not look at her once after he'd stored
her bags in the backseat. He stared straight ahead and
chewed a wad of tobacco, and she prayed he would not
use the interior of the tiny car for a spittoon as evidenced
by the dark, rancid-smelling stains on the seats and dash-
board.

Because of the early hour, the road was not crowded.
There was an occasional vehicle and several buses filled
with farmhands on their way to the fields. The heat of the
sun was brutal and she was conscious of her blouse sticking
to her moist flesh, outlining the shape of her breasts.

Eve concentrated on the monotonous passing country-
side—anything to keep her mind off Matt. Biting down
hard on her lower lip, she thought of Chris. Her firstborn,
her son. She had been so close; closer than she'd ever been
before and still her arms were empty, and she wondered if
she would ever see or hold him again.

She had come to Mexico to find her child and found
love instead, love and a new husband, and now she was
leaving without any of them. She covered her face with
her fingers.

"*¿Enferma,* Señora?"

It took Eve several seconds before she realized her driver
was asking about her health. Smiling, she shook her head.
The illness she'd acquired could not be cured by any
doctor.

The journey continued along the dusty road and past

towns where the division of classes were clearly visible, as
evidenced by large sprawling homes and tiny structures
with tin roofs whose interiors never cooled even after
sunset.

At one point the dust became so thick that she was
forced to raise the window to keep from choking. Her hair,
skin, and clothes were littered with the tiny, red particles.

The driver turned off the road and headed in the direction of the mountains. Eve then knew he wasn't taking a
direct route because he wanted to avoid being followed.
She clenched her teeth as the Volkswagen bumped over
uneven surfaces. Weak springs under the seat stabbed her
bottom and legs with every jolt.

Miraculously, the car made the climb up the steep hill,
wheezing whenever the gears shifted. The trees and under-
growth thickened, closing around them until dense foliage
slapped at the windshield. They bucked for another half
mile, then stopped.

"Señora."

Eve looked around her, then at the driver. He gestured
for her to follow him. She opened the door, squeezing
through the small opening. If the car had been any wider
it never would've been able to navigate the narrow trail.

She had no choice but to follow the man as he carried
her bags and scrambled up the side of the mountain like
a nimble goat. She took several steps, then she heard a
pinging noise. She recognized the sound immediately.
Someone was shooting in their direction.

Eve hit the ground, covering her head with her arms.
There were two more shots, then silence. The sound of
running footsteps reverberated in her ears. *It can't be, it
can't end like this,* she thought.

The figure looming above her shielded the rays from
the sun, but she didn't move. She thought of her son and
how his life would mirror her own. She had grown up
without a mother, and so would he. But she had survived.
Chris would also survive.

She was going to die and she was not afraid. She had lived and found love, and for that she was grateful.

Strong fingers curved around her upper arms, lifting her from the ground. "You're in no danger, Señora."

Her head came up quickly. The man spoke English. Shock, not fear, filled her eyes as she found herself face-to-face with Alejandro Delgado.

He tightened his grip as she attempted to free herself. "I can't allow you to go home. Not yet." His dark brown eyes narrowed. "You, Señora Arroyo, are my ticket out of this country with my head intact."

"Go to hell!" she yelled at him.

Alejandro's face was a mask of fury. "Get her out of here," he shouted in Spanish to the man who came toward them, a high-powered rifle slung over his back. "And pay him," he ordered, gesturing toward Eve's driver.

Eve's temper exploded and she turned on her driver. "*¡Cabrón!*" The stinking goat had delivered her to her enemy.

"Take her!" Alex shouted, turning his back and making his way up the incline.

The man with the rifle threw a wad of money at the driver, then extended his hand to Eve. "Señora, *por favor.*"

Eve saw compassion in the man's eyes. Something in his gaze pleaded with her not to cross his boss. She jerked away from his outstretched fingers and walked past him, following Alex.

She made it up the hill without assistance, stopping short. On the other side of the rise was a strip of flat land where a twin-engine aircraft stood waiting for her.

She had come to Mexico looking for her ex-husband, but he had found her instead. She stared at the silvery shape of the small plane, the sun reflecting off its surface, and she knew someone had alerted Alex of its location and who was to be the passenger.

Following Alex to a dark sedan parked under the sweeping branches of a copse of trees, she gave him a penetrating look for the first time. He hadn't changed at all. In spite of the heat, his straight, black hair was neatly combed, and his clothes were impeccable.

There were times when she wondered what it was that had drawn her to him, and it was always the same: his British-accented English, perfect features which made him almost too pretty to be a man, and his endearing smile and charm that concealed a vain, selfish, and vindictive personality.

She glanced at the plane, and Alex saw the direction of her gaze. "Don't worry, Eve. I'll let you go as soon as I obtain clearance for my own safety."

"What about my son? Will you let him go, or will you continue to hold him hostage?"

Frowning, Alex removed a handkerchief from his trouser pocket and dabbed his forehead. "What are you talking about?"

Her hands curled into fists at her sides. "Don't play dumb, Alex! My son. Of course you remember Christopher Delgado."

He put the handkerchief away, the natural color draining from his face. "I sent him back."

Eve felt faint and she reached out, capturing his arm. "When?" She could hardly contain her relief.

"I put him on a plane Christmas Eve. I wanted him to be home for his birthday."

"No!" she screamed once before Alex's hand tightened on her wrist.

"Where is he, Eve?"

She began to shake as fearful images paralyzed her mind. He'd sent her baby back, and Chris never arrived. "I don't know." The three words slipped out in slow motion.

Alex pushed Eve into the back of the sedan and sat beside her. "Let's go," he ordered his driver.

"Who knew you were sending him back?" Eve mumbled, pressing her head against the back of the seat. Her pounding, runaway pulse made it difficult for her to draw a normal breath.

"Harry Blackwell."

Uncle Harry, Matt Sterling, and Alex Delgado. Had the three men conspired to drive her crazy?

"I don't believe you, Alex."

He covered her left hand with his right. Delicate eyebrows arched on his smooth forehead. "I know I've given you cause not to like me very much, Eve. And because you didn't love me as much as I wanted you to, I tried to hurt you. I tried every conceivable way that I could to destroy you." He closed his eyes and long lashes shaded his cheekbones. "I wanted to be a good husband to you, but I didn't know how.

"You were the only woman I'd ever wanted to marry because I thought having you as my wife would make everything I'd strived for complete. But you were so aloof that you became a challenge. A challenge I couldn't resist." His eyes widened and the dark orbs danced wildly with passion. "I tried so hard to make you love me. Even when I heard you say it, I didn't believe it."

Withdrawing her hand, Eve clasped them together on her lap. "More lies?"

"No. For once in my life I'm not lying to you. I contacted your uncle and told him that I was sending the boy back. Blackwell said he would pick him up at the airport. That was the last time I spoke to Harry Blackwell."

Eve felt as if something stopped her from breathing. Why had her uncle used her? For what reason had he deceived her? And how could he use an innocent child?

Alex put an arm around her shoulders, pulling her to him. "I'm sorry. There's nothing I can do about the child."

"Why do you call him 'the child'? Don't you care? He's your son," she said against his chest.

Alex's expression was closed, impassive. "He's your son, Eve. I may have fathered him, but he has always been your son. Never mine."

* * *

Eve was back in Puerto Escondido and in Alejandro Delgado's house, and even though she was informed that she wasn't a prisoner she was shown to a bedroom and locked behind the door by the stoic man who was her ex-husband's bodyguard.

She lay on the bed, unseeing eyes staring up at the ceiling, failing to understand her uncle's behavior—if Alex had told her the truth. And where did Matt fit into the scenario? Had her uncle also set him up, or did Matt know where Chris was?

The questions tumbled over themselves inside her head, and after a while she was ready to scream.

She didn't stir as she heard a key in the lock. The aroma of food filled the room and she closed her eyes.

Alex stood next to the bed, staring down at Eve. She had matured. When he left her she was still a girl. Now she was a woman—all woman.

"Lupe tells me you won't eat."

"Get out." There was no emotion in her voice.

"I can't do that, Eve. You must eat something."

"For the last time—I don't want to eat."

Alex placed the tray on a bedside table. Reaching out, he pulled Eve into a sitting position. Her eyes opened and she glared at him. There was no mistaking her hatred for him.

"I don't want you dead, Señora Arroyo. And that's what you might be by the time your uncle gets around to granting me amnesty. I need you alive and healthy."

Eve's eyes narrowed into slits. "Amnesty for what? For kidnapping your son?"

Alex released her, straightening. He turned his back, slipping his hands into the pockets of his slacks. "It has nothing to do with my taking the child."

"What are you involved in?"

His shoulders slumped under his crisp white shirt. He

couldn't tell her that he'd been marked for death by corrupt officials within the Mexican government; corrupt officials he'd identified who had stolen millions of dollars from U.S. companies doing business in Mexico.

"I can't tell you."

"Then don't expect me to save your deceitful hide. Whatever you're mixed up in, then I wish you get what's coming to you. The way you live will be the way you'll die."

Alex spun around, glaring at her. A wildness she'd never seen before distorted his classical features. "I'll remind you of your words moments before I kill your husband." She gasped. "I'd hate to kill Mateo Arroyo, especially since he'll become quite useful to me."

Eve felt her heart in her mouth. "What are you talking about?" she questioned breathlessly.

"You really know how to pick them, don't you, Eve? I heard about how he swept you off your feet only days after you arrived in Mexico. Arroyo's reputation as a confirmed bachelor was shattered completely when he managed to wed and bed you within a month. And knowing Arroyo, he probably did not have to fight with you to take your clothes off for him, the way I had to on more than one occasion."

"You're sick and twisted," she spat out in disgust.

"And what is Mateo Arroyo? He's scum. The man pretends to be a legitimate businessman while amassing a fortune trafficking in drugs. And that makes him garbage."

She stared up at Alex while her heart pounded painfully in her chest. "Liar," she whispered.

He flashed a knowing smile. "Oh, how naive you are. Your husband will be here tomorrow morning to discuss some business with me. Business that will prove to be quite profitable for both of us."

Eve shook her head slowly. "No."

"Yes," he mocked. "Now, you'd better eat. To not please me would put your husband's life in grave danger." Leaning over, he patted her cheek. "Judging from what I've heard about you and Arroyo, you seem quite fond of each other. It doesn't make me very happy to know that he has the love from you I'd always sought. Do me a favor, Eve. Please me."

She stared at the the tray of food long after Alex left, locking the door behind him. Matt and drugs. She couldn't believe it; she didn't want to believe it.

She had fallen in love with a drug dealer; he was a man who lived in luxury by destroying the lives of people who existed only to crave the drugs which turned them into something sub-human.

And Alejandro Delgado was malignancy; everything he touched he destroyed, and not once did she doubt his threat that he would kill Matt.

She moved like someone in a trance. Picking up a fork, she speared a portion of steak. She ate mechanically until she emptied the plate. Alex had won this round because in spite of his double life, she still loved Matt.

Chapter Twenty-Three

"Mateo, you haven't heard a word I've said," chided Antonio Arroyo.

"I'm sorry, grandfather," Matt apologized. The trouble was, he had been unable to concentrate on anything since Eve left with Cord. He had waited until the pickup disappeared, then thrown his clothes into several bags and locked up Horst's house. He couldn't spend the night at the house without her.

"You miss her, don't you?"

He focused on his grandfather's lined face, nodding. "I feel as if I've lost a part of my body." He hadn't thought he would get so used to her.

Antonio flashed his grandson a knowing smile as Matt rose to his feet. "It doesn't get any easier, Mateo. Even after all of these years I still miss your grandmother when she's away from the house."

Matt reached over and laid a large hand on Antonio's frail shoulder. "I must leave for my appointment. I'll be back later tonight."

* * *

Matt watched Alejandro Delgado the way a cat watches a bird; he sat motionless, only his eyes betraying his intent. Delgado was only five-nine and weighed one hundred sixty-five pounds. He mentally assessed that he could sever Delgado's spinal cord with one fatal blow to the back of his neck.

His jaw tightened as he recalled how the slender, elegant man had caused Eve years of pain, and continued to inflict pain, because he still held her son captive.

Alex smiled at Matt. "I must congratulate you on your recent marriage."

"Thank you," Matt, returned, his voice deceptively soft, masking his loathing of Eve's ex-husband.

Alex draped his left leg over the arm of a side chair, his leather-shod foot dangling with deliberate slowness. A feral smile parted his lips. "It appears as if we have many things in common, Arroyo. We share an interest in similar business ventures and we also share a woman."

Matt's golden eyes glittered like a brilliant yellow topaz. "I share Eve with no man."

Alex lowered his leg. "You misunderstand me. I didn't mean to imply that I'm involved with Eve. I merely meant that she was married to me first."

Matt fought to control his temper. "I'm here because a mutual acquaintance said you wanted to meet with me to discuss business. But I want to warn you that discussing *my wife* is not a part of my business, Señor Delgado. It never has been, and never will be. Let me know now if you wish to proceed with business, or continue to waste my very valuable time."

If Mateo Arroyo had been any other man Alex would have had him killed where he sat lounging arrogantly on his chair. It was as if the man was testing his manhood.

"A thousand pardons, Señor Arroyo," he apologized,

successfully disguising his rage. "I know it is early, but may I offer you something to drink?"

Matt glanced at a delicate clock ticking softly on a nearby table. It wasn't quite the noon hour, but he was willing to share one with Delgado. "Some sherry, please."

Alex rose and walked over to a door. He spoke quietly to someone standing behind it. In the few seconds it took for Alex's attention to be diverted elsewhere, Matt examined the room quickly.

Its contents were representative of wealth and centuries of priceless possessions. He also hadn't missed the number of men guarding the imposing property. Alejandro Delgado had surrounded himself with a private army.

Alex closed the door, smiling politely. "Perhaps you would like to share a light repast on the loggia?"

Matt scrutinized Delgado's straight, neatly-combed black hair and white silk shirt and linen slacks. If he didn't know better, he also would've been taken in by the man's fastidious appearance and impeccable manners. He could see why Eve had been charmed by Alejandro Delgado.

"Thank you." He followed Delgado from the room and returned a smile from a young, attractive woman who lowered her gaze quickly before her employer caught her flirting with his guest. The woman spread a cloth over a wrought iron table in the shaded coolness of the loggia.

Matt's gaze lingered on her slender figure and the dark hair flowing from a ponytail down her back. His open, blatant stare caught Delgado's attention.

Delgado waited until the woman walked away. "I see you still can appreciate a beautiful woman even though you're married."

Matt nodded slowly, drawing his lower lip between his teeth. He continued staring at the doorway where the woman disappeared. "I'm married, Señor Delgado, not dead."

Alejandro Delgado smiled, gesturing where Matt should

sit. "You're a wise man, Arroyo. If you so wish, I can have Lupe visit you when you take *siesta.*"

"That would please me very much." He shifted an eyebrow and inclined his head, then sat.

Lupe returned with two glasses and a matching crystal decanter filled with sherry. Alex whispered close to her ear and a flush darkened her cheeks as she lowered her chin and flashed Matt a shy smile.

Another young woman joined Lupe, this one carrying a tray of vegetable and fish appetizers. The two women worked quickly and efficiently, setting the table with china and silver and filling the glasses with prized wine.

Delgado dismissed them with a nod of his head. He picked up his sherry and swirled the golden liquid around in the delicate, multifaceted glass, his gaze fixed on Matt's face. "A friend of mine tells me you intend to transfer your goods from Guadalajara to San Luis Potosí instead of Mexico City."

Matt shifted an eyebrow. The trap had been set and Delgado had taken the bait. His informant had given him the information which had been detailed in Operation MESA.

"Who is this friend?" Matt questioned, not confirming or denying Delgado's statement.

"That I cannot divulge, Señor Arroyo."

Matt took a sip of the premium Spanish sherry. "Then don't expect me to tell you about how I plan to move ten thousand tons of high-grade sinsemilla, Señor Delgado. I contribute quite generously to the Federales and the Federal Judicial Police to make certain my goods are protected. I don't need another business partner."

Alejandro's forehead furrowed. "That's not what Señor Birmingham reported to me. He claims you've hit a snag. He reported that the Federales and drug officials from the United States are ready to close in on you. And that translates into you requiring assistance. *My* assistance."

Matt gave him a level stare. "I don't need you."

A mask of fury twisted Alejandro's classical features. "You're new to this game, Señor Arroyo, and if you wish to continue you'll listen to me, because your *generous contributions* won't mean anything if I decide to close you down. Nothing or no one moves in Mexico without my knowing about it," he boasted proudly. "My connections even go as far as the Church."

"If you have that much clout, why would you want to meet with me?" Matt asked, smiling. A tinge of color touched Alejandro's delicate cheekbones.

"You insist upon asking questions I cannot answer at this time." His dark gaze was fixed on a small lizard which had attached itself to the wall of the stuccoed structure. "I'm not much for playing head games, but I will tell you this much, Arroyo." His gaze shifted, meeting Matt's. "I've been targeted for death. An execution would be a more appropriate term."

Matt froze. "Why?"

"That I don't know," he lied smoothly. His lashes came down, shadowing his eyes. "I'll help you to move your goods out of Mexico if you contact a U.S. official on my behalf to arrange for me to get out of Mexico alive."

"Why don't you use your Mexican connections?" Matt countered.

"I don't trust them."

Matt exhaled, leaned back and affected an expression of boredom. "I don't know if I can help you. I pay my people in pesos, not U.S. dollars."

"But you do have access to Harry Blackwell, don't you?"

Every nerve in Matt's large body screamed, however his reaction to hearing Blackwell's name was one of bewilderment.

"Who is this Harry Blackwell?" he asked in feigned innocence.

Alejandro leaned forward, peering closely at Matt's face. "He's your wife's uncle."

"And?"

Alejandro's shoulders slumped in a gesture indicating disappointment. "Apparently, you know very little about the woman you're married to."

"I know you've kidnapped her son," Matt retorted, his anger apparent for the first time.

"You know about the boy, but not about her uncle," Alejandro retaliated. "Harry Blackwell is an associate director of an intelligence agency."

Matt sat up straighter, his eyes blazing with excitement. Delgado was ready to talk. "CIA?"

Alejandro shook his head. "FBI."

Matt whistled softly under his breath, smothering an expletive. "Well, don't that beat all." Picking up his glass, he drained it in one swallow.

He knew Delgado was running scared. However, the man's informant had failed to let him know that he was no longer a target. The target was whoever was feeding him his information.

"I don't know this Harry Blackwell," Matt informed Alejandro. "Besides, I wouldn't know how to begin to contact him. And if I did, what leverage would I have?"

Alejandro ran his tongue over his lower lip. "Tell him I have a relative whom he's quite fond of. Also tell him he'll never see this relative again if he refuses to comply with my wishes."

Rage surged through Matt's body like an inferno, rendering him almost mindless. "I want proof that you have the boy."

"I can't give you proof."

Matt stood up, dropping his linen napkin on the table. "You want me to expose myself to an American agent for a few dollars of potent marijuana while you continue to play games with me about my wife's son? I haven't come this far because I've been a trusting Boy Scout, Señor Delgado." He bowed slightly. "Thank you for your hospitality. I'll find another way to get the boy back—with or without your cooperation. Only because I always try to give *my wife* what she wants."

Alejandro's left hand gripped Matt's wrist. "Do not rush off, Señor Arroyo. Why don't you take advantage of the *siesta* to think about what I've told you, and I'll also consider your position." He saw Matt's fierce gaze at the sight of his pale, slender fingers on his wrist. He dropped his hand and stood up. "The heat of the day does not always permit one to think and feel like a reasonable human being."

Matt did not congratulate himself on a quick victory. His mouth curved into a smile. "Perhaps you're right, Alejandro," he agreed, addressing him by his Christian name for the first time.

"Bueno, Mateo," Alejandro returned.

Matt removed his jacket, shirt, and shoes and lay across the large bed in the room assigned him for the *siesta*. He stared up at the ceiling. It had been easy, too easy. Delgado wanted out of Mexico, and he was willing to give up the child. But he had not been willing to disclose his informant. Blackwell didn't want Delgado, he wanted the informant.

There was a light knock on the door. He sat up. "Yes?"

"It's Lupe, Señor."

Matt left the bed and opened the door, grinning broadly. Lupe lounged against the doorjamb, a saucy expression on her face.

"I came to help you enjoy your *siesta*, Señor Arroyo."

His large hand curved around Lupe's waist, pulling her into the room. Closing the door, he kissed her cheek. "It's good seeing you again, *Corazon*."

Rising on tiptoe, Lupe kissed his smooth cheek. "Never mind the pretty words, Mateo. Save them for your wife."

Matt led her over to the bed, pulling her down beside him. "Word travels quickly, even in a country as large as Mexico."

Lupe nodded and smoothed out the folds in her colorful

skirt. "Even the scorpions have ears, Mateo," she whispered.

His gaze moved over the even features of the woman he'd left in Bogotá the year before. "What have you uncovered?" he whispered close to her ear.

Lupe leaned closer to his chest. "He has your wife, Mateo."

Matt went rigid, as if he had been shot. He stared at Lupe, not wanting to believe what she'd just told him. His fingers gripped her shoulders, tightening on the nerves near her throat.

"What the hell are you saying?"

"Mateo, you're hurting me," she gasped, blinking back tears. Whispering an apology, he released her, unaware of his awesome strength. "She's here. Delgado brought her here yesterday."

"Where?" The single word was ripped from the back of his throat.

"She's at the east end of the house, the last bedroom on the second floor." Lupe's fingers massaged the tender skin over her neck.

Matt tried to still his runaway pulse. Eve had not made it out of Mexico. "What happened?"

"Manny and Rene are missing."

"What about Cord?"

Lupe recognized the savage glow in Matt's eyes. "Cord dropped her off to Rene before the abduction occurred. It appears as if Rene never intended to take her to Manny. He delivered her directly to Delgado."

Matt covered his face with his hands. Rene Izquierdo was to drive Eve to Manuel Rivera, who would fly her back to Mexico City, where she would take a commercial jet back to the States.

"How did you find out? he questioned through his fingers.

"I've managed to get close enough to one of Delgado's men to get him to tell me anything I need to know," Lupe confessed as an attractive blush stained her cheeks.

Lupe Morales was thirty-four, but looked much younger. She had saved Matt's life when he barely made it out of Colombia with his head intact. Her seductive wiles had worked their potent magic when she skillfully seduced the man who was to monitor his every move.

Matt lowered his hands, a steely look igniting the fire in his savage glare. "Where's the boy?"

Lupe watched Matt as he picked up his shirt and slipped his arms into the sleeves. Her gaze moved slowly over his magnificent body.

"He's not here," she informed him as their gazes met. She'd enjoyed pretending to be Mateo Arroyo's wife in Bogotá, but regretted not sharing his body. She envied the woman who claimed him as her husband.

Matt slipped the tail of his shirt into the waistband of his slacks. "Where is he?"

"Delgado sent him back last year."

A quiet rage exploded in Matt. It had been a double setup. Blackwell knew he would not have taken the assignment unless he offered something other than money. He used the child and he used his niece. He was almost certain that Eve knew nothing about the return of her son.

A wry smile lifted the corners of his firm mouth. At least he wouldn't have to go searching for Eve or her son. Delgado had made it easy for him.

"I want you to arrange for me to get to her."

Lupe's eyes widened. "It's not going to be easy, Mateo. Delgado has her heavily guarded. At all times," she added.

Matt flashed a sinister grin. "Does your *friend* guard her?"

Lupe returned the smile. "Jaime Reyes usually has the night shift. He guards her between midnight and dawn."

Matt reached for Lupe, running his fingers over her

shiny, sable-brown hair. "Help me out, *Corazon*. Distract your friend while I visit with my wife."

"When?"

"Tomorrow night."

Lupe pressed her face to his wide chest, her arms curving around his waist. "Be careful, Mateo," she whispered softly. "Delgado is scared and dangerous. He knows that something is in the wind, and he's become like a cornered animal. He'll strike and ask questions later."

Matt kissed Lupe's forehead. "I'll be careful."

Lupe pulled out of his embrace and stared up at him. "There's something else you should know."

"What is it?"

"Jorge has been meeting with Delgado."

His expression never changed. What he'd suspected was now apparent. "Is there anything else I should know?"

She blushed again, her eyes telling him the secret which lay in her heart. It was apparent that she had fallen in love. "Jaime Reyes is on our side."

His smile was dazzling. "I'm happy for you, Lupe. I'll see you tomorrow."

Alejandro rose to his feet, extending his hand as Matt strolled into the loggia. "I hope you enjoyed your *siesta.*"

Matt clasped the proffered hand, smiling. "Yes, thank you." He took a chair at the table where he'd sat only hours before. "I've thought about your offer, Alejandro. I accept."

Alejandro's eyes glittered with excitement. "Splendid," he replied softly.

Lowering his chin, Matt stared at the man he longed to torture, using the most primitive methods. But that was no longer necessary, because Lupe had disclosed Delgado's informant.

"After I meet with my business associates, I'll head up

to Mexico City. The U.S. Embassy seems like as good a place as any to place a call to Blackwell.''

"I don't just want Blackwell's word. I want the man to come to Mexico himself.'' Alejandro exhibited a bravado Matt had not noticed before.

"You're asking a lot, Señor Delgado,'' Matt retorted, slipping into the formal manner of address.

"I value my life, Mateo.''

"Don't we all.'' He rose fluidly to his feet and stared down at Alejandro's bowed head. "I'll be in touch.'' Spinning on his heel, Matt walked out of the loggia.

He was escorted to his car and off the Delgado property by the same man who had met him on his arrival. The man gave him a half-salute when he reached the boundary line which separated the Castillo and Delgado estates.

Matt returned to his grandparents' hacienda and was informed that Señor Birmingham had been waiting for him in the courtyard.

Cord did not rise from his sitting position at Matt's approach. His expression was tight and closed and as unwavering as the automatic he held in his right hand.

"Keep your hands in plain sight or I'll blow your brains out where you stand.''

Matt obeyed, raising his hands in front of his chest. "Are you going to kill me the way you tried to kill Joshua? And what did you do with Manny and Rene?'' he continued, bluffing.

High color suffused Cordero Birmingham's face, but he didn't lower the gun. "I didn't have anything to do with the hit on Joshua, and you know it.''

Matt lowered his hands, slipping them into the pockets of his slacks. "I don't know a damn thing! All I know is that Eve never made it out. Delgado has her.''

The automatic came down slowly and disappeared behind his back under a lightweight jacket. Now Cord's

face was a sickly shade of yellow. "What the hell is going
on down here, Mateo?"

"Why the gun, Cordero?" Matt questioned in a dangerously silken tone.

Combing his fingers through his dark red hair, Cord
shook his head before he glanced up at Matt. "I've been
ordered to kill you."

"Because of Eve?"

Cord nodded. "It came straight from the top," he admitted. "You didn't follow orders. Blackwell expected his
niece yesterday."

Exhaling audibly, Matt turned his back. "Well, I think
it's about time *I* gave a few orders." He spun around. "Get
in touch with Blackwell and tell him to hustle his ass to
Mexico pretty damn quick! I want you to also tell him that
I know that Eve's son is *not* in Mexico.

"Tell him that Delgado wants a personal escort out of
Mexico, with the blessing of the United States. And you'd
better tell him that if anything happens to Eve he'll never
live to enjoy his government pension, because I'll become
his personal judge, jury, and executioner."

Cord didn't realize he'd been holding his breath. "Anything else?"

"Yes. Tell Blackwell to bring diplomatic passports for
Mateo Arroyo, Lupe Morales, and a Jaime Reyes. Please
include yourself, Cordero."

Cord swallowed several times before he spoke. "Who's
Jaime Reyes? And what about Jorge?"

"Let me give you a piece of advice—check and double
check your people. This leak is big enough to pass Niagara
Falls."

Twin pools of blue hypnotized Matt with their vibrancy.
"Jorge," Cord whispered. "Why, Mateo? I don't understand it. Why would he turn? It can't be the money."

"Whatever his motivation, it's now out of our hands.
Jaime Reyes appears to be a Delgado defector. You won't

know if he's turned until you're ready to pull out. If he stays, then he'll have to be neutralized.''

"Are you going to neutralize him?"

"Don't you think you'd better get going? Mexico City is not around the corner," he said, not answering Cord's question.

Chapter Twenty-Four

Matt drove to the mountaintop retreat where he was certain his telephone call could not be traced by Delgado's sophisticated electronic system.

Operation MESA was destined for failure unless he worked fast. He reached the house in record time and dialed the number to his private line at El Moro.

"*Sí,*" came a voice speaking Dutch-accented Spanish.

"Horst?"

"Yes, Mateo."

"I'm at your place. I need a quick trip to Mexico City."

"Tonight?"

"Yes, friend."

"Give me time to refuel and I'll be there pronto."

"Horst . . . you're going to need a carpenter."

"What did you do?"

"I'll show you when you get here."

He hung up, feeling as if he was going out on another rescue mission. The wars were over yet he was still fighting a war. His own personal war.

He had given Delgado his word that he would go to

Mexico City and he had to follow through; he couldn't take the chance that Delgado wouldn't have him followed, even though Cord had his own instructions to relay to Blackwell.

He would spend the day in Mexico City, then fly back to Escondido to see Eve. He had to get her away from Delgado and the danger which put every drug kingpin in Mexico in peril. Operation MESA was set to go within days, and only divine providence would stop it.

Eve's gaze was fixed on the calm blue surface of the ocean; she was unable to check the flow of tears staining her cheeks.

"I'm sorry, Mateo," she whispered. She'd tried valiantly to control her emotions. She'd told herself over and over that he would come for her, he would rescue her, but as the night faded and the sun rose to herald a new day, she weakened.

Her fingers clasped the lumps of gold hanging from the chain around her neck. "Help me," she prayed, closing her eyes and turning her face to the clear Mexican sky. "Matt, love you. Chris, baby, I miss you so much."

"What does Arroyo have to wring so much passion from you, Eve? When I see you like this it serves to remind me that I haven't gotten over you."

Eve spun around, but not before she wiped away her tears with the back of her hand. Alex leaned against the wrought iron railing of the second-story veranda, watching her. The guard who usually lounged in the chair at the far end of the veranda was missing, and she suspected Alex had sent him away.

Shifting, she presented him with her back, her eyes narrowing as she examined the palm trees lining the narrow strip of beach and gentle lapping waters of the Pacific Ocean. Alex moved closer, and she froze as the heat from his body seeped into hers.

"Lupe tells me that you're not eating again," he crooned softly.

"Lupe is a spy," she spat out angrily. Eve had come to despise the silent, attractive woman. They'd never exchanged a word, but it was apparent Lupe reported everything she did or did not do to Alex.

"Lupe is a loyal employee," he confirmed. "And I always reward my loyal employees." The fingers of his right hand toyed with the curls around her ear. "So far your husband has been loyal to me."

Eve pulled away from his hand, still refusing to look at him. "What are you talking about?"

"Arroyo went to Mexico City to contact your uncle. Harry Blackwell will become my guardian angel on a journey I plan to take to a little hideaway in South America."

"Why would my uncle help you?"

Alex stepped around her and captured her chin. "Why shouldn't he? He got me into this, and he's going to be responsible for getting me out. Besides, I don't think he'd want to lose his niece and her husband so soon after their whirlwind affair and marriage."

"You underestimate my uncle, Alex. Why should he believe Mateo? He doesn't know him," she lied smoothly. "Do you really think Harry Blackwell is so gullible that he would believe any stranger who called him with whatever flimsy story you've concocted?"

Alex's hand cradled her jaw. "Don't underestimate me, Eve. Harry Blackwell will listen to what Mateo Arroyo has to tell him, because both of them know that I will kill you faster than I would a bug who insisted on annoying me."

Eve's gaze narrowed. "Mateo will kill you."

"Mateo Arroyo will do as he's told. And if he loves his wife as much as I'm told he does, he'll follow orders."

The rising heat, the cloying fragrance of Alex's cologne and the cold, gnawing fingers of fear descended on her, and she felt sick. She swallowed back the nausea rising in the back of her throat.

Alex released her, watching her closely. "Sick so soon after the wedding?" he taunted. "Could it be that Arroyo bedded you before you arrived in Mexico? Is that why you came to Mexico, Eve? You didn't come to look for your son, but for the man who'd left another child in your womb."

"You're a sad, sick, twisted excuse for a man."

"Are you saying that I'm not the man Arroyo is?"

Eve refused to rise to his bait, walking away and returning to her bedroom. Alex was close to exploding, and she didn't trust her own temper. She didn't want to do or say anything which would put Matt's life at risk.

"Eat, Eve!" Alex screamed at her back. "Eat or I'll feed you myself."

Eve sat on her bed, eyes closed. She could still hear Alex as he shouted his orders in Spanish, and she felt sorry for the those on the receiving end of his rage. This Alex was different from the man she'd married, and she wondered what had happened to bring about his altered personality.

He'd always been selfish, but she never thought he would kill anyone. Alex was frightened, and Eve was confused by his statement that her uncle was responsible for his having to flee Mexico.

It was her third night of captivity and Eve lay in the darkness of her bedroom. This night was hotter than the one before, and she left the casement windows open to capture whatever breeze was sweeping across the scorched earth.

She was afraid to fall asleep, because with sleep came the nightmares. She had dreamt that she was being chased by someone or something she couldn't see, and as she ran she cried out for Matt. She was able to see him in the distance, but as she drew closer he moved further and further away until he disappeared.

Tossing restlessly, Eve was tempted to get up and walk

out onto the veranda. However, she didn't want to encounter the dark, searching eyes of the guards who watched her around the clock. The men who guarded her differed in height and weight, but their eyes were always the same. They all had sharp eyes that missed nothing and saw everything. And all of them were armed with semi-automatic weapons. Alex had made certain she would not escape him.

Hours later, a gentle breeze feathered over her nude body. She would try to get some sleep; she would sleep until the nightmares jerked her back to consciousness.

Something woke her, but it was not a dream. She was not alone. A large hand covered her mouth, cutting off a scream.

"Preciosa."

Matt! She barely heard his soft endearment. He *had* come for her.

"I'm going to take my hand away from your mouth," he whispered. "Don't make a sound."

Eve nodded and let out her breath after he'd removed his hand. Her fingers clutched his wrists as she leaned into his strength. His hands roamed freely over her body, and a small whimper escaped her constricted throat.

The sky was black, the room dark, and she wanted to turn on the lamp and make certain it was Matt. Maybe she was dreaming; maybe he really wasn't there with her.

"Eve," he groaned, his mouth moving over hers.

Relief merged with passion as the twin sensations made her weak with joy.

"Darling," she breathed out softly, disobeying his command.

Matt drew her to him, her back pressed to his chest. His lips touched the softness of her hair and he inhaled the sweet scent of her bare skin. He fought the heaviness in his own body, wishing he could make love to her.

"I had to make certain you were safe," he rasped in her ear.

Eve relaxed in his embrace and closed her eyes. All she wanted to do was sleep. "I'm safe now," she whispered. A soft sigh escaped her parted lips, and within seconds she was asleep.

Matt held Eve until a tinge of violet broke through the moonless sky. It was time for him to leave.

He shook her gently. "Eve." She blinked slowly, then sat up. "I have to go." Her fingers touched his mouth. "I can't take you with me. Not now," he added. Her fingers were trembling. Taking her shaking hand, he held it over his heart. "When I return I'll take you with me."

She nodded and tried to see his face in the emerging light. "When will you be back?"

Pulling her onto his lap, Matt looped his arms around her waist. "In two days. I want you to be ready. The night I come for you someone will leave you what you'll need to wear. I don't want you to change your routine. Do what you normally do every night. The moment you hear the guards change, get dressed and wait."

Her fingers clutched the black T-shirt stretched over his back. "What about Chris? Alex claims he sent him back."

Matt didn't know whether to tell her the truth or lie. He decided on the truth. "He did send your son back. Your uncle said the boy was abducted en route. He left Escondido, but never made it to Mexico City."

"What happened to my baby?" she sobbed softly against his chest.

Matt held her until he knew it was too risky to remain any longer. "I'll find him, Darling." He prayed he wasn't lying to her, but he had to make the attempt.

He slipped out of the room as quietly as he had entered it. His footsteps were silent as he made his way to the opposite end of the veranda. He froze, flattening his back against a wall. Several voices drifted up from the lower level. The voices were muffled, not permitting him to overhear who was speaking or what was being said. His right hand inched toward the knife in a scabbard concealed under his shirt.

Ribbons of light from the rising sun inched over his rigid outline. Within minutes it would be daybreak, and he would become a target. His fingers tightened over the handle of the knife. A figure emerged from one of the bedrooms at the end of the veranda.

Cursing under his breath, he realized that he'd lingered too long. Jaime's watch was over and another guard had come to replace him.

Matt's dark clothing blended with the shadows but he knew with the encroaching light he would become a distinct target against the sun-bleached walls. He waited for the guard to lay his rifle on a table next to the chair before making his move.

The short, powerfully-built guard hitched up his pants, then yawned loudly. He raised his arms upward, turning his back. Matt moved with the stealth and swiftness of a cheetah.

The edge of his right hand came down on the back of the guard's neck. There was only a low moan from the man, coupled with a whoosh of air from his slack mouth.

Matt eased him into a sitting position on the chair, positioning his hands over his stomach and covering his face with a sweatstained straw hat. Delgado would have the man's head for sleeping while on watch.

He scanned the grounds quickly, then made his way around to back of the house to the bedroom where he was to have spent the night. He tapped lightly on the window, waited and tapped again. The casement window opened and he smiled down at Lupe.

Lupe yawned delicately. "I hope you enjoyed yourself, Mateo," she scolded. He stepped into the room and closed the windows behind him. "I get to sleep alone while you—"

"Think of it as a selfless sacrifice," he interrupted. He

pulled the black T-shirt over his head. "How about letting me get some sleep now, *Corazon?*"

Lupe picked up a robe and slipped it over her night-gown. "What's the matter? Didn't you get any?"

Matt ignored her teasing and turned his back. By the time he'd divested himself of his clothes, Lupe had left the bedroom, closing the door behind her.

He'd returned to Alejandro Delgado with the news that Harry Blackwell was willing to come to Mexico and serve as a personal escort for the former diplomat. But Blackwell was scheduled to arrive in Mexico City the day Operation MESA was to go into effect. No amount of arguing could persuade him to come sooner.

Harry Blackwell wanted to make certain he would have the protection of both the Mexican and U.S. governments once he stepped foot on Mexican soil. And that meant Matt would have only twenty-four hours to get Eve away from Delgado and out of Mexico.

For security purposes, Joshua Kirkland had formulated a cryptographic key which could be decoded only by himself and certain bureau chiefs, and Cordero and Lupe would receive their orders twenty-four hours before the sweep was to begin.

Jorge. The name twisted in his gut. His childhood friend. What made him sell out his country? Had he associated with the unscrupulous for so long that he had also become corrupt?

Lilian. Matt thought about her and her small, dark-eyed children with their adorable, smiling round faces. What would happen to her after the arrest of her husband?

So many things had happened to him since Eve had come into his life: he had become a husband, fallen in love with his wife, and had exposed a senior DEA agent who had violated the laws of his agency and country.

Closing his eyes, Matt let out his breath slowly. He had only a few hours before he would meet with Delgado again.

It was apparent Alejandro Delgado was anxious to leave Mexico.

Matt made his way out to the loggia, smiling at Alejandro Delgado's thunderous expression. He had purposely kept the man waiting for their breakfast meeting.

Alejandro rose to his feet. "I trust you spent a restful night, Mateo," he said facetiously.

"Quite restful," Matt confirmed, politely extending his hand.

Alejandro shook Matt's hand, then smoothed back his neatly brushed hair. "Good." He waited until Matt sat before retaking his own chair. "I've planned to return to Mexico City tonight. I want to make certain that nothing keeps me from meeting Blackwell."

He added a splash of cream to the thick, strong-brewed Mexican coffee, then brought the fragile porcelain cup to his lips, his dark eyes never leaving Matt's face. "I've heard that your hotel offers some of the best amenities the city has to offer. I've shown you the hospitality of my house, and I'd hope you would do the same."

The corners of Matt's mouth lifted in a sardonic smile. "I don't mind that at all. But I would like to know when you intend to release my wife's son," he stated softly, aware that Alejandro had sent the boy back to the States.

"I'll tell Blackwell where he is when I meet him."

"No deal, Señor Delgado," Matt snapped. "You'd better tell me *now,* or you'll meet your ancestors instead of Harry Blackwell."

He needed information, any lead, that would tell him where Chris Delgado could possibly be hidden, because once he left Mexico he would never be able to return.

Alejandro stared at the savage expression on Matt's face, and his ex-wife's words attacked him: *Mateo will kill you.* For a instant he glimpsed his own death in the eyes of the man sitting across the table from him.

"I don't know where the child is," he confessed.

Matt went still. Lupe confirmed that Alejandro had arranged for Christopher Delgado's return, but what he had to do was find who had intercepted the child.

"You lied to me," Matt stated in a calm voice, surprising himself with his rigid control. "If you lie about one thing you'll lie about another."

A flush darkened Alejandro's face. "I never said I had the boy. You did. I said that I have a relative whom Blackwell's quite fond of."

Matt knew it was past time for playing cat and mouse games. "You have my wife." The question was a statement.

Alejandro nodded. He stared down at the delicately woven tablecloth. "She is safe. I will not harm her."

"Where is she?"

"Somewhere safe."

Every nerve in Matt's body vibrated with tension. He'd planned to come back and get Eve within forty-eight hours, but that wasn't possible because Alejandro Delgado wanted to leave for Mexico City within a few hours.

He knew he couldn't walk out of Alejandro's house with her unless the man himself sanctioned it, and he did not trust Alejandro enough to go to Mexico City with him and leave Eve behind.

"I'll go to Mexico City with you, but not without my wife," Matt stated firmly.

Alejandro's expression grew hard and resentful. "That is not negotiable."

Matt rose and reached across the table, his fingers snaking around Alejandro's neck and pulling him from his chair. China, silver, and serving dishes crashed to the brick-lined floor as Alejandro struggled against the death-like grip on his throat.

The loud clatter alerted one of the guards and he raced into the loggia. The rifle slung over his shoulder was quickly leveled at the two men.

"Get my wife," Matt ordered against Alejandro's flushed

face. His fingers tightened on the man's throat until his face turned purplish-black. Alejandro made gurgling sounds while clawing at Matt's hand.

The guard cocked the rifle at the same time Matt pulled Alejandro across the table and lifted him off his feet, using him as a human shield.

"Drop it!" he snarled savagely. The man complied immediately. "Now, get the hell out of here!" Within seconds he disappeared. Matt's fingers eased slightly. "Are you ready to be reasonable?" he whispered in Alejandro's ear. He nodded weakly and Matt released his throat.

Alejandro Delgado collapsed on the table, gasping loudly. The tears filling his eyes flowed down his cheeks. A violent trembling shook him when he realized how close he'd come to death. He stared up at the vaulted roof of the loggia, trying to focus his glazed eyes.

"Okay, okay," he repeated hoarsely. "Eve will come with us."

Chapter Twenty-Five

A light knock on the door and the scrape of a key in the lock brought Eve to her feet. She stood rigidly as Lupe entered the bedroom with a pile of dark-colored garments over her arm and a pair of black hiking boots in the other hand. She placed the items on the bed, a slight smile softening her full lips. Lupe's smile widened until it became a full grin.

Eve felt her pulse quicken with excitement, and she remembered Matt saying someone would bring her clothes the night he would come back for her. But he'd mentioned he would be back for her in two days. He'd only left her early that morning.

Lupe nodded briefly and backed out of the room. Seconds later, Matt walked in and Eve stared at him, unable to believe she'd been released from her tiny prison without bars.

She held out her arms, and he closed the distance between them, pulling her tightly against his body. Pressing her nose against his chest, she inhaled his warmth, the natural scent of his skin and his aftershave. He had come for her; last night had not been a dream; he was real.

Matt lowered his head and covered her mouth with his, taking from Eve what she offered so willingly: her love and her passion. Breathing heavily, he pulled back. Gold-green eyes mirrored the deep feelings for the woman he'd married.

"I love you, *Preciosa.*"

Eve smiled for the first time in days, but it faded as quickly as it had formed. Anxiety spurted through her as if some invisible force had wrested the joy from her. She watched the play of emotions cross Matt's lean, dark face and she knew something was wrong. Had he heard about Chris? Had something happened to her child?

"What's wrong, Matt?"

His hands tightened briefly on her waist before he released her. "I have to escort Delgado to Mexico City. Your uncle will meet him in a few days."

Her spirits sank even lower. He didn't have any news about her son. "What's going on between Alex and Uncle Harry? Alex told me that my uncle is responsible for something he's involved with here in Mexico."

"What else did he say?"

"Nothing else except that *you are* involved with drug trafficking." Her black eyes raced quickly over his impassive expression. "Tell me he lied, Matt. Tell me it isn't true."

Matt longed to divulge every detail of Operation MESA, but couldn't. As it was, Eve also was in too deep. "I can't confirm or deny it."

Turning away from him, Eve wrapped her arms around her body as if to hide from him. "How many other ways must you devise to kill? People who smuggle drugs are no better than those who sell them. How could you, Matt? Drugs are the scourge of the earth." She spun around. Anger, not pain, dulled her eyes. "What have I fallen in love with, and pledged my future to?"

Matt refused to let her see his pain as her words sliced through him as deeply as a knife. "Let's get ready to leave." His voice was cold, detached.

Matt felt more like a stranger than her husband as Eve changed into a pair of midnight blue twill trousers, heavy cotton socks and the hiking boots. She turned her back to him when she exchanged her blouse for the matching, long-sleeved twill shirt.

Before staring at Matt she took one last glance around the bedroom where she'd spent the past three nights. He was also dressed for traveling: black slacks, shirt, and jacket.

"I'm ready," she stated firmly.

Matt extended his hand and she crossed the room and grasped it. His fingers closed protectively around hers, and he led her out of the bedroom, down the hall and down the staircase to the courtyard.

Alex approached them, and unconsciously Eve moved closer to Matt's side. His fingers tightened slightly on hers and she flashed him a knowing smile. There were still too many unanswered questions surrounding Matt's double life, but there was one thing she knew she could validate— Matt would protect her from anything and anyone.

Alejandro, also dressed in black attire, nodded. "We are ready to leave," he rasped, his voice still hoarse from Matt's attack.

Two men, both armed with concealed weapons, stood by Alex's Mercedes Benz sedan. One opened the rear door and Alex stepped into the car.

"Get into the car, Eve," Matt ordered quietly.

She glanced up at him and again she encountered a mask of stone. Bending slightly, she slipped into the car and sat beside Alex. Matt sat down next to her, and she was sandwiched between her former and present husbands.

Matt's right arm rested on the back of the seat, his fingers grazing her shoulders. The possessive gesture was not lost on Alejandro Delgado, who turned slightly and stared out the window.

The drive to Mexico City would take hours, and it was better for the three backseat occupants to refrain from any manner of communication.

Eve spent her time alternating between dozing and staring out the window until it became too dark to see anything but the steady beam from the car's headlights. She tried not to dwell on the son she might be leaving behind. She blinked back bitter tears when she thought that perhaps he was buried somewhere in an unmarked grave, or taken in by some family who didn't mind another mouth at their table. Matt had promised he would find her son, and even that promise had turned sour.

The car swerved, and Eve, Matt, Alejandro, and the guard beside the driver were suddenly alert.

"What the hell . . ." Matt cursed softly, as the driver maneuvered wildly to avoid the obstruction blocking the road.

Eve blinked, trying to see why the driver had stopped. Without warning, Matt pulled her from her seat and prevented her from rising. His fingers were bands of steel on her shoulder.

"Mateo," she whispered.

"Stay calm, Eve," Matt ordered, "and do exactly what I tell you to do." It had only taken a quick glance to count the number of armed men surrounding the car before he chanced a look at Alejandro. His face was pale, his features frozen with fear.

"They're going to kill me," Alejandro croaked painfully.

"Get a hold of yourself, Delgado," Matt countered. He unlocked his door, then held his hands high above his head as the door was jerked open. "Be careful with the woman," he warned as a man motioned to Eve.

A strong hand curved under Eve's elbow as she stepped from the car. Alejandro was handled less delicately as he was hauled from the vehicle.

After Matt's stern warning to their captors, there was complete silence. The five occupants of the Mercedes were blindfolded, their hands tied behind their backs, and then herded up a ramp into the cargo area of a pickup truck.

Eve felt the blackness closing in on her but refused to panic. She knew Matt had sworn to protect her and she believed he would. She braced her back against what appeared to be a sack of grain and stretched out her legs, sensing Matt was only a few feet from where she sat. The smell of his aftershave wafted near her nose whenever she swayed to her left.

The truck began moving, and each time it rolled over an uneven tract of unpaved road, Eve clenched her teeth and struggled to keep her balance, refusing to think of what lay ahead.

What had been a twenty minute ride in the back of the truck seemed like hours to Eve. Every muscle and bone in her body was strained and bruised when strong hands lifted her to the ground.

There was only the shuffling of booted feet as they were led out of the truck. Eve stumbled and was righted quickly by a pair of strong hands.

"Be careful," a rough voice warned in Spanish.

"How can I be careful when I can't see," she retorted in English.

"¡Silencio!"

"Don't yell at me."

"Eve," Matt said quietly. In the single word was the tone of iron authority that expected immediate obedience. He didn't want her to complicate their situation with her antagonizing their captors.

Her jaw snapped loudly and she concentrated on putting one foot in front of the other while her rage simmered just below the surface. Her child was missing because of Alex; she was in Mexico because of Alex; she was being held captive because of Alex, and she would probably die in Mexico because of Alex.

After what seemed an interminable amount of time, Eve found herself in a room, her hands freed. A solid door closed behind her and she reached up and removed her blindfold.

The sight that greeted her made her stomach drop. The room was small and contained one barred window, a crudely constructed bed, and a rickety chair with most of the seat cushion stuffing missing. It appeared as if she'd traded one prison for another. The only difference was this one was less luxurious than the one at Alex's house. She glanced down at her watch, then began pacing the worn boards covering the uneven floor.

Matt, Alejandro, and his driver and bodyguard, sat on chairs, blindfolded and with their hands still bound tightly behind their backs. He'd estimated that they had been there more than an hour, and he wondered how much longer they would be held captive before they were interrogated, released, or possibly executed.

There was silence except for the sound of raspy, labored breathing coming from the other captives. Matt did not dwell on his own predicament, because he knew instinctively their captors were not interested in him, but in Alejandro Delgado-Quintero.

On the other hand, his thoughts were constantly on Eve. She did not pose a threat to the men who wanted Delgado but she was a woman—a beautiful woman who just by looking the way she did could heat and stir a man's blood. He knew he had to protect her—at all costs!

The sound of chorused breathing was shattered by the stomping of booted feet on the wooden floorboards. Armed men, standing silently around the room, came to attention.

"Who have we plucked from the golden net?" asked a

deep, masculine voice speaking cultured Spanish. "Hmm-mm," the man continued, "Alejandro Delgado-Quintero, his trusty driver, and a flunky goon who also doubles as his bodyguard. *Señor bodyguard, you are fired!*"

Sauntering around the room, he stopped in front of Matt. "Who do we have here?" He leaned closer. "I don't recognize what I can see of the face."

Matt sat up straighter. "Mateo Arroyo. And may I ask, Señor, whom am I addressing?"

The silence that ensued was deafening before the man threw back his head and laughed a full-throated laugh. "Mateo Arroyo," he roared, "I like you. However, I would like you even more if I hadn't found you in the company of Señor Delgado."

"That can't be helped," Matt continued. "Señor Delgado was traveling with me to Mexico City. I've invited him to spend some time at El Moro as my guest."

"You have bad taste in guests, Arroyo,"

"And you have even worse manners, Señor," Matt retorted. "I asked you who you are and—" He never completed his statement, as a leather-covered fist connected with his jaw, sending white-hot pain radiating along the side of his face. His head snapped back from the force of the savage blow.

The man leaned over Matt, his breath hot and moist against his throbbing jaw. "I ask the questions, Señor Arroyo, not you! *¿Comprende?*"

"I understand," Matt ground out between clenched teeth.

"Bueno. Now, answer another question for me, Señor Arroyo. Who is the woman?"

"She's my wife."

"Now there's where your taste is impeccable. She is quite a beauty."

Matt forced a pained smile. "I agree."

There was a marked pause in conversation. "Señor Arroyo, I'm sorry that you are involved in this, but such is life. I've been looking for Señor Delgado for quite some time now, and fate has delivered him to me. He is a traitor to his country. He spies on our officials, then reports back to the Americans, who pay him very well for his information. I'm sure you're aware of the story of Judas and what happened to him after his betrayal."

"He hung himself," Matt confirmed.

"Exactly. Señor Delgado has just hung himself."

"It's Delgado you want, and now you have him. Let the woman go," Matt urged.

"I'm sorry, but I can't allow you or your wife to go."

"Señora Arroyo has nothing to do with any of this. Why can't you release her?"

"That decision has been taken out of my hands." There was another lengthy pause. "Because I, too, am a married man and I treasure the sanctity of marriage, I will permit you to be with your wife, Señor Arroyo. But if either of you try to escape, then you'll die together as you've lived together."

Matt was hauled roughly to his feet by two men and led away from Delgado and the other two captives. The pain in his jaw shot up to his left eye and with every step the agony increased, and if the two men anchoring him hadn't aided him in walking he would've fallen. Between spasms of pain, he promised himself that he would exact his revenge on the man who had injured his jaw.

One man supported Matt while the other opened the lock to a room. The door swung open and they pushed him into the room. Seconds later, the door slammed shut and locked securely.

Eve stared at her husband's fallen body. She rushed to his side and cradled his head on her lap. A small cry of horror escaped her when she saw his rapidly swelling jaw. Pulling the blindfold from his face, she surveyed his face.

"Oh no, Mateo," she crooned softly.

"Untie me," he ordered, his breathing heavy and

labored. He had to lie down and sleep. With sleep he would forget about the pain.

Eve untied him and Matt sat up. Smiling lopsidedly, he pulled her to his chest. "It's going to be all right."

Those were the last words he spoke before he fell across the bed. Eve lay beside him, cradling his head to her chest. After a while Matt's pain vanished, and everything around him faded as he drifted off to sleep.

Chapter Twenty-Six

Matt woke hours later, his jaw frightfully swollen and discolored. He examined it tenderly, applying pressure with his fingertips.

"Is it broken?" Eve asked, watching him intently.

"No," he replied, wincing.

Eve moved closer to him on the bed; the fear she'd felt when she first saw his injured jaw turned to rage. "The egg-sucking cowards! They must feel like real men. Hitting a man when he's blindfolded and trussed up like a holiday bird."

Matt, opening and closing his mouth and testing his tender jaw, wanted to howl in laughter but couldn't. "It's okay, *Preciosa.*"

"It's not okay, Matt! They could've broken your jaw," she argued.

"If they had, then I wouldn't be able to bully you. I don't think I'd be too effective issuing grunts through wired teeth," he teased.

Eve crawled onto his lap, her arms going around his waist. "You'd still find a way to bully me." Pulling back, she stared up at him. "Do you think they're going to kill us?"

"If they'd planned to I don't think we'd be sitting here talking to each other right now."

"What about Alex?"

"I don't know," he answered truthfully.

"When is Uncle Harry expected to arrive in Mexico City?"

"He'll be here Friday."

Eve closed her eyes. Three days. Seventy-two hours. "What's going to happen if Alex doesn't meet my uncle?"

"Only Delgado knows that. He claims he's been marked for death, but he won't say who it is that wants him dead."

She swallowed back the question she longed to ask. *What about my son?*

"What do we do, Matt?"

He gave her a long, penetrating stare. "We wait."

After twenty-four hours in the small room, Eve thought she was going to lose her mind. She'd spent most of the time either pacing the floor or sleeping. Matt, on the other hand, stood by the window, staring up at the sky. It was as if he was waiting for something or someone.

"What are you looking for?" she finally asked.

"I'm not looking. I'm listening."

She exhaled loudly. "Then what are you listening for?"

Matt didn't move. "It's not what, but who."

Eve felt her control snap. "Dammit, Mateo, who are you listening to?"

Matt turned his head and she saw the dark purple bruise along his left cheekbone. "I'm trying to pick up bits and pieces of conversations. I just heard someone mention Delgado. He must still be alive," he whispered.

She crossed the room and stood next to him. There were two, maybe three men, standing close enough to the window to be overheard, but they spoke in rapid Spanish and she could only pick up a few words.

She watched Matt's face for a change in expression. His impassive mask of stone told her nothing.

Bored, she walked away and flopped down on the bed to wait. A day had passed. Her uncle was due to arrive in another forty-eight hours, but would he find them? Would Alex be alive? Would someone have answers to where Chris could possibly be?

She had no idea where they were or how far they were from Mexico City. Matt didn't know who the men were who held them prisoner. However, he was certain that except for Delgado, they would be released. But when?

There came two thuds on the door and she sat up. It was the signal that she and Matt would be allowed to leave the room for a quarter of an hour for a small, antiquated lavatory at the end of the hall; in their four allotted trips to the bathroom they'd managed a modicum of tolerable personal hygiene.

Matt turned from his position near the window and made his way to the bed. *"¡Entre!"*

The bolt slid back and the door swung open. A short, stockily-built man walked into the room. Nodding slightly to Matt, he lapsed into a rapid string of Spanish, addressing him as Señor Arroyo.

Matt inclined his head, thanking him. The man backed out of the room and closed the door. This time there was no distinctive sound of the bolt sliding into place.

"We've just received an invitation to dinner," he explained to a perplexed Eve.

"With whom?"

Matt managed what could be called a smile. His injured jaw had temporarily marred his strikingly attractive face. "We'll find out soon enough. Put your boots on, Darling. It appears as if we're about to check out of this most reputable establishment."

* * *

Matt and Eve sat in the back of the pickup truck with the same man who'd come to their room and told them they were leaving. There was no sign of Alejandro Delgado, his driver or his bodyguard.

Eve sat close to Matt, resting her head against his solid shoulder. She knew he was in pain because each time the truck dipped and swayed over the rutted road the muscles in his shoulder tightened involuntarily.

There were so many questions she wanted to ask, but didn't. It seemed as if she'd been asking questions ever since she stepped foot on Mexican soil. Questions she didn't have answers to, and questions Matt would not or could not answer.

The truck left the rutted road and continued up a steep incline, its gears grinding loudly. With the higher altitude Eve experienced a popping sound in her ears.

Then, it appeared out of nowhere. A sun-bleached, white, two-story structure stood in the midst of a carved-out portion of a jungle of towering trees and trailing vines.

"Matt," Eve whispered, sitting up straighter. The truck screeched to an abrupt halt seconds after his name was out of her mouth.

The front door opened and a cadre of green-fatigued men flanked by a dark-suited Harry Blackwell walked out into the late-afternoon sunlight. Matt held Eve firmly as she attempted to scramble over the side of the pickup unaided.

"Uncle Harry!" she gasped in shock.

"Careful, *Preciosa,*" Matt warned softly. "Your uncle will have my head if you break your neck."

Standing, he swung her over the side of the truck and handed her to a waiting Harry Blackwell. A twisted smile tortured his injured jaw as he watched his wife's tearful reunion with her uncle.

Matt climbed out of the truck, his gaze firmly fixed on

the phalanx of specially-trained men closing in around Blackwell and Eve. Even though their uniforms bore no identifying insignias, he was certain they were members of the elite Delta Force.

Harry hugged and kissed Eve. Pulling back, he nodded, and a man from his escort team stepped forward and extended his hand.

"Come with me, Ma'am."

Eve took a step backward, shaking her head. "No."

Harry's lined forehead furrowed deeper. "Eve, you have to—"

"I don't have to do anything," she said, cutting off her uncle's entreaty. "All *I* have to do is find my son."

Harry stared over Eve's head at Matt. A silent undercurrent of realization passed between the two men, and Harry was aware that Matt knew what he was going to say before he verbalized it.

"Christopher is safe," he confirmed after a lengthy silence.

A cry of joy broke from Eve's lips. Her baby *was* safe. "Where is he?" she questioned, her heart pounding wildly against her ribs.

"He's with your aunt."

Eve lifted her face to the sky and mumbled a silent prayer of gratitude. Tears welled up behind her lids, turning her eyes into brilliant, sparkling onyx.

Matt felt her joy as surely as if it had been his own. He took a step toward her, but his efforts were thwarted as two men from Blackwell's team stepped between him and his wife.

The almost imperceptible motion was not lost on Eve. She moved away from her uncle and found her target restricted by the men, who took orders only from Harry Blackwell.

"Excuse me," Eve said politely, even though there was no mistaking the coldness in the two words.

"It's over, Eve," Harry barked out. His face was marked with a barely restrained loathing.

Rage replacing her joy, Eve glared at her uncle. "It's not over until I'm back on U.S. soil with my son *and* my husband."

Harry Blackwell, his dark face set in a vicious expression, nodded. The two men in front of Matt moved as one, capturing Eve's arms.

Matt, who had been silent and motionless, sprang with the speed and agility of a cat and grabbed Harry Blackwell from behind. There was only the sound of steel slapping leather as automatic weapons were snatched from holsters.

Harry froze in the deathlike grip on his neck. He knew Mateo Arroyo could snap his neck in less than two seconds. And two seconds was enough time for his men to extinguish Matt's life in a hail of bullets.

"If you kill me, then you'd better prepare to join me in death." Harry's voice was strong and unwavering.

"You don't want to die anymore than I want to," Matt whispered savagely in Harry's ear. "But I'll take your life as sure as you stand here, you lying, lowlife bureaucrat. You set me up, then you expect me to walk away after you get what you want. Wrong, Blackwell, because this time I'm going to get what *I* want. I'm leaving Mexico with *my wife!*"

Harry struggled to control his temper. "You'll leave Mexico—in a body bag!"

"No!" Eve screamed, the piercing sound floating upward and lingering in the humid air. Her lower lip trembled uncontrollably. "You can't kill him," she pleaded in a soft voice. "How will you tell your grandniece or nephew that you killed its father?"

Matt's arm fell from Harry's throat, and seconds later the guns pointed at him were holstered. Eight pairs of eyes were trained on Eve's face.

The shock of what Eve had admitted hit her full force and she swayed slightly. What she'd suspected for the past week had been confirmed that morning. The wave of nausea had hit without warning, her stomach rejecting her breakfast. She didn't need a doctor to confirm her pregnancy. Her body had undergone the same changes when she became pregnant with her son.

"Are you certain?" Matt asked in a quiet voice.

She stood straighter in quiet, regal dignity. "As sure as I am that I love you."

Harry stared at his niece, then Matt, stunned. He'd asked Matt to marry Eve, not get her pregnant. His shoulders slumped in resignation. "Let's go inside," he suggested. "This new revelation changes everything."

Chapter Twenty-Seven

Matt extended his arms and Eve walked into his embrace. He held her gently, tenderly, as if he feared crushing her. He was so overwhelmed with emotion that he didn't know what to do or say.

A bright smile creased his bruised face. A father. He was going to be a father!

"Sterling!" Harry bellowed. "We have work to do."

"And you, husband, have a lot to explain," Eve said quietly.

"I'll explain everything once we get back," he promised, curving an arm around her waist and leading her into the house behind Harry.

A spacious entry opened to an expansive living room. The room was empty except for a portable rack filled with metal folding chairs.

Turning, Harry smiled at Eve. "A room has been set up for you, honey. It's the second one on the left at the top of the stairs."

Matt's right hand cradled the back of Eve's head, his fingers caressing the soft curls on the nape of her neck.

"I'll be up as soon as I can," he said quietly. Lowering his head, he kissed the tip of her nose. He released her, watching as she climbed the stairs and disappeared from sight. The tender expression softening his features vanished. "I want her out of here immediately."

"She'll leave with me an hour before Operation MESA is launched," Harry stated in a firm tone.

Crossing his arms over his black-shirted chest, Matt gave Harry a withering stare. "Let's settle something right now, Blackwell. My first priority is seeing that my wife and unborn child are safe. I don't give a damn about you, Operation MESA, or how Alejandro Delgado figures into your covert border politics, but I do know that Eve and I were released because you deemed it. And I also know that you still need me."

Harry's expression remained unchanged, not denying or confirming Matt's accusation. "Talk to me, Blackwell," Matt taunted. "You were quite vocal just a few minutes ago when you threatened me with something which sounded like—uh—a body bag." He leaned closer to Harry. "You do remember the B words, don't you?"

Harry cursed under his breath, the words savage and coarse. Glancing away, he nodded. "You're right. I still need you."

"How soon can you get Eve out of Mexico?"

Harry hesitated. "How about tomorrow morning?"

"How?"

"Military helicopter."

Matt placed a large hand on Harry's shoulder. "Let's talk."

Harry exhaled loudly, and he didn't care if Matt knew of his relief. There weren't too many occasions when associate directors of intelligence bureaus were directed to personally oversee an international maneuver.

He removed two chairs from the rack and handed one to Matt. They sat down, very close to each other. Harry stared at the man who stood near the front door, and the soldier turned his back.

"Jorge Martín has been funneling DEA information to Delgado," Matt whispered.

Harry snorted, shaking his head. "Martín is a fool, because he had no way of knowing that Delgado's our link to Raul Cordero-Vega."

Matt glared at Harry. The man had known all along who headed the rebels. The retired army colonel who had become Costa Rica's interior minister extracted enormous sums of money from foreign companies by increasing tariffs on their exports.

"It appears," Harry continued, "that the Costa Rican government confiscated a very lucrative Delgado-Quintero holding, and Alejandro wanted revenge. He came to us with the story, asking for our help. We cut a deal—we would help him get his holdings back if he fingered certain Mexican officials who were extorting from American companies."

"When did this happen?"

"A couple of months before he married Eve."

Matt's expressive eyebrows shifted. "And knowing what Delgado was involved in, you let Eve marry him?"

"Delgado never mentioned that he was seeing Eve, and I only found out *after* they were married. I was very persuasive when I told him to annul the marriage, but it was too late. Eve was already pregnant, which meant I couldn't touch him. He wouldn't leave Eve, so we set it up for her to leave him. Delgado's reputation as a womanizer was common knowledge, and we helped him along with a number of his infidelities."

"What about his involvement in all of the drug and weapon smuggling?"

"We created the foil for Operation MESA. Delgado lured a lot of spiders into our net."

"You set the man up," Matt said incredulously, shaking his head. "And now he's caught in his own trap."

"He came to us willingly."

"You still set him up," Matt repeated accusingly.

"I would've done anything to get him away from my niece," Harry retorted. "I didn't want her involved in an international—"

"But she is," Matt interrupted. "Who kidnapped us?"

"A few Federales whom Vega has on his payroll. They intercepted Christopher on Christmas Eve and held him until they snared his father. We're responsible for Delgado, so what I want you to do is negotiate with these rogue Federales for his life."

"How much are you prepared to pay?"

"Up to a million," Harry stated firmly.

Matt smiled and leaned back on his chair. "I wonder if Delgado realizes how valuable a snitch he is." He sobered. "How much time do I have?"

"You have until an hour before Operation MESA begins. After that we won't be able to protect you or Delgado."

Leaning over and resting his elbows on his thighs, Matt stared down at the highly polished wood floor. He had less than thirty hours to win a life and death game of chess.

He glanced up, giving Harry a long and penetrating stare. "I'm going upstairs to my wife, and when I come down you can tell me where I'm to go and who to see. I'll leave the moment the helicopter lifts off with Eve on board."

"You're wasting precious time. She's not leaving until tomorrow morning."

Rising to his feet, Matt stared down at Harry. "My way or no deal, Blackwell."

Harry also stood up. "I'm glad you're getting the hell out of this business," he grumbled. "I give orders, not take them. Especially not from someone *I* pay."

"Don't bother firing me, Blackwell. I quit."

Matt crossed the floor and took the stairs two at a time to the upper level. He and Eve would have one more night together before they parted.

He rapped lightly on the closed bedroom door, then stepped into the room. The familiar fragrance of Eve's perfume lingered in the air. His gaze swept around the space, missing nothing. The last time he saw Eve's luggage it had been in the trunk of Delgado's Mercedes. It was apparent that Blackwell had come to Mexico earlier than planned to negotiate for his niece and her husband's release.

Eve lay on a large bed draped with mosquito netting, asleep. Removing his clothes and shoes, he walked over to the bed and lay down beside her. She stirred briefly as he pulled her against his chest, but she did not wake up.

"I love both of you," he whispered to Eve and the tiny life growing in her womb.

Matt closed his eyes and thought about the time Harry Blackwell had invaded the private world of Matthew Sterling to plead passionately for him to look for Eve's son, with the promise that they would annul their marriage of convenience after the child's return. Christopher Delgado was now back on U.S. soil, where he would soon share his mother with a stepfather and a brother or a sister.

In thirty hours it would be over, and if he didn't succeed he and Delgado would forfeit their lives. Eve would lose not only an ex-husband, but also a husband and the father of her unborn child.

No, he said silently. This was his last mission, and he would come out a winner. He lay motionless, then lapsed into a deep, dreamless slumber.

The lashes shadowing Eve's large, dark eyes lifted, and she encountered a pair in gold and green watching her. "Hi," she whispered shyly.

"Hi," Matt returned with a wide grin. He kissed her forehead. "Why didn't you tell me that you were pregnant?"

She stretched, raising her bare arms above her head and

reminding him of a sleek cat. "I only realized it for certain this morning. "I'd missed my period two weeks ago and my breasts are quite tender, but when I couldn't keep my breakfast down this morning, I knew."

His brow furrowed in a frown. "I didn't see you throw up."

"It happened during one of my trips to the bathroom. The guard had been smoking and the smell of stale smoke on his clothes and breath sickened me."

Matt gathered her close to his body. "I promise I'll never smoke again, *Preciosa*. Well—maybe the day the baby's born," he added cheerfully."

"There will no smoking in my house."

"*Sí*, Señora."

There was a moment of silence before Matt spoke again. "You're going home tomorrow morning."

Pulling out of his embrace, Eve sat up. "When are you leaving?"

Matt decided not to lie to her. "I'll be delayed a few days. "I have to get Delgado out of Mexico."

Her eyes widened. "No!"

"Yes, Eve."

She buried her face in her hands. "When is it going to end?"

"It's over when I get Delgado out." He touched her shoulder. "You have to believe me, Darling. Please, Baby, let's not fight about what is inevitable. We have so little time together before you leave."

Eve melted against his large body, crying quietly. She loved him—loved him so much.

"I need you to be strong for me, Eve. Before you know it I'll be back and we can begin the rest of lives together."

"Where are we going to live?" she questioned, her voice muffled against his bare chest.

"New Mexico."

"I've never been to New Mexico," she admitted.

"You'll love it. It's a wonderful place to raise a family."

"Speaking of a family, are you upset about the baby?"

"Are you kidding?" He eased her back and stared down at her beautiful face. "Each and every time I made love to you I prayed you'd get pregnant, because I wanted something more between us than just the memories if you decided you didn't want to stay married to me."

"You deliberately got me pregnant?"

Matt shrugged a broad shoulder. "If you didn't want a baby there *are* things a woman can do to prevent pregnancy."

"I thought there was no need for that because you said you wouldn't make love to me."

He shifted an eyebrow as a boyish expression crossed his strong features. "I lied, darling."

She brushed her lips over his. "As long as you don't get into a habit of telling lies, I think I'll keep you."

Matt's lips pressed against hers, then devoured her open mouth. The kiss ended and both of them were breathless.

"Matt," Eve crooned. She pressed a slender hand to her flat middle.

"What, love?"

"I need to eat something before I pass out."

He swung his legs over the side of the bed and picked up his clothes. "What do you want?"

She smiled at him. "Anything, as long as it's not spicy."

Matt dressed in record time and raced down the staircase, and Eve's smile vanished. She had to put on a brave face. There was no way she would let Matt know her fear— the fear that she would not only lose her husband, but also the father of the child he'd placed in her womb.

She would remain stoic, return to the United States, and then her waiting would begin again.

Chapter Twenty-Eight

Eve, strapped into a seat in the Blackhawk helicopter, stared at the ground as the aircraft rose powerfully above the earth. She waved to her uncle and the military team who had accompanied him to Mexico. Matt was nowhere to be seen, but she knew he stood at the window in the bedroom where they'd spent the night together. Their good-byes were unspoken because they'd silently demonstrated the depth of their love to each other.

She was too numbed to acknowledge her fear of flying as twin emotions of joy and sadness warred within her. She knew she would not experience the peace she sought until Chris and Matt were at her side.

The helicopter flight to Mexico City was accomplished in record time, and within half an hour Eve found herself on a jet bound for the United States.

She slept during the non-stop flight to Dulles International Airport and only awakened when the flight attendant shook her gently.

She deplaned and was met by a man who flashed a badge from the Justice Department. His identification got her through customs and he directed her to a car bearing official plates.

A driver expertly navigated the late afternoon Washington, D.C. traffic, and Eve stared at a lighted sign atop a bank flashing the date, time, and temperature.

She had left Washington March twenty-fifth and returned June second, and in only ten weeks she'd married, found herself pregnant, and gotten her firstborn back.

The driver turned down the quiet street where her aunt and uncle lived, and a shiver of excitement rushed through her. Chris! Her baby was home!

The driver stopped in front of an elegant townhouse. Eve was out of the car before he turned off the engine. The front door opened as soon as her finger touched the doorbell.

Dorothy Blackwell held out her arms to her husband's niece, holding her tightly against her ample, scented bosom. "He's been waiting for you," she whispered softly.

"Where is he?" Eve's voice shook with raw emotion.

"Mama."

The word was the single most precious word Eve had ever heard. Stepping away from her aunt, she stared down at the small child who'd been snatched from her.

Christopher Delgado looked more like his father than Eve remembered. He was the image of Alex, except for his eyes. The child had inherited her eyes.

Holding out her arms, she sank to her knees, and she was not disappointed when Chris flung himself against her body. He was only three years old, but he hadn't forgotten her.

"You still smell nice, Mama," he said in Spanish.

Eve, blinking back tears, ruffled his curly hair. "And I thank you, Darling."

"He speaks very little English," Dorothy Blackwell stated.

"That shouldn't be a problem, because my Spanish is a lot better than it was before I left.

"Did you eat on the plane, child?"

Eve rose to her feet, still holding her son's hand. "In fact, I didn't. I slept the entire trip."

"I prepared a special dinner for you."

"Thank you, Aunt Dot. This is a very special night and I have some very special news."

Dorothy put an arm around Eve's slim waist. "The news can wait. You've lost some weight, so that means we'll eat first."

Eve winked at Christopher. "Can you show me where the bathroom is so I can wash up?" she questioned in Spanish.

The young boy puffed out his narrow chest. "*Sí*, Mama."

She followed the child to the bathroom, experiencing a peace she hadn't felt in years.

Eve pressed her nose against the window as she had done as a child, watching the summer sun slip down beyond the horizon. It was the end of July, and Matt still hadn't come for her.

Harry Blackwell had returned to the States two days after her arrival, with the news that Alejandro Delgado had fled Mexico for an undisclosed country in South America.

His only mention of Mateo Arroyo was that he'd disappeared without a trace. Harry would not confirm or deny that he'd been killed.

Eve walked out of her bedroom and made her way down the stairs to her uncle's study. She knocked on the closed door, then pushed it open.

Harry turned on his chair, frowning. "I know you were brought up with better manners than to enter a room without permission."

She ignored Harry's reprimand. "Where does Matt live?"

Harry cleared his throat several times. "I think he's from Texas."

"Not Texas," she countered, walking slowly into the room with her hands on her hips. "Where does he live in New Mexico?"

"I don't know, Honey."

Eve stood over a seated Harry Blackwell. "Find out, *Uncle Harry*. And you don't need me to tell you that you have your ways of finding out, do I?"

Harry saw the determination in the eyes of the woman who'd pledged her future to Matthew Sterling. "Eve, why don't you just wait and let nature take its course? He'll come to you when he can."

Her eyes narrowed. "Something tells me that he *can't* come to me, so I'm going to him." She flashed a saccharine smile. "I'll be back tomorrow. Same time, same place."

Eve glanced down at the odometer, biting down on her lower lip. The attendant at the service station had said she had to drive another twelve miles before she reached the Sterling ranch. She'd driven eleven, and in another mile she would see it.

Stealing a quick glance in the rearview mirror, she smiled. Christopher had fallen asleep the moment she'd driven away from the Las Cruces airport.

Since becoming reunited with her son, Eve had told him that she had remarried and there was a baby growing inside of her. The child was overjoyed when he realized he was going to have a brother or sister.

The brutal southwestern sun beat down on the windshield and she adjusted the air-conditioning. A pickup truck passed her and Eve caught a glimpse of a familiar profile. The man with the dark, wide-brimmed hat looked like Matt!

Eve brought the car to a screeching halt, and put it in reverse. The man in the pickup had maneuvered over to the side of the road, stopping at the same time she drew abreast of his vehicle.

The door to the pickup opened, followed by a sturdy cane. Then a booted foot emerged. The head and shoulders came next, and Eve knew without a doubt that it was Matt.

She found herself in his arms, not knowing whether she was laughing or crying. "Matt, Matt," she repeated over and over between his passionate kisses.

Matt crushed her to his chest, then remembered she was carrying a baby. "What are you doing here?"

Eve stared up at the rugged face of the man she loved beyond belief. "You didn't come for me, so I came to you."

"I was coming for you."

"When, Matthew Sterling?"

"Now," he admitted. "I was on my way to the airport."

Pulling back, she looked him up and down. He wore a western-style, dark suit with a white shirt and a shoestring tie.

"What took you so long, Matt?"

"I broke my ankle," he admitted. "Today was the first day I could pull a boot on."

She stared down at his black, snakeskin boots, then returned her gaze to his face. "Why didn't you call me, Darling?"

"I wanted so much to call you, but I wanted to give you time to become reacquainted with your son. I spoke to Harry at least three times a week, and he kept me updated on everything." What he didn't say was that he had to wait until *all* of his injuries healed; the Federales had exacted a high price for Alejandro Delgado's freedom.

"*Our* son," she corrected, her arms going around his neck.

Leaning heavily on his cane, Matt curved his free arm around her thickening waist. Lowering his head, he captured her mouth, drinking deeply again.

Sated, he pulled back, his eyes a deep, verdant green. "*Our* son," he repeated.

"Would you like to meet him?" Matt swallowed painfully, nodding. "He's asleep in the back seat."

Matt limped over to the car and stared at the child, who was now awake and staring at his mother and the tall man beside her.

Eve unlocked the door and beckoned to Chris. "Come and meet your stepfather." Chris scrambled from the seat and stepped out into the arid New Mexico heat.

Matt leaned down as far as his injured leg would permit him. Extending his free hand, he smiled. "How are you, Christopher?" he asked in Spanish.

Chris glanced briefly at his mother, then took the proffered hand. "Fine," he replied in the same language. "Mama said you're going to be my stepfather. What do you want me to call you?"

"What did you call your father?"

"Daddy," Chris said without hesitating.

"If that's the case, then I wouldn't mind being your papa."

"I like papa, Papa." Chris and Matt laughed while Eve blinked back tears.

Matt swept the hat from his head and placed it on Chris's, and Eve noticed several streaks of gray in the raven black hair. "It gets pretty hot out here and you're going to need a hat to keep the sun off your face and neck." The hat slid down over the boy's forehead.

"It's too big," he mumbled under the wide circle of straw.

"Then we'll have to see about getting one that will fit." Chris handed Matt back his hat. "You like horses, Chris?"

"I don't know."

"How about you ride in the truck with me, while your mama follows us in her car, and I'll tell you about some horses who live at the place that's going to be your home."

"Can I ride the horses?"

Matt stared at the child who would never get to see his

natural father again. He would become the father Alejandro Delgado could never become.

"Of course," he finally answered, staring over the boy's head at Eve. "I'll teach you to ride, shoot, and how to live off the land. But most of all I want to help you to become an honorable man."

"Thank you," she whispered softly.

Chris tugged at Matt's hand. "Can we go now, Papa? I want to see the horses."

Matt winked at Eve as he helped her into her car, then he limped back to the truck with Chris, knowing that he'd been given another chance; like the phoenix, he'd risen from the ashes of death to live with the woman he'd promised to love and protect for the rest of his life.

Dear Readers:

Now that the curtain has come down on the performances of Matt and Eve in **HIDDEN AGENDA,** it is expected to go up again for another member of **HIDEAWAY'S** cast of characters.

I am currently working on Joshua Kirkland's story, tentatively titled **HALLOWED VOWS.** The brilliant and enigmatic half-brother from **HIDEAWAY** will take center stage as a shadowy figure in the clandestine world of industrial espionage.

Look for Joshua and the woman who will claim his love and make this memorable hero a man for all seasons in a future Arabesque novel in December, 1997, and for David Cole's **HEAVENSENT** in July 1998.

I'd also like to thank you for your overwhelming response to **HAPPILY EVER AFTER, HIDEAWAY, FIRST FRUITS** (a Kwanzaa novella in **HOLIDAY CHEER**) and **HOME SWEET HOME.**

I welcome and appreciate your comments, so please write. Enclose a self-addressed, stamped envelope for a reply.

Rochelle Alers
P.O. Box 690
Freeport, New York 11520

ABOUT THE AUTHOR

Rochelle Alers is a native New Yorker who now resides in a picturesque fishing village on Long Island where she draws inspiration to write her novels and short stories. Her interests include music, art, gourmet food, mediation and traveling.

Look for these upcoming Arabesque titles:

May 1997
SOUL DEEP by Monique Gilmore
INTIMATE BETRAYAL by Donna Hill
MAMA DEAR, A Mother's Day Collection

June 1997
RHAPSODY by Felicia Mason
ALL THE RIGHT REASONS by Janice Sims
STEP BY STEP by Marilyn Tyner

July 1997
LEGACY by Shirley Hailstock
BEYOND ECSTACY by Gwynne Forster
A TIME FOR US by Cheryl Faye